The Man

Met His Maker

By

George Chittenden

Shield   Crest

© Copyright 2015 George Chittenden

ISBN: 978-1-910176-98-6

MMXV

A CIP catalogue record for this book
is available from the British Library

Published by
ShieldCrest,
Aylesbury, Buckinghamshire,
HP22 5RR England
Tel: +44 (0) 333 8000 890
www.shieldcrest.co.uk

To all my readers out there. You make it all worth it.

Many thanks.

Chapter One

Oct 17th 1765

The icy wind swept across the Atlantic Ocean as four tall ships were blown across her choppy surface in the closing stages of a race that would decide if men would live or die. After six hard days that had tested every sailor on board the Royal Navy frigate HMS Destroyer, she finally gave up her futile effort to escape the three sloops giving chase. Originally the Destroyer had set out for the British colonies in Jamaica and safety, but everything was against them. The sloops were designed with speed in mind and easily outmatched the frigate whose heavy cannon weighed her down. The sloops were closing in on them with the weather on their side and would attack within the next few hours, easily sinking the frigate in open water and drowning all hands. All three sloops had been built in the same shipyard, originally for the navy, before they'd been attacked and appropriated by a man who'd quickly turned them against their masters, a ruthless pirate who posed a greater threat to England's navy than any country on earth.

On the Destroyer's crowded decks men scurried about dropping her mighty sails and admitting defeat. Others simply stared at the horizon towards the rising sun as they made their peace with God and prepared themselves for what was to come.

The previous day when the sloops had first appeared on the horizon the Destroyer's Captain, a wiry and bad tempered man named Robert Carter, had disappeared, seeking refuge in his cabin. Hours later the ship's First Lieutenant had found his superior drunk on rum and mumbling about the devil finally collecting his debt.

With a terrified crew, many of whom were new recruits on their first outing at sea, First Lieutenant Alexander Saunders, a skilled sailor, had been forced to take command of the ship. Captain Carter's only concern seemed to be drinking his own weight in rum. As the Lieutenant left the Captain's cabin he'd heard the man mutter the name Alfred Mudd: this caused him to stop in his tracks as he was hit by waves of surprise and fear.

The First Lieutenant had heard the horror stories about Alfred Mudd, few in the navy hadn't. He'd even heard the stories about the cruel events on the island of Antigua years earlier, but he hadn't believed them. Some said that Captain Carter and a number of other young officers had set out to teach a daring young thief a lesson, but instead had turned him into the most ruthless pirate on earth. The Royal Navy had completely denied the events had ever taken place, and the only source of these stories was the mouths of drunken men at dinner parties.

Now though as he stood on the ship's quarter-deck and peered through his telescope at the sloops sailing closer – the plain black flags that blew in the wind confirming the pirate's presence – he swallowed down his fear. Whilst the sloops navigated into a pincer position on each side of the frigate, at a distance that posed no threat from the Destroyer's arsenal of cannon, he prayed the stories were not true. Saunders had read reports of previous attacks on Royal Navy ships, all marked 'Top Secret', and knew only too well that the pirate leader Mudd was already a master of naval warfare, though not yet thirty years old. The reports described a man who was patient, determined and incredibly ruthless.

Standing on deck surrounded by men who were relying on him for their lives, the young Lieutenant waited through 'the calm before the storm'. His mind wandered to his wife and boy back in England, and he prayed he'd see them again. Suddenly the sailors on deck began to stir, pulling him from his thoughts.

"We need to launch an attack!" one of the midshipmen shouted in a panic, as he looked around at his comrades who were unwilling to offer their support. The First Lieutenant stepped forward to take control, knowing only too well what the outcome would be if they fired on the sloops.

"That's what he wants!" he barked at the sailor, "If we attack him he'll kill us all. Now raise the white flag in surrender."

A few moments later the white flag was hoisted and the sailors watched as several row boats were lowered to the water before making their way over to the frigate. The cold wind gusted and the sailors on deck pulled their jackets tighter as they waited to receive their punishment for sailing under the Union Jack. Then the First Lieutenant watched in horror as two dozen of the roughest looking sailors he'd ever seen climbed up onto the frigate's main deck and proceeded to take control of the ship. In their hands they gripped muskets and cutlasses, but it was clear by the way the crew held their hands up in surrender that no battle was going to take place, and the pirates looked disappointed at this prospect. After securing the deck several of the savages turned to a man named Digby who had a deep scar running down his left cheek from a knife fight in his early teens that he'd barely survived.

Taking a deep breath to steady his nerves the young Lieutenant stepped forward.

"I would like to speak to Captain Mudd," he stated as calmly as he could, before Digby turned on him.

"You'll get your chance, boy!" the pirate barked whilst flashing a glare that forced Lieutenant Saunders to fall into silence and stare down at the worn timber at his feet.

Meanwhile a handful of pirates had slipped below decks and had begun rounding up the rest of the crew.

Alexander Saunders finally summoned the courage to glance back up and survey the scene on the deck, *'Be brave, you owe it to the crew,'* he told himself. The pirates had complete control of the vessel now and stood covering the sailors from all angles with their muskets. The Lieutenant recognised the weapons. They were top of the range and made by the manufacturer that the Royal Navy used. Saunders had no doubt that they'd been stolen from his comrades during previous attacks on navy ships.

The atmosphere on deck changed in an instant as a pair of boots hit the deck, and silence fell over the ill-fated ship. Lieutenant Saunders turned and watched as Alfred Mudd arrived on the crowded deck. The pirate leader was easily distinguishable, being incredibly tall, and so skinny he looked like he hadn't had a hot meal in many years. His face was skeletally gaunt and framed by red hair that flowed down to his shoulders, but it was his eyes that scared Saunders the most: they were bright and seemed to shine, giving him the look of a lunatic.

Any courage the sailors had mustered vanished leaving the Destroyer's crew genuinely terrified. Some were shaking uncontrollably whilst others actually wept. The Lieutenant watched and, much to his own surprise, he felt angry. Most of the sailors at his side were barely men, and didn't deserve this.

Captain Mudd stood taking in the scene before finally addressing the crowd, "Where is your captain?" he asked, and Saunders stepped forward.

"I am now master and commander of this ship. If you would like to punish someone then punish me, but I beg you to leave this crew alone. Many of these sailors are only boys experiencing their first stint at sea," the Lieutenant stated, as many sets of eyes turned and stared his way, Alfred

Mudd's among them. The pirate fixed his gaze on Saunders before nodding slowly and contemplating the young Lieutenant's words.

"You're a noble man, sailor and your bravery serves you well. What is your name?" the pirate demanded. The Lieutenant was terrified, but held it well. "My name is Alexander Saunders," he replied.

Captain Mudd marched up and down the main deck for a moment, lost in his thoughts and completely oblivious to the crowds of men who were cowering in fear around him.

"Alexander Saunders." he finally said, "I admire you. You have honour, which is a rare trait in your country's navy. Now, where is Captain Carter?" he demanded, catching Saunders by surprise. The briefest of moments passed whilst the Lieutenant wondered how the pirate knew who was captaining the ship, but judging by the crazy look on Mudd's face Saunders concluded that he wasn't a man you kept waiting. So the Lieutenant quickly explained that the Captain had turned to the bottle and had been relieved of his duty.

The pirate gritted his teeth and rubbed the ginger stubble on his chin. "Once a coward always a coward…" he muttered before turning to a handful of his men. "Load these sailors into row boats with more than enough food and supplies for the rest of their journey," he ordered, turning his attention back to Saunders.

"You married? Any children?" the pirate asked, and the navy man nodded

"Yes, Captain Mudd. I'm married with one child, a boy. His name is Philip and he is eight years old," he managed to reply. The pirate nodded and a smile crept up on his gaunt face. It was a strangely tender moment that Alexander Saunders would remember for the rest of his life, Mudd's name bringing it back for many, many years to come.

"You look after them!" the pirate warned, and the young Lieutenant found himself staring back down at the ship's deck as he realised that the horror stories about the island of Antigua were all completely true and the anger he felt for the pirate in front of him was equalled by pity.

Suddenly the smile on Alfred Mudd's face vanished and his calm expression changed in an instant as Captain Carter was dragged out onto the ship's deck, drunk on rum and already pleading for forgiveness.

Mudd gritted his teeth as his red hair blew around his gaunt face and he stared at the drunk Captain with the eyes of a madman at full moon.

"I'm so sorry, Captain Mudd. I knew this day would come!" the man slurred as several of Mudd's crew threw him into a row boat and attached a shackled cannon ball to his leg. By now most of the sailors had looked up from the deck, partly out of relief that the pirates weren't planning on killing them and partly out of curiosity, staring at the scene taking place in front of them.

"I know she didn't deserve it, nobody deserves that, but it wasn't just me. It was Louis Francis' idea," he pleaded to Mudd, who appeared to be completely lost in a world of his own as his pirate crew lowered the row boat towards the sea where it hit the surface with a thud and drifted a few feet from the Destroyer.

"I was there, but so were dozens of others" Carter shouted as he stared twenty or so feet up towards the ship's deck.

Alfred Mudd's pirate crew began pouring paraffin over the Destroyer's stern where it splashed all over the drunk Captain and the small rowing boat. Coughing and spitting out a mouthful of paraffin, Carter stared into Mudd's crazy eyes as it dawned on him what was about to happen, and he tried to free the heavy shackles on his legs.

"Well," the pirate shouted down at one of the many men who'd contributed to the destruction of his soul on a small Caribbean island several years before, "If it makes you feel any better, I will kill those others just as painfully," he promised. "Now you can choose: drown or burn!" he said, as he threw a paraffin lamp over Destroyer's starboard side.

A moment later it landed with a smash on the floor of the row boat and flames raced over her surface engulfing Captain Carter in a fireball. The man stood for split second waving his arms around…and then the first agonised scream filled the air. The sailors on deck looked away from the terrible scene. Carter's hair disappeared and then the skin on his face began to peel away, before his screams were finally cut short as he leapt overboard, dragging the heavy cannon ball fastened to his leg with him, which swiftly pulled him down into the murky depths.

Alexander Saunders stood in shock and watched the smile of satisfaction on Alfred Mudd's face, before the pirate turned to him and handed him a scroll of paper.

"On this list are sixteen names of men I want dead," the pirate said, fixing those crazy eyes of his on Saunders, before turning and staring out to sea, "When you get back to England you tell your superiors to stick these men on a ship and sail it around the Horn into the Pacific: only then will I stop waging war against your countrymen," he stated.

A short while later Alexander Saunders was forced into a row boat and dropped into the Atlantic. He watched as Alfred Mudds crew raised the sails on the Destroyer and sailed it away, adding yet another ship to the pirate's ever growing fleet. It was several long days drifting on the vastness of the Atlantic Ocean before the navy men were picked up by a small fleet of merchant vessels, and weeks more before they reached dry land. Saunders, who was considered a hero by his crew, spent many bitterly cold nights staring at the stars and thinking of his encounter with the most ruthless pirate on earth. When he arrived back in England he was sworn to secrecy regarding the incident. The Royal Navy were scared of the damage that would be done to their reputation if the world knew they were being outmatched by a common pirate. Finally Alexander reached his home and gripped his wife and young boy tightly, never wanting to let them go. His son, a little boy named Philip, was destined to follow in his father's footsteps and become a legend in the British Royal Navy.

Chapter Two

The English Channel 1792

The boy had grown into a man and, like his father before him, Philip Saunders was both brave and noble, traits that had served him well and helped him advance swiftly through the navy's ranks as he'd enlisted in his early teens. Now nearing the age of thirty-five Admiral Saunders stood on the deck of his seventy gun warship the HMS Windsor angry and confused as he took orders from a ruthless politician who'd commandeered his ship in the port of Sandwich and ordered him to chase a small sailing ship out into the English Channel. The politician, Cecil Blackheath, was a corrupt man whose only interest was personal financial gain. He'd used all his sway in the Houses of Parliament to gain permission to launch an attack against the country's most successful smuggler, a young man people called 'The Boy', whose criminal empire was costing the government enormous sums in lost revenue, a young man who Admiral Philip Saunders respected highly and considered a friend.

Saunders had argued with the politician, but it was a battle he was destined to lose. Blackheath held a document signed by the Prime Minister, William Pitt himself, giving the politician permission to use 'all the resources necessary' to catch or kill the young smuggler. In the end the politician had pulled rank.

"That's an order, Admiral, and if you don't want to face the gallows for treason you'll carry it out immediately!" he'd barked at him. This forced Saunders to attack the small sailing ship attempting to escape through the notorious sandbanks 'The Goodwins' in the English Channel, an attack that would haunt him for the rest of his life.

"Full broadside," he'd finally ordered as his ship swung around into an attack position, his gunners awaiting the order to touch off their cannon.

"Fire," Saunders muttered, the order immediately repeated by his lieutenants who bellowed the command. When the destroyer's starboard cannon let go, the ship shook with such force that both sailors and soldiers of the crown held on for dear life as she pitched to port before levelling out.

Admiral Philip Saunders was feeling enraged and deeply distressed, and struggled to conceal his emotions. Over the years Saunders had fought numerous battles at sea and squared up to face his enemies, even when he'd been outclassed and outgunned. Never had he felt like this. The Admiral had just assisted in executing a man he thought of as a good friend, on the orders of the government. Orders that were in complete opposition to his own secret mission. Consumed by a sick feeling deep in his guts, Saunders took a deep breath and racked his brain in an attempt to figure out how disastrous the consequences of what had just occurred would be for the country as a whole. He was recalled from his thoughts as he was ordered to sail back to Sandwich. Gritting his teeth he complied, eager to get the man off his ship.

During the journey back to the Royal Port of Sandwich Philip Saunders concealed his true feelings from Cecil Blackheath who pranced up and down the deck wearing a smug expression, an expression the Admiral struggled not to wipe off the politician's face.

Finally, as the ship docked and the gangplank went down, Cecil Blackheath marched off with his soldiers in tow and the Admiral breathed a sigh of relief, dropping his head as he gathered his thoughts. He tried not to think of the brave young man who had once risked his own life to save that of the Admiral. It had been a chance encounter that had brought Philip Saunders face to face with the country's top smuggler, a man his superiors had described as a dangerous criminal. But on that day out in the English Channel when Jacob Swift had jumped overboard in treacherous waters to save a complete stranger in distress, the Admiral had seen the young smuggler for what he was. Swift led an army of men who'd have risked everything for him. Each man knew 'The Boy' risked everything for them, making sure their families never missed a meal or worried where their next one would come from.

Soon after this happened, the Admiral had discussed the encounter at length with his superiors, specifically the spy-master Rupert Knightly whose huge network of informers drew information from all over Europe and beyond. Knightly advised the Government, and his information often averted conflict. Some of this information was fed directly to the Royal Navy who were then able to modify their strategies. Rupert Knightly listened intently to the Admiral's story as he puffed on his pipe and nodded from time to time. Knightly was a supremely intelligent man whose job was to protect Britain at all costs. The man knew information was a weapon. To Rupert Knightly revenue lost due to smugglers in no way compared to the country's safety. What Rupert Knightly wanted was information and he sought it constantly, like an opium addict looking for another fix.

The country's relations with France had deteriorated yet again following the revolution on the continent. War had been declared, Britain was nearly bankrupt and the spy-master was hearing all sorts of unusual stories. Knightly had ordered Admiral Saunders to cut a deal with Swift giving him safe passage in the English Channel, in return for information regarding activities on the French coast. The young smuggler interacted with French merchants all along the coast of France on a daily basis, and was in the perfect position to glean information.   As the smuggler operated illegally, Knightly possessed complete deniability if anything went wrong.

Meanwhile, on the deck of the Windsor, Admiral Saunders let out a lungful of sea air and sighed as his anger began to slowly subside.   Finally he turned to several of his men. "Prepare my coach.   I will be leaving for London as soon as possible," he ordered, before his mind drifted back to Rupert Knightly: the only man he knew who might be able to offer an explanation of what had led to Jacob Swift's death.

Chapter Three

Igh up on a chalk cliff overlooking the estuary of the River Stour two men were seated on horseback observing the small clipper as it tacked from left to right making its way out into the English Channel.

The men were smugglers in Jacob Swift's network and confident their boss would make good his escape. Both men had fled on horseback across the open fields of Kent by Jacob's side only hours earlier, but the young smuggler had led their pursuers off course away from the pair in an attempt to save their lives. Now as they observed Jacob's clipper making progress they both breathed a sigh of relief. Both were all too aware that very few men were capable of catching Jacob Swift out on the English Channel. The young smuggler's knowledge of the treacherous Goodwin Sands and all the other dangerous wrecks out there was second to none.

Suddenly something else caught their attention: the pair watched with curiosity as Admiral Saunders huge man o' war came out of the estuary in the wake of the small clipper. The taller of the two smugglers was named Alfie, and he rubbed at his ginger beard, puzzled, as he watched the HMS Windsor giving chase. He quickly dismissed any notion of a threat to the clipper from the warship. Both Alfie and the man at his side, a tough youngster named Jim Robson, had worked with Jacob Swift for many years. Both men were aware of the agreement their boss had made with the Admiral after Jacob had saved Saunders' life during a storm out on the English Channel, the pact that Saunders would turn a blind eye and allow Jacob Swift to smuggle with impunity. When the HMS Windsor began to turn into an attack position it was

Alfie who noticed it first. As his shoulder length red hair and his bushy beard blew in the wind, the rough and ready smuggler watched in horror. Alfred Bicks was one of Jacob Swift's most trusted men. The skinny copperhead smuggler oversaw 'The Boys' gang, collecting debts and making sure nobody stepped out of line along the way. Bicks had grown up thieving on the streets before his skill with a blade and his willingness to use it had earned him employment in the lucrative smuggling trade.

The shorter of the pair, Jim Robson, was Jacob Swift's oldest friend. Jim had known the country's most successful smuggler before he'd even taken up the trade. The pair had worked on the same fishing lugger before Jacob had set out to make a name for himself in their small town.

Alfie Bicks turned from the scene unfolding in front of his eyes to his companion, but before he could utter a word Admiral Saunders man o' war lit up as her starboard cannon fired a full broadside at Jacob's small clipper. Both Alfie and Jim saw the flash of light first and watched in horror as their boss' sailing ship was hit by nearly three dozen cannon balls. Many missed their target spraying plumes of water into the air, but the vast majority found their target and smashed the clipper into hundreds of pieces. Then the crash of the cannonade finally reached the pair and they stared at each other in shock as Jacob Swift and his clipper sank to the bottom of the English Channel and were buried in the very sands 'The Boy' had used to such good effect during his smuggling career.

Jim Robson slid from his horse in the silence after the explosion and staggered a few steps before collapsing in a heap on the ground. Alfie reacted differently. The tall smuggler's eyes clouded over, giving him the look of a man possessed. He stared at the Windsor as her huge bulk moved into the mouth of the estuary and cursed Admiral Saunders, the traitor he'd just seen kill his friend.

"Oh, you'll pay for this," Alfie promised, as his mind raced and he wondered how to avenge Jacob Swift's death. After a moment he was pulled from his dark thoughts by the sound of Jim Robson sobbing and he climbed down from his horse.

"Jim, I'm sorry, but we need to leave. Our lives are in great danger. It appears that it isn't just that scoundrel Blackheath who is against us!" Alfie said through gritted teeth as he dragged Jim Robson to his feet.

"We need to make haste out of this area," Alfie continued. "We can go to one of the safe-houses towards London. Blackheath will never get us that far out of town; but we need to move now!"

Rubbing tears from his eyes Jim's expression turned from grief to anger as he stared toward the wreck of his friend's clipper for the last time.

"Promise me one thing, Alfie," Jim said, as Alfie turned his way. "Promise me that Saunders will pay for betraying us!" he said, mounting his horse. Alfie Bicks stared out towards the HMS Windsor through those crazy eyes of his and gripped the handle of the dagger he carried everywhere in his pocket.

"Oh, I promise that dog Saunders will die slowly for what he's done," he swore as the pair galloped off into the distance.

Chapter Four

The sun had fallen from the sky by the time Admiral Saunders began his long journey by coach from the docks in Sandwich to the city of London. The journey itself passed quickly for Philip Saunders, who was completely lost in his thoughts and grieving for the smuggler he'd helped kill. He tried to sleep, but that solace eluded him. Saunders needed answers: as he gazed out of the coach window into the night he watched as countryside turned to shanty towns littered with beggars and opium dens. He knew he was on the outskirts of the city and that those answers would soon come.

Daylight arrived and the sun was high in the sky when Admiral Saunders' coach finally reached Greenwich and pulled up outside Naval Headquarters. Alighting, Saunders breathed in a lungful of smoggy air and frowned as he turned and gazed at the River Thames towards Deptford, making out the masts of dozens of ships of the line in the distance.

Shaking off the effects of the long journey, the Admiral marched towards the main gates of Naval Headquarters where two sailors stood on guard. Both men looked shocked at seeing Saunders and saluted the man who was already a legend in the greatest navy on earth. Created by the country's most ruthless King, Henry VIII, the Royal Navy had dominated the seas for over two hundred years, serving as the country's first line of defence.

Reaching his private quarters, the Admiral speedily washed and changed. Saunders was feeling exhausted, having spent the night pondering the situation, but he had no time to waste on sleep when his mind craved answers. A sharp knock on the door of his quarters startled him. Opening the door he saw an officer from the Royal Navy's intelligence division who saluted him.

"Good morning, Admiral. I'm pleased to see you, but surprised that you made it here so quickly," he said, as Saunders stared at him baffled by the man's words.

"So quickly? I don't follow your meaning, officer. I've come to the city on private business," Saunders replied, at which the intelligence officer's face contorted into a mask of confusion matching his own. "Am I missing something?" Saunders enquired, forcing the man to stare at his feet awkwardly.

"A messenger was sent to fetch you at first light. The order came from the very top and even the staff of our division are being kept in the dark," the intelligence officer replied. Philip Saunders stared at him for a moment longer, but the man could offer him none of the answers to his many questions. The Admiral nodded curtly to him and marched out of his luxurious apartment towards his waiting coach.

"Take me to the Somerset Club in King's Cross," he ordered the driver, who wasted no time whipping the horses into a gallop as the Admiral sat back in his seat and rubbed his eyes. His thoughts quickly drifted to a young lady named Elizabeth Swift, who had recently been made a widow because of his own actions. Philip Saunders' heart sank and tears ran down his cheeks. Only weeks ago he'd watched with pride as the young lady had married his smuggling friend. Now that friend was dead and the marriage ended far too soon.

When the carriage pulled to an abrupt stop forcing him out of his dark thoughts, Saunders glanced out at the Somerset Club, a grand building decorated with mighty stone pillars and polished marble. The building was a symbol of what it stood for: power. It was where the rich came to drink and dine as they brokered deals and lined their own pockets. The Somerset was a members' only club, an invitation only establishment, and if you were not a somebody then your presence wasn't welcome.

Normally Saunders despised such places. He was born in to a high class, and was an Admiral which opened many, many doors, but Saunders was just another sailor at heart. Philip had followed his father into the navy, not because of a lust for power, but because of a deep rooted love of the sea. At the age of thirteen Philip had gone to sea as a servant for a captain who was a friend of his fathers. Admiral Saunders had worked his way up through the ranks, but unlike many of his fellow officers he felt most at home on the deck of a ship amongst the common and inarticulate men who were the backbone of the Royal Navy. Philip Saunders felt like a fish out of water in such lavish places as the Somerset Club.

Climbing out of the carriage the Admiral strolled through the main entrance and was swiftly scrutinised by a number of handy looking men who were stationed near the doorway. They were smartly dressed, but obviously ready to launch into action to expel any unwelcome guests.

"Admiral Philip Saunders, it's always a great honour," the house manager said as he rushed over and took the Admiral's coat. Suddenly Saunders was of no interest to the door staff who returned their gaze to the street. Strolling into the main hall Saunders walked past dozens of familiar faces who were enjoying breakfast as they read the daily papers, or huddled in groups smoking, deep in conversation. Many were politicians, bankers or merchants keeping up to date with what was happening in the city. Saunders could have easily joined any table he chose. He was powerful enough to be welcomed into any circle, but he kept his head down as he strolled towards a small bar in the corner, trying not to draw attention to himself.

Reaching the bar he ordered a large brandy and asked the barman if the geese were flying north. It was an odd question, but the barman simply nodded and asked Saunders to take a seat. A few minutes later he approached the Admiral's table.

"Please follow me, sir," the barman requested and the Admiral climbed to his feet and was led through several of the Somerset Club's many rooms. All were decorated in the finest of tastes with polished marble floors and walls adorned with oil paintings depicting the country's most famous battles on both land and sea. From the ceiling hung chandeliers above men playing billiards, so completely lost in the game that they were oblivious to the Admiral's passage. Eventually they reached a small room which was empty. Saunders watched as the servitor pressed a small mahogany panel above the fireplace. A secret door sprang open and the barman gestured for the Admiral to enter, closing the door to the secret passage behind him. He then returned to his duties at the bar.

Chapter Five

The secret door opened into a small meeting room. Like the rest of the Somerset Club it was tastefully decorated. In the middle of the room stood four leather chairs surrounding a small table. Sitting on one of the chairs was the man he'd come to meet, one of the most powerful men in the country, the spymaster Rupert Knightly. Out of the corner of his eye Saunders observed a second man and as he turned he froze in his tracks for the briefest of moments before offering a salute. The man was none other than Sir Robert Burns, 1st Sea Lord, and the most powerful man in the world's most powerful navy. Normally he was the life and soul of any gathering, but today he sat twirling the ends of his grey moustache deep in thought. Saunders had known him for many years, but had never seen the man looking so troubled. Both men rose to their feet and shook hands with Saunders before returning to their positions around the table, where Philip joined them.

Rupert Knightly was smartly dressed as always, his bespoke garments in his favourite charcoal. He sat silently staring, waiting for Saunders to explain why he'd called the meeting. Saunders was more than confident that Rupert Knightly already knew, as there was little he didn't know, but the spymaster would not give anything away.

"Jacob Swift is dead!" Saunders stated, looking towards the spymaster and then at his own superior for their reaction. "One of Pitt's men turned up and commandeered my ship."

Rupert Knightly nodded as he watched the emotions cross his friend's face through the small spectacles he always wore. The spymaster had a great deal of respect for Philip Saunders and he didn't like to see the man upset.

"I'm sorry, Philip, but I'm glad you've come here. A messenger had already been sent to call you in for an emergency meeting," Rupert stated, as Saunders sat upright curious to know what the spymaster meant. When Knightly thought the country faced an emergency situation it meant the gates of hell were about to break open. A moment passed before the spymaster spoke, which moment seemed to last a lifetime for Saunders who had spent all night speculating.

"With regards to your friend Mr Swift, I'm sorry for your loss, Philip. I know that you considered the smuggler a friend. I was unaware of these events until it was too late: as we are at war with the French I'm sure you understand that national security keeps me fairly busy. The politician you speak of is Cecil Blackheath, a despicable man. A few days ago he led a vote in the House of Commons to wipe out smuggling once and for all," the spymaster said. He paused and poured all three men a generous brandy from the crystal decanter on the table. Sir Robert Burns picked up his glass and with shaky hands lifted it to his mouth and drained it in one savage gulp. The man was looking pale. He had deep bags under his eyes and the sweat beads breaking out on his forehead suggested he wasn't a well man at all.

"Why would he lead such a vote?" Saunders asked, "besides the obvious loss in revenue from smuggling, why now?"

"Why indeed..." Rupert said as he sipped his brandy. "To be honest with you, Admiral, I believe it has nothing to do with smuggling. Have you ever heard of the Eye of the Serpent?" he asked. Saunders took a sip of his brandy but it didn't seem to make anything clearer.

"The Eye of the Serpent? No, I can't say I have," he replied. The spymaster explained that a civil war had erupted in India because of a priceless ruby that had been stolen from a temple six months earlier.

"And where does the vile Blackheath come into this?" the Admiral asked, confused about what relevance this had to the death of a smuggler on the Kent coast of England.

"Cecil Blackheath was stationed in the province during the time the gemstone went missing. He was out there on diplomatic duty, but my sources tell me he's as crooked as they come. To be honest I don't know where Jacob Swift comes into the equation, but I promise you that as soon as Blackheath tries to sell the gemstone he'll pay for his crimes with his own life. I have people in place and nobody could sell that stone anywhere in Europe without me knowing. The theft of the stone has caused quite a stir in India and has been incredibly damaging to our plans there, but with all due respect, Philip, this really is the very least of our problems at the moment," the spymaster said as he adjusted his spectacles and sipped at his brandy.

"Meaning?" the Admiral asked. His fatigue left him unable to play guessing games. The spymaster turned to the First Sea Lord, who cleared his throat before addressing Saunders.

"At the moment we're facing a situation that could have devastating consequences for our country," Sir Robert warned. "As I'm sure you're aware it's not just the French who pose a threat to Britain. Relations with several European countries are at an all-time low and if the Portuguese, the Spanish, or even the Dutch had the finances to wage war against us they would without a second thought. The French fleet is in a poor state, but given sufficient financial resources they could destroy us."

Philip Saunders shrugged "Building a fleet of ships to outmatch our own would cost an absolute fortune and nobody with that much money would risk it, surely?" he asked. His question, rather than eliciting answers, was met with silence. The spymaster sighed and took a long swig of his brandy. Saunders watched him and waited for an answer.

"Have you ever heard of a pirate called Alfred Mudd?" Rupert Knightly finally asked, and the Admiral laughed to himself before taking a sip of his own brandy.

"Yes, of course I have. I've heard all of the stories about the great Captain Mudd. How he cut a deal with the devil for control of the seas and possesses supernatural powers," the Admiral said with a smile, "but these are just stories that sailors tell their children."

Now it was the spymaster's turn to talk and unlike Saunders he wasn't smiling, "Mudd was incredibly ruthless. He spent a lifetime spinning stories that scared his enemies and they worked. To be honest, I admired him for that. In many ways he used information as a weapon, much like myself. However, stories aside, he spent a lifetime raiding the ships of any and every country. The vast majority of attacks on our own fleet were never even reported. Our navy worked hard to make sure that Mudd never received the notoriety he wanted. Over the course of his lifetime he amassed an immense fortune in stolen treasure. If the public knew the truth: that our Navy, the most powerful Navy in the world, was too scared to sail into certain oceans our country would be a laughing stock."

Admiral Saunders was listening to the spymaster and struggling to believe what he was hearing. His mind couldn't help but wander back to the story his father had told him when he was a boy, about how Mudd had shown leniency to his entire crew.

"Well, Alfred Mudd is dead now," Rupert said, pulling the Admiral back from his memories.

"What? When? How?" Saunders asked, and the spymaster explained that his body had been found on a small pacific island several months earlier.

"And the treasure?" Saunders asked, before Rupert exhaled a lungful of air and took another gulp of brandy. The Admiral watched his friend raise the glass shakily: he'd never seen the spymaster show such unease. Saunders turned to Sir Robert Burns, who was rubbing his temples and looking troubled and frail, and Philip knew in that moment that Britain was facing a serious threat.

"The treasure. Well, there lies the problem," the spymaster said, "Mudd's body was found by a British merchant vessel with a handful of native tribespeople who, under interrogation, gave the location of the great pirate's treasure haul," the spymaster said, and a smile broke out on Philip Saunders' face.

"So we know where the treasure is?" he asked excitedly and Rupert nodded.

"We know enough. The treasure is buried on an island in the South Pacific. We now possess the co-ordinates and could locate her. Unfortunately we're not alone. Do you know a man named Louis Francis? He's navy," the spymaster asked and Saunders nodded.

"Yes, he's long in the tooth now though. He was my father's generation. He's the man Alfred Mudd wanted to kill his entire life. The man who topped the pirate's infamous death list. Louis Francis spent his entire life in Europe, never daring to sail out into the unknown, so they say. He was educated in Paris, right?" Saunders asked, and the spymaster nodded.

"Yes, Louis was educated in Paris. He is half French on his mother's side. He speaks the language and has always worked for us trying to maintain a positive relationship with our neighbours across the channel, but when Louis heard his nemesis had died he was taken over with fantasies about Mudd's treasure," Rupert said, "and four days ago he failed to report to us. Within twenty-four hours word began to reach me from multiple sources that the French were preparing to sail out of Bordeaux with a small squadron on a hunt for Mudd's treasure. Louis Francis has betrayed our country. He knows that if the French get their hands on the treasure they'll have a war chest so large they'll conquer the whole of Europe," Rupert said, as Saunders sat silently letting the shocking news sink in.

"But why would he do that?" the Admiral finally asked, and Rupert smiled.

"It's hard to say. Possibly because he knows, as I do, that war is inevitable with the French and he wants to be on the winning side. Or, more likely, he wants to get the last laugh over Alfred Mudd. Who really knows?"

Admiral Philip Saunders drained the last of his brandy. "So the French already have several days head start?" he enquired. Rupert Knightly adjusted the spectacles on the bridge of his nose.

"My spies inform me that they put out to sea yesterday. They'll sail across the Atlantic on the trade winds before navigating around Cape Horn and making for the South Pacific," the spymaster said, before turning to Sir Robert Burns.

"We've been making preparations ourselves," Robert Burns stated, "We would like you to take charge of a squadron of half a dozen ships, made up of two frigates to act as reconnaissance and four seventy-four gunners. Unfortunately most of our fleet is either out in the Indian Ocean or committed to protecting our shores, so we can only spare six ships. It will be a long hard stint at sea, make no bones about it. A journey that will take you around the world and back. Sailing the Horn will be difficult enough, and then you'll face the most testing seas on this earth. I've known you since you were a boy in your father's arms, Philip, and I've watched your progress in the navy with pride in my heart. You're respected below decks more than any Admiral I've ever known. In my opinion your father was the best sailor I ever put out to sea with. Like him, it's in your blood. This is without any doubt the most dangerous mission I've ever asked you to accept, Philip," he finished. The room went quiet and the three men thought hard about the situation their country faced.

"How strong will Francis' fleet be, Rupert? Did your spies on the continent report on the number of vessels he sails with?" Saunders asked. Knightly looked the Admiral in the eye.

"Reports mentioned half a dozen ships sailed from Bordeaux, but I can't guarantee that vessels from their Mediterranean fleet will not join the quest," the spymaster replied.

"And we cannot spare any more than six ships, Sir Robert?" Saunders asked, turning to his superior officer. Robert Burns shook his head, but it was Rupert Knightly that answered the question. As always it was the intelligence officer calling the shots.

"Any more and we'd risk losing control of the English Channel. The French fleet on their north coast is weak, but they have many allies and we have too many of our vessels currently overseas. I wish that we could offer you more, my friend, but losing the Channel would lead to an invasion. You have helped keep that risk at bay by working with the late Mr Swift for a long time, so you're fully aware of how crucial control of the Channel is to the safety of this country," the spymaster stated. The room fell silent once more and each man considered the difficulties they faced and the possible consequences the pirate's treasure haul posed.

"Will you accept the mission, for King and Country?" Robert Burns formally requested as he stared at Saunders.

"Sir Robert, it would be an honour," Saunders replied, and both Rupert Knightly and Sir Robert Burns smiled at the young Admiral with pride. The spymaster poured another round of brandy, and Sir Robert explained to Saunders exactly what was expected of him and his small flotilla.

"If you can intercept them in the Atlantic and attack them, then do so. Remember, Philip, that your mission is to retrieve Mudd's gold and bring it back home to England. Sinking the French and killing that traitorous scum Louis Francis is secondary, you understand?" Sir Robert demanded, and Saunders nodded.

"You can select your own men, within reason, so you have much to do. Your squadron will sail out of Deptford tomorrow." Sir Robert Burns finished, and Philip Saunders rose to his feet excited and eager to return to Navy Headquarters and start making preparations for the expedition that lay ahead.

"Did one of Jacob's men called Alfred Bicks survive?" Knightly asked suddenly, catching Philip Saunders completely off guard. Saunders stared at the spymaster completely lost for words.

"How do you know about Alfie Bicks? I've never mentioned him," the Admiral asked, feeling confused. Rupert Knightly smiled and adjusted his spectacles again. "I'm an intelligence expert, Philip. I work very hard to make sure there is very little I don't know. I suggest you return to your seat. There is much more that you need to know," Rupert advised.

An hour later Admiral Saunders began the coach trip back to his private quarters in Greenwich. During the journey he stared at the small item that he held in the palm of his hand, an item that had been found on a corpse months earlier and proved beyond doubt that the infamous pirate Captain Mudd was finally dead. The Admiral needed sleep, but he doubted it would come even if he tried. His mind was swimming with the shocking news Rupert Knightly had just delivered. Whichever way the circle of his thoughts rolled they kept returning to the boy who'd brought him to the city of London in the first place. He thought about the smuggler's men, who he'd made friends with over the years, with a pang of guilt knowing they were being hunted down like animals by soldiers of the crown. Saunders let out a sigh and rubbed at his temples taking comfort in the knowledge that he'd help them as much as he could, at least by getting them out of the country and to safety. He just hoped they would forgive him for their leader's death. Many of them were dangerous criminals, Alfie Bicks included, and Saunders hoped he wouldn't feel the cold sensation of Bicks' blade against his throat like many others before him.

Chapter Six

Meanwhile down on the Kent coast in the rough and ready smuggling town of Deal, chaos was erupting in the cobbled streets. Since Blackheath's arrival in town, accompanied by several dozen armed soldiers, the townsfolk had been scared, and not just for themselves. 'The Boy' was a local hero and people were genuinely concerned for his safety, but all their lives were about to change.

For decades the profits from the smuggling trade had supplied the poor with food in their mouths and clothes on their backs. Jacob Swift had returned the vast majority of his profits back into the town, particularly to the people who needed them, like the man who'd taught him his trade: the notorious Billy Bates.

Word soon swept through the town that Jacob Swift was dead, news that left many people distraught. The young smuggler had survived wars with rival gangs and trouble with Customs and Excise for many years. This time he'd finally landed himself in water so deep that, skilled as 'The Boy' was at navigating the English Channel, even he could not sail to safety.

At the news of Jacob's death, many of the townsfolk locked themselves up in their houses. They were scared out of their wits and already worrying about how they'd survive the difficult months ahead. Others had braved the streets and were guzzling liquor in some of the town's countless taverns toasting the bravest smuggler they'd ever known. Only a stone's throw away, in the local church, the vicar was using his sermon to pay his final respects to the town's young friend whilst his congregation wept in the pews.

The majority of Jacob's hundred or so strong gang of smugglers had fled Deal town. A handful of safe-houses where smuggled merchandise was stored had been raided by the soldiery, ordered by the venal Cecil to burn them to the ground. Jacob Swift had safe locations littered throughout the Kent countryside all the way to the city of London, and many of them survived. Over the years his men had found shelter at such places during their long trips 'running' cargoes. Though now empty-handed, the men scattered to these refuges. They were wanted men but they still stood a fair chance of escape, unlike Jacob Swift's most ruthless enforcer who had already been captured.

The fearless man that locals knew only as Thomas was kneeling on rotting straw in a filthy prison cell at the local barracks. Jacob's close friend and bodyguard was as tough as they came. As a child he'd been an orphan and had been sold to a cotton mill where he'd been tortured on a daily basis. In the end he'd managed to escape and flee London, but the damage had been done. The orphan was an empty shell barely able to feel any emotion, and completely fearless. Thomas was short in height, but made up for that with his brawny physique. After years and years of carrying heavy tunb of brandy his wide shoulders rippled with muscles.

Hearing a clink Thomas turned and watched his cell door open and Blackheath enter. His escort of several soldiers remained in the doorway. Reflexively, Thomas pulled on the chains that fastened both of his arms to the walls with all his might, but they held firm. The politician watched with a smirk on his face until Thomas gave up and stared his captor in the eyes.

"The mighty Thomas. They say you've killed countless men with your bare hands. You know what I want, don't you?" the visitor asked. Thomas merely grunted in reply.

"Will you tell me where you hid it? And save yourself the agonising pain that's to come?" Blackheath asked. Thomas shook his head.

Cecil Blackheath smiled. He was a sadist and over the years he'd tortured many men.

"Oh, you'll tell me in the end!" he said, turning to the soldiers in the doorway.

"Get me the rest of Jacob Swift's gang, in particular his father. Let's see if that old fisherman is as tough as you," he said, turning to Thomas who gritted his teeth in anger and tried desperately to break free of the chains binding his arms.

"The local magistrate has already informed us of Swift senior's address, so off you go!" Blackheath ordered, before laughing evilly.

Chapter Seven

A short while later two soldiers reached the townhouse where Jacob Swift's father lived. The old man had spent a lifetime fishing the English Channel before ill health had forced his retirement. Stepping forward one of the soldiers banged hard on the door before he stepped back and gripped the rifle in his hands. Along the street several tough looking men stood glaring at the soldiers in their bright red uniforms. Like most of the town, they knew who lived in the house the soldiers were visiting, and in common with their fellow townsfolk they were totally loyal to Jacob Swift, whether he was dead or alive.

The townhouse's door slowly opened and one of the soldiers wasted no time barging in, grabbing Benjamin Swift by the collar, and pulling him into the street where the old man staggered forward and fell to the ground.

The onlookers had seen enough and rushed forward ready to attack the soldiers, but one of the soldiers spun round and hit the first of the pair with the butt of his rifle, knocking him down. Then he levelled his rifle at the other men who stopped in their tracks and glared at the soldiers shackling Benjamin's hands and feet.

"This isn't right. That man's never smuggled a cargo in his life!" one man shouted at the soldiers who simply shrugged.

"If you want to live to see tomorrow you'll get moving," the soldier told his prisoner as the first local got to his feet and helped his friend do the same. A cord was tied around the chains on Jacob's father's wrists and the soldiers swiftly mounted on their horses. They then began to trot through the town while Benny Swift staggered behind them trying to keep up. Occasionally he would fall to his knees but these soldiers of the crown had no sympathy for the father of the country's most notorious smuggler.

Benjamin Swift was dragged through the streets in front of most of the town who stared in shock knowing the old fisherman was as innocent as they came. Benny himself had never felt so humiliated in his entire life.

Eventually the town fell away and the soldiers reached a copse where they paused for a moment to rest their horses. Benny collapsed to his knees struggling to catch his breath as the soldiers dismounted. One of them spat at Benjamin and half pushed half kicked him, leaving him on his side lying in the dirt and struggling to breathe, whilst both soldiers stood mocking him.

Benjamin tried simply to catch his breath which was often a difficult task for the old fisherman, who'd barely survived a case of pneumonia a few years earlier. Benny cared little for himself, the only thing that mattered was his only son Jacob, and he wondered where he was and whether he was safe.

"You're scum! Like the rest of that rat's nest of a town," one of the soldiers shouted at him. Lying on his back Benny stared at the soldiers whose red uniforms made them stand out against the green backdrop of trees and vegetation, and then he saw something among the trees directly behind the soldiers: and he knew someone was about to die.

Hidden in the foliage and slowly creeping towards the group was a man he recognised. The man was tall and incredibly thin, but it was his bushy ginger beard that had given him away. Benjamin lay there feeling humiliated as he rubbed the soldiers' spit off his face, but he could see the crazy look in Alfred Bicks' eyes even when the man was half a dozen paces away, and suddenly the only feeling he had towards the soldiers was pity. Both soldiers had been well trained, but their training was nothing in comparison to Alfie's whose childhood living on the streets had prepared him for a life of battling for survival.

"Hello," Alfie finally said warmly, and as both men turned suddenly towards him he lashed out with the dagger he carried everywhere. The first of the pair received a slash to the throat that sent him backwards where he stood clutching his neck, and, from the expression on his face, he was wondering how to stop the sudden flow of blood that was pouring out between his fingers. The other soldier stood watching in horror before he heard a branch break at his side and he turned to face Jim Robson.

Jacob Swift's oldest friend was built like a barn door and very handy with his fists. The first punch he threw knocked the soldier onto his back. Jim quickly leapt onto his foe pinning him to the ground where he proceeded to strangle the man. Alfred Bicks and Benny Swift watched in silence, the only sounds those coming from the woodland animals and the horses that were still breathing heavily.

Suddenly Benny snapped into action and sprang forward to stop the murder, but Alfie grabbed the old fisherman before he could interfere. Clutching him tightly Alfie muttered just a few words, but they were enough.

"I'm sorry, Benny, but Jacob's dead," he said, and the old fisherman collapsed to the ground in shock. He neither cried nor made any other sound as he watched his son's school friend strangle the last vestige of life out of the soldier. Eventually Jim looked up at Alfie and then over at Benny, offering his condolences too. Both Alfie and Jim had tears in their eyes as they watched Benny Swift's entire world crash. The old fisherman who had taught his son everything he knew about the English Channel and its treacherous sandbanks was completely silent. He knelt on the muddy ground and stared towards the treeline in a daze.

"We need to move, and now," Alfie ordered. Jim nodded and helped Benjamin Swift to his feet.

"Listen to me, Benny," Alfie shouted, pulling the fisherman out of his trance. "We need to make speed towards London. There is a safe-house that Blackheath and his soldiers definitely don't know about. We need to reach there by nightfall. Understand?"

Benjamin Swift just stared at Alfie. The news of his son's death had been so profound a shock that Alfie took him by the hand as the strange looking trio made their way through the woods to where Alfie and Jim's horses were tethered. They had considered stealing one of the soldier's horses for Benny, but had concluded that the fisherman wasn't in a fit state to ride by himself. Instead Alfie pulled him up onto his mare, and for the rest of that day the old man didn't say a word as they galloped at full pace, trying to put as much distance between them and the cobbled streets of Deal as possible.

Hours later they finally reached the safe-house which was in the country only a dozen or so miles from the banks of the River Thames in London. Much to the smugglers' relief they were greeted by a handful of friendly faces. One of these belonged to a man named Carp, a long standing friend of Alfie Bicks. The pair had worked side by side for many years in the smuggling trade. Carp had been responsible for landing the smuggled goods and organising the teams that transported the contraband off the beaches and into the safe-houses. That evening a few dozen men, the remnants of the greatest smuggling gang the country would ever see, sat around a small fire contemplating their futures. They were all scared knowing that they needed to flee the country or face the gallows. None of them could have guessed that an adventure lay before them.

Chapter Eight

own on the Kent coast in the town of Deal Cecil Blackheath was busy torturing Thomas. The former Civil Servant had spent six months of his life in India, a country he despised and considered filthy. Cecil had coped for one reason only: he knew the country held great treasures that were there for the taking.

Originally he'd been dispatched to India on diplomatic business to calm the trouble brewing between local factions who opposed the East India Company and British colonisation. Cecil Blackheath was a greedy man, as his corpulent figure suggested. Instead of concentrating on the task at hand and working to secure peace on behalf of the British Government, he plotted to steal a priceless ruby the size of a man's fist from a temple where it was worshipped by the poverty stricken Indian people.

Blackheath had succeeded in the theft, but he was as sly as they came and had decided not to run the risk of smuggling the stone back to England himself, a mistake he was now cursing himself for. Instead he'd made a deal with a ship's captain to transport the ruby: unfortunately when the ship had anchored off the Kentish downs it had been raided by thieves and the priceless ruby had been stolen.

Blackheath gritted his teeth in anger as he waved a red hot poker in the smuggler's face.

"I know that my ruby was given to Jacob and I know he gave it to you to hide," he said, as the smuggler stared silently at the small cell's brick walls. As usual, Thomas displayed absolutely no emotion, which was already annoying Blackheath.

"What I don't know is where you hid it, and you will tell me," Blackheath promised as he held the poker close to Thomas' face. Suddenly a sharp knock on the cell door interrupted him and Blackheath glanced up as a soldier entered.

"Sir, the local magistrate is here to see you. He says it's of the utmost importance," the soldier said, grimacing at the smell of burnt flesh and trying not to stare at the smuggler shackled to a chair whose bare torso was already covered in burn marks and blood.

The politician smiled and put the poker back down into the fire before looking Thomas in the eyes. "I'll be back shortly, and we'll start where we left off," he promised as he marched out of the cell and down a dingy corridor into the small office at the end.

The town's local Magistrate, another corrupt official named Theodore Rawlings, who formerly had been happy to take bribes off the young smuggler Jacob Swift, looked up and nodded a very nervous greeting to Blackheath.

"Where are the soldiers I sent to collect Jacob's father, Magistrate?" Blackheath demanded, and Theodore Rawlings looked down at the floor and cleared his throat.

"I'm afraid their bodies were found earlier this evening in some woodland a short distance from here. I'm confident they were killed by Jacob's men," the Magistrate was saying, but he was cut short as Cecil Blackheath screamed in anger and with one swipe of his arm cleared everything off the desk in front of him, most of which smashed on the floor.

"I'm sure we have nothing to worry about, Mr Blackheath, we have Thomas in there. He is one of Jacob's most trusted men. There is little he doesn't know about Jacob Swift's criminal empire. I'm sure given the right motivation he will tell you exactly what you want to know."

Cecil Blackheath glared at the Magistrate. He was beginning to realise that he had made a grave mistake in killing Jacob Swift. The man craved his ruby and would kill anyone to get his chubby hands back on it. Taking a deep breath, Blackheath tried to calm himself down before addressing the Magistrate.

"That thing in there," he spat out, pointing in the direction of Thomas' cell, "is barely even human. I've already spent hours torturing him and he hasn't given up a thing. Now you listen to me, Rawlings! I killed Jacob Swift as you wanted, but I have yet to get my end of the bargain, so I suggest you take as many soldiers as you like and start rounding up the rest of Jacob's gang. Find out where they're hiding and capture them. I'll kill them all if I need to. Now get the hell out of my sight!"

Theodore Rawlings was looking down at the floor and didn't even glance up as he sheepishly made his way out of the office. Once he'd left, Blackheath took a few deep breaths. "Don't worry, you'll get it back," he told himself before strolling back into the small cell.

The sadist stared at Thomas and the wounds that already covered most of his bulky torso for a long moment. "So, where is my ruby?" he demanded as he pulled on thick gloves and retrieved the poker from the brazier in the corner of the room, admiring its red point. Thomas simply grunted and suddenly anger overcame Cecil Blackheath, driving him to step forward and press the poker against the skin on the smuggler's back. Thomas howled in pain and bucked in the chair struggling with all of his might to break the shackles which held him firmly.

"Oh you'll tell me in the end! They always do," the torturer promised.

Chapter Nine

The safe-house where the smugglers were hiding out was an old barn with a thatched roof hidden in a small patch of woodland, miles from any village. The previous day when the men had arrived they were exhausted both physically and mentally, and grateful to still have their freedom.

After a long night drinking from one of the barrels of brandy that had not been delivered yet and reminiscing about their lost friend Jacob Swift, the men fell into a deep slumber. They were convinced that this safe house was not known to any enemies and didn't even post a guard. They slept as the sun made its first appearance on the horizon and were still asleep an hour later as the barn was completely surrounded by a small army carrying the finest firearms available.

The soldiers knew that time was of the essence and a siege scenario needed to be avoided at all costs, however, much to the soldier's amazement, they found the barn door had been left unlocked allowing them to very slowly and silently pull the door open, creep in and take up positions.

The soldiers had been briefed that the men wouldn't go silently and each man didn't doubt it as they clutched their weapons and waited for the first to stir out of slumber. Every soldier present had heard about Jacob Swift and his gang, and were all too aware of what the smugglers were capable of. Nobody was underestimating these men even if they were sleeping off their grog: one of the soldiers leant forward and prodded Alfie Bicks in the face with the sharp end of the bayonet fixed to his rifle.

The red headed smuggler opened his eyes and simply stared at the scene in front of him without uttering a word. The man who had a vicious reputation for using the small dagger he carried everywhere glanced from the end of the rifle in his face to the soldier carrying it and then around the barn at the other soldiers, before deciding that he wasn't in a position to put up any resistance. Alfie Bicks knew that, unlike many of his friends who were still asleep on the barn's cold and hard floor, he faced certain death. Only a day earlier he'd murdered a soldier of the crown. If Alfie had been alone in the barn he'd have gone out with a fight, but he wasn't willing to get his friends, whose biggest crime was running smuggled cargoes, killed in the process.

Time passed slower than at any other moment in Alfie's entire life and his mind raced with a thousand questions as he watched his fellow smugglers awake to find themselves in exactly the same predicament. Alfie Bicks knew the group of smugglers hadn't stood a chance. Their captors had moved in stealthily and were very well trained. The red headed smuggler wondered how they'd discovered the safe-house so quickly, and much to his frustration came up with no answers.

"Nobody move a muscle and you won't get hurt!" one of the soldiers ordered, as one of his colleagues began collecting the smuggler's weapons strewn across the barn floor. The smugglers were then shackled one at a time and dragged outside where they all knelt on the dirt squinting from the bright morning sunshine. Most men would have been shaking with fear at the thought of facing the noose, but the smugglers had lived very different lives where danger was lurking at every turn.

As Alfred Bicks was dragged out of the barn he glanced over at Jim Robson who was climbing to his feet. Jim was in his early twenties and had faced the gallows before. Several years earlier he'd come so close to death he had experienced a noose around his neck, but Jacob Swift had arrived with his own private army and freed him. Jim knew that wasn't going to happen this time.

Turning and glancing over at Benjamin Swift, Alfie could see the old man was still completely lost in a world of his own, and his heart went out to him. The other men gathered had broken the law smuggling goods into the country and avoiding the exorbitant tax. Benny Swift had been arrested simply for who his son was. Alfie watched the old fisherman, and couldn't help but wonder about the stories Billy Bates had told him many years before.

Suddenly several carts arrived, looking like cages on wheels. Still groggy from the brandy he'd consumed late into the night Alfie squinted in the daylight as he turned to one of the soldiers.

"Are we due to hang in Deal?" he asked, "If I'm going to die somewhere I'd like it to be there."

"You'll never see that town again. You're headed for London," was the answer he got. Before Alfie could reply a sack was pulled over his head and fastened around his neck. He struggled and tried to break free but the shackles binding his hands and feet held firm. He was thrown into the back of one of the cages where he fell to the floor and, from what he could hear, his friends were being treated in a similar fashion. Alfie Bicks lay there breathing heavily as the horses began to trot away, pulling the prisoners towards their meeting with destiny.

Chapter Ten

Following his secret meeting at the Somerset Club with his spy-master friend and the Royal Navy's 1st Sea Lord, Philip Saunders had never worked harder. A thousand things needed to be done in order to ready his squadron for sail.

Saunders' most difficult task had been selecting the captains and crews to sail under his command. The Admiral wasn't short of names. Over the years he'd sailed countless missions and earned a reputation as a fair man. Whilst other captains had ruled their ships with an iron fist via routine floggings on deck, and regular hangings from the yardarm, Saunders had ruled through fairness, discipline, and above all else great leadership. After long stints at sea in the past many men had bought him gifts and begged to join him on his next voyage. Individuals entered service in the Navy via different routes. Some volunteered, some were forced in by press gangs, others were 'quota men', miscreants sent to sea as sentenced by a Magistrate. The Admiral knew he had to choose wisely, and selected as many volunteers as he could, keeping numbers of both quota men and pressed sailors as low as possible. This mission was the most important the Admiral had ever commanded, and mutiny or desertion were complications he couldn't afford. The one element Admiral Saunders had on his side was the prospect of prize money, which was every sailor's dream and an effective way to control a crew at sea.

Following the secret meeting the Royal Navy had burst into action as orders had been issued and thousands upon thousands of sailors and shore personnel had begun the huge task of readying the half dozen ships for sail, embarking on one of the longest and most dangerous voyages possible. None of the personnel involved knew anything about the mission or the route they would take. Even the captains and officers were left in the dark partly for fear of information reaching enemy agents, but mainly to avoid the probable panic once Alfred Mudd's name was mentioned. Cape Horn at the tip of South America was one of the most dangerous seas on earth, where swells of seventy feet or more were common and outcrops of rocks broke the surface and consigned sailors to the icy deep. Every sailor knew Cape Horn was a graveyard for ships, a nightmarish seascape where many sailors had tried and failed disastrously to navigate her, leaving only wreckage as a reminder of the lives lost.

Admiral Saunders stood on the balcony of his private quarters and watched the men who would work under his command for the next year or so loading the vessels with mighty winches. He noted the good spirits amongst them and knew he had made the right decision in leaving them blissfully ignorant of the dangerous journey that lay ahead.

Every division of the navy was pulling their weight. The victualing board personnel, whose role it was to organise and load the food on board each ship, were working tirelessly moving tons upon tons of biscuit, salted meats, cheeses, oatmeal, sugar, beer and countless other commodities from dozens of wharves along the Thames. Meanwhile the ordinance board prepared cannon, powder, shot and muskets to arm the squadron.

The Royal Navy base appeared to be in chaos as sailors rushed from pillar to post. Saunders was feeling exhausted but as he watched these legions of his countrymen working like ants for the good of the country he felt a deep sense of pride. Further, as his mind turned to the pirate Captain's treasure and the adventure that lay ahead, his heart raced with excitement, butterflies flew in his stomach, and the exhaustion faded in to the background.

He found himself thinking of his father, and the tale his father had told him. He remembered with vivid clarity the conversation they'd had after hearing of the horrific way Alfred Mudd had been treated by his fellow navy men on the island of Antigua a lifetime ago. He recalled his father looking down at him and ruffling his hair and muttering "Wouldn't any man want revenge?"

Suddenly a cold wind blew pulling Saunders out of his thoughts. He stood on his balcony staring at the countless masts of ships inhabiting the docks and his mind began to drift once again, this time to his new enemy: the traitor and coward Louis Francis, the man Alfred Mudd had spent a lifetime dreaming of killing, and Saunders vowed his own revenge on Francis.

Earlier that day the young Admiral had met secretly with members of the government and many of the ruling elite. The meetings had confirmed what Saunders felt in his heart. The betrayal of Louis Francis and his assistance to the French Navy posed an incredibly serious threat to the future of Great Britain. The wealthy were more frightened than he'd imagined and Saunders thought he knew why. The name Alfred Mudd sent shivers down people's spines. The little boy who'd listened to stories about the most ruthless pirate on earth wasn't alone: everyone had heard them.

Alfred Mudd posed a risk no more, but the man had left a deadly legacy. The pirate had spent a lifetime plundering ships and building up an immense treasure hoard and nobody doubted it. Many of the rich and powerful had worked equally hard covering up the pirate's attacks. The government had struggled to maintain the image of Great Britain having the most powerful navy on earth.

The rich and powerful had absolutely no doubt about the massive wealth Captain Mudd had accumulated. Over the years the pirate had often raided merchant ships and had cost them all one way or another. If the treasure remained buried the British Government were confident the Royal Navy would eventually defeat the French in Europe. That same treasure in the hands of the French was a different story entirely. The power distribution on the continent would slowly change as the French expanded their fleet, a fleet that would dominate the seas for years to come. Many current allies would turn against Britain and side with the French. Saunders had no doubt that within a decade France would control the whole of Europe.

Thankfully Admiral Saunders didn't have long to dwell on the difficult situation the country faced. His commanding officer, Sir Robert Burns, had ordered the squadron to leave as soon as possible. The French, under the guidance of Louis Francis, had already despatched their ships and would be well into the Atlantic; it was of the utmost importance to attack that lead. The spy-master Rupert Knightly had also warned that the French would of course have their own spies watching the English Channel. Even a small squadron would arouse suspicion. The six ships were to leave individually and re-group in the Atlantic away from prying eyes.

The first ship to raise anchor and sail out of the Royal Navy docks was the HMS Orion, a twin decked seventy-four gunner with a crew of nearly six hundred hand-picked and experienced sailors. As it navigated its huge bulk along the Thames making for the Estuary, Admiral Saunders felt a rush of excitement through his bones. The next ship was the second seventy-four gunner, the HMS Illustrious, which was followed by HMS Brunswick. Admiral Saunders was aboard the last ship to leave Deptford. The HMS Romulus was a frigate, a single decked ship that carried thirty-six cannon and was designed with speed in mind. Romulus was due to dock at the Royal Dockyards at Chatham early the next day in order to collect further crew members, and sail out alongside her sister ship, the frigate HMS Sandown.

Once the Romulus had raised anchor Admiral Saunders took his position on deck and watched the familiar sights of London drift astern. He thought of Louis Francis and what the man had done on Antigua all those years ago, and hoped the traitor would fail and he would triumph, and prayed the French force would be small in number. Fantasising about the adventure that was to come, Admiral Saunders hoped for King and Country that the mission would succeed, but the boy who had followed his father into the Royal Navy couldn't have imagined the dangers that lay ahead.

Chapter Eleven

lfred Bicks, Jim Robson, Benny Swift, Carp and another dozen of Jacob Swift's men experienced hell on earth after leaving the safe-house that morning. Some of their hangovers had been pretty bad prior to being blindfolded and thrown into the back of the caged wagons, and they only got worse as they bumped around crashing into each other as the wagons were hauled towards the River Thames. Alfie Bicks heard his good friend Jim Robson pleading for answers. Jacob Swift's young enforcer had always looked up to Alfie Bicks, but as Alfie lay on the wagon floor he couldn't find the right words to put his young friend at ease. Like Benjamin Swift, shackled and blindfolded at his side, Alfie was in a state of shock. The tall red headed smuggler who'd spent a lifetime living on the wrong side of the law and watching his back had finally been caught.

Feeling defeated as he lay there in the back of the wagon, sure that he'd be dead within a week, his mind wandered to the huge red ruby Jacob's gang had found in the hands of a thief only a few days earlier and he wished from the bottom of his heart that Jacob and his gang had never come into contact with it.

"They'll kill me, just like Jacob… hell, that politician will kill us all!" Alfie muttered to himself, as he closed his eyes and tried to sleep.

He awoke with a thud a short time later. Alfie didn't quite know how long he'd been asleep, but judging by his thumping headache and relentless hangover from the several pints of brandy he'd consumed the night before it hadn't been long. He could hear his fellow smugglers shouting, questioning their captors, and for the first time since being thrown in the back of the cage he found some words, "Men, we need to remain calm," he advised. "We've been caught, and caught proper. Whatever will be, will be."

Alfie Bicks concentrated on listening in an attempt to obtain some answers to the many questions rattling through his mind and could hear sobbing, but he could also hear something else. He could hear the wind blowing and waves lapping against the shore. Turning his head he felt the rush of air blowing through gaps in the sack fastened over his head. Alfie also smelt salt in the air, and for a moment his heart rose as he thought of his home town, but then he remembered the soldier's remark that he'd never see Deal again and his heart sank lower than it had ever been before.

Alfie was sure he knew where they were. The cages had finally reached their final destination, the dreaded Tower of London. The tower itself was a fortress nestled next to the Thames in the heart of London. Letting out a lungful of salty air Alfie accepted his fate. If it hadn't been for Billy Bates who'd taken him in off the streets many years before and employed him in his prospering smuggling network, Alfie Bicks wouldn't have survived to adulthood. The smuggler knew this all too well, and despite the situation he now found himself in felt thankful to have had the life he'd had.

"Alfred Bicks, for what it's worth, I wouldn't want to die next to any other man, it's been an honour to serve by your side!" he heard his good friend Carp shout with emotion in his voice and suddenly tears ran down Alfie's cheeks. He tried to reply, but for the first time in his life he found himself so caught up in his own emotions he could not answer.

Suddenly a firm hand grabbed his shoulder and began pulling him out of the cage. He offered no resistance and staggered forward taking small slow steps due to the shackles binding his feet. As he was steered from left to right almost as if he was in a maze, Alfie wondered if they were leading him straight to his death. How many steps did he have left before he'd feel the noose around his neck? Would they remove the sack over his head and let him see the world for one last time before his life came to an end?

He was still considering these questions five minutes later as he was led, still blindfolded, into a small cell. Hearing the voices of several of his companions Alfie realized his friends were close by and felt a ripple of relief. A moment later he felt the shackles binding his hands being fastened to a long bar, and the ones on his feet being removed. Suddenly the sack covering his head was pulled free. The smuggler squinted his eyes in anticipation of daylight, but the room he was in was very dark. Alfie could only just make out his friends by his side, also chained to the bar that ran the length of the room. He breathed a sigh of relief as he felt the walls and realized that they were made of wood, and not stone.

"Well, at least we're not in the Tower," he muttered, wondering if this option was any better.

"Alfie, what's going on? Where are we?" Jim Robson demanded. Turning to the young man who was barely in his twenties though built like a barn door, he noted the look of fear on his face.

"The walls are wooden, we're on a ship," he managed. Jim Robson's look of fear suddenly grew to a look of absolute terror as he glanced around the cramped space the smugglers occupied.

"We're aboard a slave ship, aren't we? They're going to sail us to the colonies for a life of hard labour, aren't they?" Jim Robson asked, his face turning a shade paler. Alfie's heart sank as he looked at his friend.

"I'm afraid so," he muttered, and Jim Robson slid to the floor of the cell and broke down in tears.

Chapter Twelve

B ack at the town's barracks the toughest of all of Jacob Swift's enforcers was slumped in a chair. If it hadn't been for the shackles binding his hands and feet he would have slipped and landed in a heap on the cell's filthy floor many hours before. Thomas was barely conscious now. Every few seconds his head jerked up from where it slumped on his chest, as if he was awaking from a bad dream, but his worst nightmare had turned into reality for the man who, as a young boy, had fled similar conditions in another lifetime at the Whitegate Cotton Mill.

Cecil Blackheath stared at the object in front of him wearing an expression somewhere between disgust and amazement, wondering how it was even possible for him to still be alive. The politician, who only cared about his precious ruby, had tried every method in his torture arsenal to get the tough smuggler to talk. Now Thomas' mighty body was covered from head to toe in slashes and burn marks. Blood had poured from the open wounds and mixed with the cell's grime to produce a dark red substance that stained the chair and most of the floor around him.

The politician felt furious, angrier than he'd ever felt in his life, but he knew it wasn't just anger. Deep down Cecil Blackheath felt scared, and that fear made him even angrier. In the pit of his stomach the politician knew that the man in front of him offered the only solution to finding his missing ruby, the priceless gem he'd bet his happy and financially glorious retirement on. Now he realised how stupid he'd been executing Jacob Swift so casually whilst on board Saunders' HMS Windsor. Blackheath had been certain that

Jacob's tough bodyguard knew the location of his ruby, and had mistakenly assumed that he'd talk. Up until now he'd believed that men were all the same. Looking at Thomas who had endured days upon days of torture he now knew they weren't.

Feeling the anger rising within him to the point when he thought he was going to explode Blackheath stepped forward and screamed at his victim "How? How can you deal with such pain?"

As Thomas mumbled a reply that was barely audible Blackheath grabbed the enforcers head and lifted it off his chest so that he could stare the man in the eyes. Thomas returned the politician's gaze for a moment, and in that exchange the politician saw not an ounce of fear on the smuggler's bruised and bloody face and it scared Blackheath more than anything he'd ever previously seen.

Suddenly Cecil Blackheath felt a strong urge to let go of the smuggler and flee. He wanted to run as far from the filthy dungeon-like cell as he could. To forget the ruby and everything that went with it.

"This is my destiny," Thomas finally muttered, catching the politician's attention once more. As blood poured from his mouth he said, "I was prepared for this from a very young age."

Cecil Blackheath ground his teeth furiously and let out a deep breath, attempting to calm himself. "Why don't you just tell me where the ruby is and end this now?" he demanded.

By this time Thomas was drifting in and out of consciousness, but he was still fighting.

"A long time ago somebody saved me. He offered me a hot meal, a bed and something I never thought possible, he offered me a life," Thomas said, pausing as more blood gushed from his mouth. Cecil stared at the smuggler, shocked to learn that there was honour amongst thieves.

"He wanted nothing in return," Thomas continued, barely able to talk, "but I would have given him anything and everything. Betraying Jacob Swift would be betraying the only person I've ever considered family, the man who raised me, Billy Bates. I'd sooner live a lifetime of this torture than do that!" the smuggler finished, and, much to his tormentor's surprise, Thomas looked at him and actually managed to smile.

Suddenly the politician was overcome by his emotions. He let go of Thomas' head which dropped to his chest and stepped backwards, grabbing at the poker which had been his main torture device. Feeling anger like he'd never felt before, anger fuelled by fear, he lashed out and buried the poker deep in Thomas' chest. The smuggler struggled with all his might in a last ditch effort to break the shackles binding him, but Blackheath had dealt a fatal blow and after his body bucked for nearly a minute his head fell to his chest for the last time. Thomas was finally dead. The most ruthless man in Jacob Swift's smuggling empire, a man who had killed with his bare hands on countless occasions, had finally left the world and was now with his old friend Boseda and the man who had raised him, Billy Bates.

Cecil Blackheath screamed with frustration as anger overcame him and proceeded to smash everything within his grasp. His ruby was lost forever, or so he thought.

A short time later Blackheath left the cell, entering the corridor where two soldiers were waiting. Both men avoided eye contact with the politician. They'd been stationed outside the cell for nearly two days and had heard things they already wanted to forget. Instead they looked down at the floor nervously as they awaited new orders. The ruthless politician scared them, much more than any smugglers could.

"Take his body and dump it down in that town's streets. I want everyone to see him and to know the consequences for smuggling contraband!" he ordered, nodding towards the cell.

As the first soldier stepped forward through the doorway the colour drained from his face at the sight of Thomas' body and he struggled to compose himself. His colleague reacted in much the same way and it took a moment before the pair were able to begin removing the padlocks and chains fastening the dead smuggler's feet. Thankfully their red uniforms matched the colour of the blood that smeared over them as they grabbed hold of the body and struggled with all their strength to drag it outside and dump it in the back of a cart.

Neither soldier was looking forward to the next stage of the task. Both men had heard of the man whose body they were about to dump: he was a legend in the town's underworld. They quickly mounted their horses and galloped towards the town, eager to get rid of the body before the locals rallied and punished them for the insane politician's action.

A short time later they reached the town's main thoroughfare, receiving glares from dozens of shady looking individuals even before their horses slowed to a stop. Wasting no time they threw the body from the cart where it landed with a dull thud on the cobbles. Then they were gone, galloping out of the town as fast as they could.

The locals crowded around in shocked silence staring at the body of the man who had protected their leader Jacob Swift, and Billy Bates before him. Many had known the quiet and emotionless man for many years. They stood in silence taking it in. Thomas' body reinforced one thing for them all; the smuggling trade had finally come to an end in the town and nobody knew how they'd manage to feed their families in the tough years that lay ahead.

It was the Reverend of the local church who finally broke the silence as he stepped forward and glanced over at a local man he knew had worked for 'The Boy'.

"Take the body to the church. We'll give him the burial he deserves," the Reverend ordered, as Michael Swan and several other smugglers wiped tears from their eyes.

Late the next day Cecil Blackheath arrived back at his townhouse in Westminster. Feeling exhausted both physically and mentally and still distraught from the loss of his priceless gem, the politician thought that life couldn't get any worse, but he was very wrong. Climbing out of the coach he didn't waste time tipping the driver who sneered in disgust and trundled off. Marching through his front garden he unlocked the front door and strolled through his house, which was luxuriously decorated, at the expense of luckless souls who at some stage of their lives had experienced the misfortune of dealing with him. Kicking off his shoes he poured a generous brandy from a crystal decanter to console himself, before striking a match to light a lantern and that was the moment when Cecil Blackheath's circumstances took a significant turn for the worse.

The light from the lantern illuminated the room and suddenly the politician's heart missed a beat. Standing in the shadows were three tough looking men. Frozen to the spot in fear he wondered how they'd broken into his house and why they hadn't stripped it bare in his absence. Then suddenly he found his voice and with it all the fury and anger he'd felt the day before. "How dare you!" he screamed at the men, "Do you have any idea who I am? I'm a Minister of the Government! I'll have you all face the noose for this outrage!" he screamed.

In the moment of silence that followed he heard someone chuckle behind him: he spun around and once again froze, having recognised the chuckling man immediately. The colour drained from his face and the brandy glass slipped from his hand and shattered on the marble floor at his feet.

Now Cecil Blackheath was absolutely terrified, far more scared than he'd been at any stage the previous day. "You can't do this to me," the politician managed to say, but it was no longer a shout. Now it was a mere whimper.

"Do you know who I am?" the newcomer asked and Blackheath nodded looking as pale as milk.

"You're Rupert Knightly," he finally mumbled, and the spymaster chuckled again.

"Then surely you know that I can do this to anyone," he stated matter-of-factly before turning to his thugs. "Clap him in irons," he ordered before adjusting his spectacles.

Wasting no time the men quickly pulled out shackles and fastened the greedy politician's arms and legs as he stood speechless.

"So, where is the ruby?" Rupert Knightly asked, and tears began to pour down Blackheath's face as his shoulders shuddered. The spymaster watched with interest but no sympathy, and smiled.

"Don't worry: you'll tell me everything I want to know given the right incentives. People always break in the end," Knightly promised. A moment later, as the thugs dragged the terrified man out of the townhouse's rear entrance all Cecil Blackheath could think of was Thomas, the smuggler he'd tortured to death; and the politician thought of Knightley's words and knew that in fact some people never broke. Would he?

Chapter Thirteen

The Atlantic Ocean

The French were now sailing in convoy, and making good progress on their hunt for the dead pirate's treasure. The squadron had left the Portuguese coast in their wake and were approaching North Africa. The seas were choppy and the squadron's flagship Severe climbed yet another wave and dropped into the following trough. An eerie scream of resistance followed as the force of the ocean shook the ship's timbers.

Earlier that day Louis Francis, the man who was leading the French on their round the world treasure hunt, had stood on the Severe's quarter-deck watching as an additional four warships had sailed through the Straits of Gibraltar to join his squadron. The man had sniggered to himself, knowing that within months he'd finally get the last laugh over his lifelong nemesis.

Seated in his private cabin Francis watched the fine brandy in the glass he was clutching slosh from side to side, and he dreamed. The traitorous British Navy officer had secretly worked for his mother's homeland for many, many years, passing information about the British navy to their greatest enemy, the French. Thinking back on his life Louis knew that the events on Antigua all those years ago had changed the course of his life just as much as they had Alfred Mudd's. Even thinking Mudd's name frustrated him. Once the young pirate had started openly attacking British navy ships, word had soon spread about what Louis and his friends had done to provoke him. His father had silenced the majority of murmurs within the Royal Navy, but people had heard the story. He always knew, by the way his colleagues had glanced away from him and avoided his eye contact. As the years trickled on and Captain Mudd continued to assail British navy ships the feeling just got worse and worse. Hatred had seeped into the cracks in Louis Francis' heart and had grown. Slowly he began to secretly despise his British countrymen as he spent long periods in France on behalf of the British Navy.

The common thief he'd set out to punish slowly became a living legend as he continued his ruthless campaign, and the more people talked of Captain Mudd, the more Louis Francis believed they talked about him. In his imagination they laughed and sneered at him. The aristocratic young man felt that the blame had fallen at his feet. Nobody in the British Navy had ever pointed the finger in his direction, or even mentioned the island of Antigua, but they didn't need to, it was written all over their faces.

Over time Louis Francis began to hate his English compatriots more than he hated the pirate. Eventually the disgruntled man faced the conflict in his loyalties. In the end it was simple: with his father in England, a drunk of a man who he despised, or with his mother, who had retired to her homeland, France. The decision was simple, and though Louis Francis didn't realise it at the time it was driven solely by revenge. Siding with the French allowed him to punish the men he thought mocked him, the British Navy.

Being as cunning as he was it didn't take him long to negotiate himself into a lucrative position playing double agent in France. Years passed as he traded intelligence: from fleet movements to rumours in the city of London, convincing himself that he was best positioned within Europe. He also turned down any mission which might take him towards a showdown with Alfred Mudd. Over the years Louis Francis had heard on many occasions of the dreaded death list and the pirate's demand for revenge, and every time his enmity towards the English grew.

As Louis Francis sipped the fine French brandy and gripped the table in front of him while the ship rocked he smiled to himself. The pirate had steered the course of his life, but now he was dead, Francis would finally get the last laugh on Alfred Mudd.

A thousand or so nautical miles in his enemy's wake, Admiral Philip Saunders stood on the deck of his frigate the HMS Romulus under a night sky strewn with a thousand stars steering his ship and barking countless orders at his men. Saunders believed in leading by example and was always willing to get his hands dirty. Amongst the sailors he was held in high regards and was considered one of them, his attitude being vastly different to that of many of the navy's other admirals who had earned their standing through birth-right without ever proving their worth at sea.

The Romulus was sailing off the coast of Portugal now and was making good time. A few dozen ship's lengths ahead of her the HMS Orion was battling the ocean which in the last few hours had begun to chop up as the wind picked up. In the Romulus' wake was the HMS Illustrious. As the squadron's Commander and Admiral, Saunders had ordered the other ships to sail in close line astern once they'd left the French coast, an order that was conveyed through hoisted flags to the other two Captains who peered through telescopes aimed the HMS Romulus' way.

With the wind at his back Saunders watched the Orion rising and falling on the waves ahead and, at least for the time being, felt confident about the task at hand. The young Admiral knew that the French squadron was ahead, by how far exactly he was unsure, but with the weather gauge on his side it mattered not. The French wouldn't dare drop sail and engage him with the wind blowing in his favour which offered him peace of mind. The battle was still a long way off, but with every gust of wind it drew closer.

At his side stood his First Lieutenant, a man named Lucas, who was inclined to reminisce about adventures they'd shared at sea whilst sailing together in the West Indies. Many of the younger sailors on deck listened intently. Saunders let him talk, though he wasn't in the mood for stories. The young Admiral was still grieving the loss of his friend Jacob Swift, and was all too aware that the smuggler's men were locked up below his feet. He let out a deep sigh and stared up at the stars. He knew he couldn't put it off forever. Tomorrow he would have to face them. Saunders had known many of them for a long time and knew he'd have to handle them delicately. Alfred Bicks was a dangerous man, not to mention Jim Robson who, like his red headed friend, wouldn't hesitate to stick a knife in Saunders back given half the chance, but neither of them really scared the Admiral. Aboard ship Admiral Saunders held the powers of a king over his domain, and if punishment was needed he'd order it, as he would for any member of his crew. What Saunders dreaded was looking Jacob Swift's father in the eye. He just hoped the old fisherman would understand that he'd had no choice but to follow the crooked politician's orders.

Meanwhile, below decks in the HMS Romulus' brig the dozen or so smugglers were rattling around as the ship sailed through the choppy sea. Once she'd navigated out of Chatham Docks the brig's door had swung open and a number of handy looking sailors had entered the small room with muskets raised.

"Don't do anything rash," Alfie Bicks had warned both his criminal friends and the strangers bearing arms, but he needn't have worried. The sailors shuffled around and unchained the locks fastening the smugglers to the long bar that ran the length of the wall, then they produced hammocks for each man that they helped fasten to the brig's walls.

Finally the smugglers were offered some food and water which they devoured in a matter of minutes.

"You don't give me any problems, and I won't give you any," one of the sailors had warned the group, but it was Alfie Bicks he directed his attention to. The tall smuggler nodded in agreement before the sailors shuffled out of the brig and the solid timber door swung shut and was locked once more.

Nearly two days had passed since that first encounter, and they were going stir crazy in the cramped dark space, still none the wiser as to their circumstances. They struggled even to sleep, as every four hours bells would ring, orders were shouted and men would shuffle loudly on the decks above them. Many of the smugglers also suffered sea-sickness during those first few days.

The guards who brought them food, water and, once, some beer had offered no explanations, despite the smugglers' pleas. Some of the smugglers were lying in the hammocks rocking back and forth as the ship tackled waves. A few preferred the floor. Benjamin Swift, the man who'd been imprisoned for being a smuggler's father, still hadn't uttered a word since learning of his son's death. He had sat in the corner for most of the day, and had eaten very little even when Jim and Alfie had both encouraged him. Now he stood staring at a crack in the brig's ceiling which offered a glimpse of the night sky. Jim Robson was pacing up and down the small room in the dark.

"How long will it take to reach the colonies in Jamaica?" he asked Alfie. The smuggler who had assumed the role of leader stared up at his young friend from where he lay on the timber floor, twisting the end of his ginger beard.

"Jim, I have no idea. I've never been to sea. The closest I've ever come was crossing the English Channel on a handful of occasions with Bill," he said, and Jim Robson continued to pace.

"You know, I half expected to one day face the gallows, but never end up slaving in a colony!" Carp added as most of the other smugglers voiced their agreement.

"This ain't no slaver," a voice stated from somewhere in the dark and suddenly the brig fell silent as every man slowly turned towards Benjamin Swift. The old fisherman had turned his attention away from the crack in the brig's ceiling and was staring at the men who had worked for his son.

"How could you know that?" one of the smugglers asked, and Alfie Bicks turned to the man and silenced him immediately with one glance from those crazy eyes of his that even in the darkness were enough to scare most men.

"Because he is Benjamin Swift," the red head said, turning towards the old man "Oh, I've heard the stories, Benny. Billy Bates once told me he'd kill me himself if I ever repeated them, and I didn't doubt him. You know I spent most of my life looking up to Billy Bates," Alfie said, "and for what it's worth you're the only person that old rogue ever admired."

Silence fell once again and the ship rocked back and forth as most of the smugglers stared at the older man. A man whose once blonde hair had turned grey, but whose blue eyes still shone brightly.

"So, where are we headed Mr Swift?" one of the smugglers asked, and Benny glanced over at the man, barely making him out in the darkness.

"A number of things don't make any sense, and I don't claim to have all the answers. Firstly, why were we blindfolded before we reached the docks? Whatever ship this is they want us to believe it's a slaver, but a slaver it's not," Benny informed them.

The ship rocked back and forth once more and one of the smugglers finally asked the question most of them were wondering.

"Why not, Mr Swift?"

Benny rubbed at his chin for a moment and contemplated his words. "For a few reasons. Firstly this timber," he said knocking on the brig's solid wall, "It's too young. Slavers are more often than not old ships that are nearing the end of their life at sea. More importantly, this ship is sailing in a battle formation with another tall ship up ahead and one chasing the rear. If you look for long enough through this crack in the ceiling you'll see the tops of the masts, and that's before you consider those damn bells that ring through the night. Slavers don't keep watch with such precision."

The smugglers thought about these points before clambering over each other to peer through the gap, and then muttering agreement. Alfie Bicks didn't even bother staring through the gap for confirmation. Billy Bates had once told him that Benjamin Swift was the greatest navigator to ever work the English Channel and had been steering ships since he was a boy. If Benny said it was so, it was so.

"So, where are we headed, Benny?" Alfred Bicks finally asked and Benny turned towards him.

"I have no idea, but I've got a very bad feeling deep in my guts. I think we may have jumped out of the pan and into the fire and we are now heading straight into trouble," was all the old fisherman said, before climbing into his hammock and letting the brig fall into silence once more. Most of the men contemplated Benny's words with fear in their hearts, but not all. Sitting on the floor in the dark Alfred Bicks smiled that lunatic smile of his and caressed his beard, for the man thrived on trouble.

Chapter Fourteen

lfred Bicks woke suddenly as the brig's door swung open and the lanky smuggler leapt up from the floor startled. He didn't know how long he'd slept, but night had turned to day according to the small crack in the ceiling that now offered a flicker of sunlight. Alfie was at the end of his tether. He was a man of action and the last few days of pacing up and down and wondering had started to drive him crazy. Standing in the doorway were three guards, two of them holding muskets that were already raised in his direction. The other held a collection of shackles that wouldn't have looked out of place in a dungeon.

"It's time you got some fresh air in your lungs and sunlight on your skin," the guard in the middle said, before passing out the shackles.

"Hands and feet, and I hope I don't need to remind you of what'll happen if you give me any trouble," he warned, staring once again in Alfie's direction, "I can promise you that you won't swim far chained up!" he finished.

Most of the smugglers were watching Alfie. He had become their leader and his reaction would determine their own, but as soon as Alfred Bicks nodded his acquiescence they began shackling themselves. Finally the guards turned each prisoner around and placed thick hemp sacks over their heads, and nobody resisted. Eventually they were marched out one at a time up to the HMS Romulus' main deck where their shackles were fastened to a post, allowing them to wander only a few paces in each direction. The guards worked quickly and before long the smugglers, who numbered over a dozen, were all assembled – some kneeling, some lying, and some staggering on the deck as the ship rocked back and forth.

Finally the guards pulled the sacks off the smuggler's heads, leaving the men dazzled by the sunlight having spent days in the relative darkness below decks. Once they'd composed themselves they stood in absolute shock staring silently at the sight that greeted them. Some stared up towards the giant masts, surprised at the sheer number of sails that held firm in the wind, blocking some of the sun's rays and leaving an unusual pattern of shadows around their feet. Others were more interested in the huge ships sailing both ahead and behind the Romulus. Benjamin Swift, though, stared out towards the horizon observing nothing but bright blue sea as he breathed in a lungful of salty air. It had been several years since he'd been on the deck of a ship, and ever since he'd been a boy it had been the only place he'd felt truly at home.

It was Alfie Bicks who broke the silence as he stared at the uniforms of countless sailors that populated the deck carrying out their work.

"What is going on, Benny?" he asked, and at least half a minute passed before Benny replied "I have no idea, Alfie, but this is a Royal Navy warship if you haven't already figured that out for yourself," Benny warned, as he continued to gaze out towards the horizon.

"But why are we aboard it?" Alfie asked as he glanced at Jim, Carp and the other men, who were equally confused.

It was a voice behind him that replied, a voice he recognised immediately. Killing the owner of that voice had been Alfred Bicks' focus for many days now.

"Because this ship is the only place in this world I could protect you, and if you were not here you'd be dead already, or worse," the voice informed them.

The smuggler spun around and faced Admiral Saunders who stood half a dozen yards away surrounded by a handful of marines who regarded the smugglers with contempt. Immediately Alfie charged furiously towards the man who he believed had killed his friend and employer, but the chains quickly caught him and he fell to his knees on the deck.

"You betrayed us!" Jim Robson screamed at the Admiral, a scream that travelled across the decks and out into the open Atlantic. "You stood at his wedding alongside us…" Jacob's friend continued, but suddenly his words trailed off as he noticed the look of despair on Saunders' face and the tears welling in the corners of the Admiral's eyes.

"I couldn't save Jacob. Whatever he got involved in, it was out of my hands as soon as that politician arrived with written consent from our country's Prime Minister to use every available force to wipe out smuggling on the coast," Saunders said.

"How the hell did you know where to find us? Nobody knew of that safe-house!" Alfie asked and Admiral Saunders let out a sigh.

"Jacob told me it's location, and a great many other things. You know, Bicks, when it comes to wielding a knife you're the best there is, but you're far from the smartest man," the Admiral stated as he tried to compose himself.

"What the hell do you mean by that?" Alfie growled, climbing once again to his feet where he stood glaring at Saunders. The Admiral returned the stare for a long moment.

"Do you honestly think that an Admiral of the Royal Navy would allow a smuggler like Jacob Swift to bring contraband over the English Channel without receiving anything in return?" Saunders asked, and Bicks just stared in shock, forcing the Admiral to continue.

"Jacob was smarter than most. He worked for me as a spy. He provided vital information about French fleet movements and in return he smuggled with impunity," the

Admiral informed the smugglers, who mostly stood in shocked silence as Saunders' words found their mark.

After a long moment the Admiral found the courage to turn and face Benny Swift who had turned his attention away from the horizon and was now glaring his way.

"Your boy saved my life, and at the time I was nothing but a stranger in distress to him," Saunders mumbled as he looked down at the deck, avoiding Benny's eyes.

"I considered him a great friend," he finally managed to say as silence filled the deck, and the only sound came from the wind as it whistled through the sails above them.

"You lie!" Bicks finally shouted, breaking the silence, but it was Benny Swift who surprisingly spoke up in Saunders' defence.

"He doesn't. My son worked as a spy in return for immunity. This I promise is true," Benny said as he stared at the tough looking group of men.

"But why?" Jim Robson asked and Benny Swift's calm façade finally slipped as anger flared within him and tears rolled down his face.

"To protect you, Jim!" he shouted, "and you, Alfie! My son risked everything to protect the people he cared about! He risked everything to feed the hungry and clothe the poor of our town. That boy would have risked it all again given half the chance. He was the most selfless person I've ever met!" he finished before turning away and staring back out to sea.

"So we're navy men now, is that it?" Alfie asked, turning to Admiral Saunders who still stood a distance away from the smugglers. It would be a long time before he ever trusted the likes of Alfred Bicks and Jim Robson again.

"For the time being, yes, you are. As far as my crew are concerned you're the latest intake of pressed men. Each of you will be given a task and you'll work at it. It was very difficult saving you all in the first place. Alfie and Jim," he said staring over at them, "You killed soldiers. You'll hang if you ever set foot on British soil. You may not like the situation you face, but believe me I've tried to do the best I can for you all. From today you'll keep watch and survive on rations like the rest of us, and if you don't like it then you'll be hung right here on deck as an example to the rest of my crew," he said, before turning and walking away from the smugglers, wondering whether he should have told them more: for this wasn't just any stint at sea, and they'd have to learn fast if they were to survive the treacherous journey.

Chapter Fifteen

As Admiral Saunders strolled away from the smugglers and climbed up onto the ship's quarter deck his marines quickly stepped in and began separating the smugglers. Alfred Bicks tried to stand his ground, but it did little good. He eyeballed the biggest of Saunders' marines with that lunatic stare of his, but the marine was far from intimidated.

"We're a long way from that town you called home, and you're outnumbered fifty to one aboard this ship," the marine advised, "Our Commander has been more than generous with you, but I promise you his generosity will only go so far."

Alfie Bicks continued his glare and suddenly the marine gritted his teeth and stepped forward standing an inch apart, nose to nose with the smuggler. Unknown to Alfie, the marine named Hendricks had fought countless battles on both land and sea for King and Country.

"So you think you're tough because you've smuggled some cargoes and stabbed a few sailors. Some of the men aboard this ship came here as punishment. Some are murderers and much worse than you and your band of criminals!"

The rest of the smugglers stood watching the confrontation, alongside the marines who clutched their weapons, eager and willing to use them.

"Aboard this ship Admiral Saunders is judge, jury and executioner. You understand?" the marine barked, "Now, there is a time and a place for battle, and this isn't it."

Alfie continued his stare for a moment longer. Bicks had stared down countless enemies over the years and was used to spotting weakness in his enemies' eyes, but with the marine there was none. Hendricks was as tough as they came. In the end Alfred Bicks' face twitched in to an eerie smile and he took a step backwards before glancing out towards the ocean. The red head had never backed down from anyone in his life, but Alfie knew when he was overmatched, just as he had when he'd awoken in the barn days earlier.

'Oh, I'll get to Admiral Saunders, you just see if I don't,' he raged deep inside as he stared towards the horizon. Finally he turned to the marine and muttered his understanding.

A moment later he was unchained and dragged away below decks, but this time it wasn't to the brig. Alfie found himself in a large room. Running along the side of this room were over a dozen small square holes, referred to as gunports, and facing these ports were large cannon that were chained in place. Kneeling on the floor and working tirelessly were a dozen or so men. They were busy scrubbing the deck, and by the smell of it they had lemon juice in the buckets by their sides. A few of the men paused in their task and glanced up at the newcomers.

"Men, you've got a fresh face bunking with you. He's a pressed man doing his first stint at sea," the marine stated, his information received with a mixture of grunts and sniggers, much to Alfie's anger.

"You're starboard watch now. They'll fill you in on what that entails, and don't think of shirking your work for a second," the marine warned, "If you don't serve a purpose on this ship you're dead weight and dead weight goes overboard," he finished, turning and leaving the room. Alfie dropped to his knees and picked up a rag as the man next to him turned his way.

"Don't worry. This life is hell at first, but before long you grow to tolerate it, and one day you'll find that you live for it," the man said, as his comrades cheered and burst into song. Alfred Bicks couldn't help but smile.

Meanwhile the oldest of the band of smugglers had been led to the rear of the ship and through doors at the back of the main deck. Benny Swift observed a long corridor which ended at a door marked Captain's Cabin. Along the sides of the small corridor were a number of other doors, of which many were open. Benny wasn't surprised at the size of the cabins. They were small, but they had actual beds and were quite cosy little spaces. But old man was puzzled at the thought of where he was being led. When the marines finally reached their destination he was pleasantly surprised.

"This is yours," one of the marines informed him as he gestured towards a tiny cabin. The space was small, but Benny was still delighted at the prospect of a bed as opposed to a hammock and some degree of privacy.

"Saunders would like to speak to you on deck, Benjamin, once you've settled in of course. There are clean clothes on the bed for you," the marine said, before strolling back along the corridor. Benny entered the cabin and sat on the bed staring at his new pile of clothes and the walls of the cabin before a voice interrupted his thoughts.

"Well, I guess that makes us neighbours," the voice said warmly and Benny looked up. In the small cabin on the opposite side of the corridor a man sat behind a desk covered with books, jars and a hoard of other unusual looking pieces of equipment. Unlike Benny's little cabin that was virtually bare, this man's space was crammed full of strange objects. Finally Benny's blue eyes settled on his new neighbour who, to his surprise, couldn't have been much younger than himself. The man wore small spectacles that hung over a large grey moustache.

"The name's Jones," he said, rising from his desk, crossing the space between the cabins and shaking Benny's hand excitedly "I'm the ship's doctor, and you – if I believe my good friend Saunders – are Benjamin Swift, a guest aboard this vessel and a man I'm supposed to make welcome."

Benny shook the doctor's hand. The old fisherman wasn't a well man, and was very pleased to have made friends with the ship's doctor.

A short while later, wearing clean clothes for the first time in many days, Benny left the cabin, wishing his neighbour good day as he did so. Walking down the corridor and rocking from left to right as the ship pitched and rolled with the swell, Benjamin Swift felt a rush of excitement, an emotion that he felt a pang of guilt for having, so close to his son's death. Many men would feel ill at the motion of the ship, but not Benny. The old fisherman had spent his life at sea before poor health had forced his early retirement, and his son had had to take to smuggling to keep a roof over their heads.

Reaching the main deck Benny stepped out and, for a moment, simply watched the dozens of men who were working away. Eventually he mounted the stairs which led from the HMS Romulus' main deck to her quarter deck.

Admiral Saunders was surrounded by half a dozen of his officers and as Benny stepped towards them a marine blocked his path, catching the Admiral's attention. Philip Saunders glanced over at the marine and nodded his consent, allowing Benny to approach the group who quickly dispersed at his arrival. A long awkward moment passed as the pair stared at each other, neither really knowing exactly what to say. It was the Admiral that broke the silence.

"I hear that you're good with charts and navigation," he said, and Benny nodded.

"It's something that has always interested me, Admiral," he replied, causing Saunders to smile at the use of his title for the first time. "But we're a long way from waters I would be familiar with," Benny concluded. Saunders considered this for a moment before signalling to one of his men who quickly arrived at Benny's side.

"Benny, this is Robert Peer who – in my opinion – is the best navigator on this earth," Saunders informed him. Benny shook Peer's hand as the navigator beamed, clearly delighted with the Admiral's compliment.

"Robert here is going to work with you during the voyage," Saunders continued "you'll work an idler watch meaning you'll get to sleep through the night, unlike most of the other men who only get four hours at a time."

"You'll be like an apprentice to Robert, and will help him navigate our course," Saunders explained. Benjamin considered this. Saunders watched the various emotions pass across his face and answered the most important question before Benny could ask it.

"You're aboard this ship now, Benny, whether you like it or not. Truth be told a man's mind needs to be kept busy. This voyage will take us to the end of the world and back, and locked up below decks you'd go stir crazy in a matter of weeks," he stated, "and whatever you may think of me, Benny, I owe Jacob more than that."

Benny stared hard at Saunders. His son was dead now, and nothing could bring him back. Swift could see the pain on the Admiral's face and he knew in that moment that Philip Saunders hadn't betrayed his son, which meant a lot to the old fisherman. Finally he nodded and turned to Robert Peer, who shook his hand.

"So, where to start? Have you ever used a sextant?" he asked, pulling a brass instrument from his pocket. Benny's face lit up: it was the first time since the fatal news that Benjamin Swift had managed to smile.

"Oh, I've heard of them, but to be honest I've never had the pleasure of using one. How do they work?" he asked Robert Peer, smiling himself at his new apprentice's enthusiasm.

Chapter Sixteen

S everal difficult days passed by aboard the HMS Romulus for the small band of smugglers as they slowly came to terms with the tough life at sea they faced. The men were split up and assigned different sleeping quarters which was a move aimed at minimising the risk of a mutiny attempt by the small gang. Any such venture would be suicidal. The smugglers would never be able to take control of the ship, but Admiral Saunders considered the possibility of such a desperate attempt none the less. The Admiral had some extra patience when it came to the smugglers, mainly out of a loyalty to his dead friend, however his crew had no such loyalty. Hendricks had warned the smugglers that Saunders' generosity only went so far, and he'd spoken true.

Any man who'd ever worn a captain's bars would tell the same tale… control on board was crucial. When a sailor stepped out of line or broke the rules, that man was flogged on deck so everyone could see, not for the sake of that man, but as an example to the rest. Saunders knew that Alfred Bicks wouldn't learn his lesson if he flogged the man all day and night. He also knew that the smuggler could be of use if things went wrong in the South Pacific, but unfortunately he could not divulge that knowledge to anyone else on board.

During those first days the smugglers struggled, that much was obvious to everyone aboard the Romulus, but every sailor had been through it themselves and they all offered their support. A life at sea wasn't easy. The ship carried hundreds upon hundreds of men who would only really be needed to man the cannon during battle, the rest of the time the Romulus could be sailed easily using only one tenth of her crew. Considering the vast crew numbers the decks seemed fairly clear as most of the day nearly half of the crew slept. The sailors took it in turns manning the ship in four hour shifts, an arrangement known as the watch system which was tough at first to adjust to. It was only twice a day at eight o'clock in the morning and evening that the whole crew stood watch for half an hour together and only during these times did the Romulus seem crowded.

At first the smugglers staggered around struggling from the lack of sleep, but they soon settled as their internal clocks became accustomed to the unusual sleeping pattern. Like all men they struggled with the lack of daylight in the cramped spaces below decks, working mainly in the dim light provided by candles and lanterns. The smugglers appreciated the food from the very start though. Many believe that sailors struggled in this department on-board, but that was far from the truth. The rations the navy issued were more than acceptable for each man, and went a long way as they were prepared by the ship's cook, and enjoyed on mess tables that were slung from the beams above and packed away after each meal. They appreciated their drink, too, half a pint of rum per day was more than generous. The smugglers quickly learnt to mix it with water and a little lemon juice to improve the taste. It helped to ease boredom for most of the sailors, but in those first few days it kept the smugglers sane as they struggled with the extreme changes in their lives. The lack of privacy was hard on them too, as even at night hammocks were slung only fourteen inches apart.

Admiral Saunders kept out of the smugglers' way for the most part. Most admirals kept the crew at a distance and only socialised with their fellow officers, who, like them, were gentlemen. Below decks the ship was sailed by a different social class. Over the years Admiral Philip Saunders had earned the respect of his crews by mixing with every man aboard, and he often thought he had more in common with the rough sailors than he did with his fellow gentlemen: men who had been born into the right family and educated at the best institutions the country had to offer. During those first days whilst the smugglers struggled with a life at sea Admiral Saunders kept to his own quarters where he was protected and safe, not venturing too far below decks. During his daily meetings with the many officers that ran the various watches, Saunders listened to reports on the smugglers with a strange combination of regret and pride. His First Lieutenant informed him that Jim Robson had already earned a reputation amongst the men after another sailor had mocked him, and the tough smuggler – who was built like a barn-door – had knocked the man unconscious with one mighty blow. Saunders smiled at this.

Everything seemed to be going well where the smugglers were concerned, but then something happened that made Admiral Saunders realise that he would never be truly safe around Jacob Swift's men. It was during the forenoon watch at around eleven in the morning when it happened in the blink of an eye. The sun was blazing in the centre of a bright blue sky and the wind was blowing fair. Saunders was standing on the quarter deck with, as usual, a handful of officers. Benjamin Swift and Robert Peer were studying charts whilst the navigator explained to Benny about depth readings and the sections of their course where danger could lie. Meanwhile, down on the main deck, Alfred Bicks was enjoying a break from his duties. The men were given leisure time for a few hours each day. Some would sit on deck and enjoy their grog, others would gamble and tell stories. Alfred Bicks was busy planning how he could get past the marines and cut the Admiral's throat. Over the last few days he'd struggled at first, but he'd quickly learnt that he had much in common with the men at his sides. The one thing the ex-smuggler realised swiftly, though, was that his fellow sailors didn't share his hatred for Saunders, and in fact it was quite the opposite. Tucked up in their hammocks his fellow sailors spoke of Saunders with such reverence that the smuggler concluded they'd slit his throat in a heartbeat if he spoke out of line or voiced his intentions towards their back stabbing leader. Alfred Bicks had made a promise to Jim Robson that the Admiral would die for his betrayal, and it was a promise he intended to keep. Alfie worked his duties on board for several days, drank his grog, ate his food and fantasised about cutting Saunders' throat. At night he dreamt of Billy Bates telling him to watch Jacob's back whilst staring at him through those jet black eyes of his, and then in his dream Jacob's body would be lying in front of him and Bill would be raging at him in that croaky voice of his. Alfie would often wake in his hammock with a jolt and wipe the tears from his eyes while checking to make sure that his fellow sailors hadn't noticed.

As he stood on deck Alfred Bicks waited patiently for his moment and when it came he took it. The smuggler knew he'd never be able to climb up to the quarter deck without arousing the marines' suspicions. They would intercept him before he got within spitting distance of the Admiral. So Alfie chose a different route. He had already acquired a small dagger that he'd bartered for with a sailor several nights earlier. It was a crude instrument and was nothing to look at, but it was sharp enough and would slice through Saunders' neck like butter. He checked the dagger was still safely stored in his waist band and continued his surveillance. The marines on deck strolled back and forth seemingly unaware, but if they saw him climb overboard they'd be onto him in a flash. Alfie picked his moment and as the small group clustered together talking he scrambled over the main deck's railing and held onto the side of the ship for dear life, before making his way to the rear of the ship where Saunders stood on deck. Every six feet Alfie had to scramble over a gun port, but he made steady progress. The men on the ship's main deck hadn't yet noticed his disappearance, but they would, this he didn't doubt. As he climbed further towards the rear of the ship the voices grew louder, and Bicks didn't struggle to pick out Saunders amongst them. Pulling the dagger from his waistband with one hand he placed it between his teeth and gripped onto the ship for dear life. Below him the ocean was passing by, an ocean that would drag him down to a murky death if he made the slightest mistake. Reaching the furthest point he needed to travel horizontally, Alfie Bicks began to climb straight up and a moment later he leapt up over the rail and onto the Romulus' quarter deck. Several of the marines glanced at him assuming he was just carrying out an inspection, but then they noticed the knife which was held between his teeth which suddenly shifted to his hand, and it finally dawned on them what was happening. It was too late though as Alfred Bicks leapt at his prey grabbing a firm fix on Philip Saunders who tumbled to the deck. A moment later Alfred Bicks had the point of the blade pressed firmly against Saunders' throat, but much to Alfie's surprise the Admiral was virtually screaming to his marines:

"Don't shoot him! He must live!" and appeared more concerned with preserving Alfie's life than his own!

Instead of sinking the blade into the Admiral's throat and fulfilling his promise to Jim, Alfie stared at Saunders and waited for some sort of explanation as his red hair dangled in the Admiral's face. The blade had now sliced through the top layer of skin on Saunders' throat and a faint line of blood was evident, but Philip Saunders remained calm. Hendricks and countless other marines were pointing muskets in Alfie's direction and screaming commands, both to each other and at Alfie, but he couldn't distinguish a single word. Alfred Bicks was staring into Saunders' eyes, and he wasn't liking what he saw. Saunders' expression told a story of pity towards him, but not fear. The instruction that 'Alfred Bicks must live' had completely confused him. Time had slowed to the point where it had seemed to stop for Alfie. He looked at Philip Saunders for answers, a man he'd known for several years and liked until recently, but they were answers Admiral Saunders could never offer.

"Let him go, Alfie!" Benny Swift was screaming at him, and finally time caught up with Alfie again and he looked up from Saunders pinned beneath him and into Benny Swift's bright blue eyes.

"Jacob wouldn't have wanted this, I promise you," the old man said, and suddenly Alfie realised what he was doing and dropped the knife. The smuggler experienced a strong wave of shame as he was dragged to his feet by four marines, who would have torn him to pieces and thrown him overboard if it hadn't been for Philip Saunders who ordered them not too. Everyone present was confused about what was going on, apart from the Admiral who very calmly climbed to his feet and rubbed at the trickle of blood on his neck.

"What shall we do with him, Captain?" Hendricks asked, and Saunders stared at Alfie for a long moment before replying, "Transfer him to another vessel, and make sure that not a word of this reaches the rest of my crew. I want every man who just witnessed this spectacle sworn to secrecy. Put him aboard the Sandown at the first opportunity. I want him locked up in their brig for the remainder of the journey," he ordered, as Alfie Bicks was dragged away. The Admiral's merciful act was to lead to serious repercussions later in the voyage.

Chapter Seventeen

Later that evening after the sun had fallen out of the sky and the wind had risen, pushing the small convoy of ships further towards their meeting with destiny, Benny Swift was summoned to Admiral Saunders' dining cabin.

At the very rear of the ship, and at the end of the corridor which Benny's cabin opened onto, was Admiral Saunders' private quarters. The fisherman had been lying on his bunk as Alfie Bicks travelled back and forth through his mind. Benny had known Alfie for many years, and knew him well. The man who'd come very close to cutting Saunders' throat earlier that day wasn't a bad man: Benny believed this with all his heart. The old fisherman thought that Alfie's attempt to kill Saunders had been wrong and he was glad that he'd failed, but he also knew that Alfie had reacted out of some crazy loyalty to his dead son, and that thought hurt Benjamin Swift. He hoped that Saunders' men would treat him fairly, and that eventually Alfie would come to accept the hand that fate had dealt them all. Benny was still considering these thoughts when a sharp knock rattled his cabin door and the admiral's private servant poked his head in the door and summoned him.

A moment later he was walking along the corridor before being admitted into the Admiral's private quarters, which opened into a fairly large room in comparison to the rest of the ship. In the centre of the room stood a large dining table where over half a dozen officers in their various uniforms sat drinking and discussing an assortment of topics. Admiral Saunders would often welcome not only the officers aboard his ship to dine with him, but also the captains and officers from other vessels sailing in his squadron. The man had a reputation for being hospitable, and from time to time even dined with common sailors, which over the years had earned him great respect below decks. Now though as Benjamin Swift glanced around at the scene, what surprised the old fisherman the most, even more than the fancy uniforms the officers gathered wore, was their age. Most of the men were young, but some were just boys. The servant instructed Benny to take a seat next to the Admiral, much to Benny's relief. The fisherman had been born into a class far below the officers present, and felt like a fish out of water as he listened to the language they used. A glass was placed in front of Benjamin and was filled with brandy before Philip Saunders turned to him and raised a toast, to which they both drank. As the table erupted into conversation once more, Admiral Saunders leant over towards him and thanked him for his help earlier out on deck: Benny nodded politely.

"You know, Benny, I don't blame Alfie, not one bit. He is doing what he thinks is right and in some ways I admire him for having the courage to act, few do," Saunders said, sipping his brandy. Benjamin Swift remained quiet for a brief moment, unsure how to react before apologising for his friend's behaviour.

"It's all he knows, Admiral. Alfie never had any options in this world. What he's achieved he's done with a knife in his hand," Benny said, causing Saunders to laugh until one of his midshipmen caught his attention.

"So, Admiral," the young officer slurred slightly, forcing most of the table to fall quiet and glare the young officer's way, "forgive me for asking, but they do say curiosity killed the cat. Can you give any indication of where we're headed and to what purpose? This is no normal voyage and I think it's time we knew what we've got ourselves into," the man finished, flushing bright red and already regretting his words. Every officer at the table stared down at the table in the silence that followed, waiting for the Admiral's harsh rebuke.

"Forgive me, Admiral, it's been a long day and this brandy is particularly potent," the officer confessed as Admiral Philip Saunders stared along the table.

"You speak out of line, midshipman, and if you were a common sailor and not a man of noble birth I would have you flogged," Saunders warned, as the rest of the table nodded in agreement.

"But you speak the truth. This is to be no normal stint at sea, but that is not news to anyone seated at this table. In time you will learn of our mission and its true destination, but that time isn't now when the brandy has loosened our lips and confused our thoughts," Saunders stated, as his men nodded. Some even glared and shook their heads at the midshipman, though he had only voiced what they had all been thinking.

"It's time we called it a night," Saunders said, and the men rose to their feet and bid him farewell. Benjamin Swift also stood, but the Admiral turned his way. "I would like to have a nightcap with you, Benny, and talk further if that suits you?" he asked, as his officers filed out of the room. Once they had gone Saunders filled both of their glasses, before lapsing into silence. Benjamin Swift could see the Admiral had something on his mind, and it wasn't just guilt from the events surrounding Jacob's death. Benny could see that whatever was troubling Saunders, the Admiral needed to talk to him about it, which roused his curiosity. So, after taking a large swig of brandy Benny finally summoned the courage to inquire.

"Penny for your thoughts, I've heard them say," Benny said, tucking a strand of his grey hair behind his ear and looking Saunders way with a smile on his face. Saunders chuckled and then sighed as he stared at the grain on the wooden table in front of him.

"I really wouldn't know where to start, Benny," he said, as he continued to stare at the table. Finally he looked up and into Benny's eyes.

"Our country is threatened by Europe, and if this mission doesn't succeed we'll be facing a war we'll be hard pressed to win," he stated, taking a gulp of brandy and watching the calm expression on Benny's face. The Admiral smiled at this. He had known Benny's son well and he now knew that the apple hadn't fallen far from the tree. Benjamin Swift's face didn't give anything away and the Admiral made a mental note to invite him to a game of cards with the officers: the man would make a fortune. Saunders admired the calm look on Benny's face as the cogs turned deep in the old fisherman's mind. Saunders was very aware that Benny hadn't ventured any comment, and was waiting for the Admiral to fill the silence. Saunders' friend Rupert Knightly had taught him the same technique. Finally the Admiral decided to take a risk where Benjamin Swift was concerned.

"On this voyage we face the unknown, and there are far too many variables for my liking. Some I can live with, and some I can't. The truth is, Benny, at some stage many months from now I may need your help," the Admiral said, looking straight at Benny who couldn't help but laugh. Saunders let him, and when the fisherman had managed to stifle his disbelieving chuckles he looked the Admiral in the eye. "You have hundreds of armed, and from what I've seen, capable men aboard this ship alone, and that's before we even consider the other vessels sailing in this squadron. What could a powerful man like you ever need from a washed up old fishermen like me? A man who gets out of breath when he climbs a steep staircase?" Benny replied, and now they both laughed.

"I would like to tell you a story, Benny. This story is a good one, and few have heard it. Once I've finished you'll know why you can help me. If you want to help you can, though, for what it's worth, I wouldn't blame you if you didn't," the Admiral said, as he picked up the brandy decanter and poured them both another drink. Turning his attention back towards Benny he made the old fisherman swear to keep the story to himself, and Benny agreed, concerned by the serious expression on Saunders' face.

"Have you ever heard of a pirate named Captain Mudd?" Saunders asked, catching Benjamin Swift completely off guard. The man who'd plied his trade on the English Channel couldn't hide his look of surprise, and it was a long moment before he could find the words to reply.

"I've heard some of the stories, few haven't. He's the pirate who traded his soul with the devil for control of the seas; well that's at least how the stories go," Benny said, and the Admiral smiled wryly.

"Fortunately, that part of Mudd's story isn't true, but in many ways the truth is even worse," Saunders stated, visibly dismayed by the story he must tell. Benjamin Swift watched feeling incredibly curious.

"So what's the truth?" he enquired, and for a long moment Admiral Saunders didn't say a word. He just stared down at the table with a look of worry on his face. Eventually he looked up at Benny once more, and some of his colour had returned.

"It's a long story, and a story that will take more than one sitting, but it's a story I think you best hear for yourself. The question is where to begin, and I suppose the only answer would be at the start," Saunders said, as he stared back down at the table and started Captain Mudd's story.

Chapter Eighteen

"The pirate who would grow to become the Royal Navy's greatest threat was a battler from his earliest days. Alfred Mudd was born in Portsmouth in 1734, but to say he was raised there would be pushing the truth. He was abandoned at a young age and quickly learned how to fend for himself. Living rough in empty warehouses – with many others in the same situation – he quickly learned to scavenge for food and survive by begging on the streets.

"Portsmouth has always been a lively place, even back then. The docks at Portsmouth bustled with trade from ships from all over the world. It was an exciting place, and a place where many boys just like Mudd began their seafaring lives.

"Alfred Mudd looks to have been destined for trouble from the very start. He was born into a harsh world where every day was a fight for survival, but the youngster had a few advantages. A born tactician, Alfred Mudd quickly realised that there were easier ways to earn a meal than begging. He made the leap from beggar to thief and was running his own gang of street urchins by the time he was ten years old, robbing sailors both merchant and navy alike. Some people back in Portsmouth say that his gang never hurt a single hair on anyone's head, but others tell a different story. One long summer Mudd and his gang conducted a relentless campaign in the port town, robbing anyone that stood in their path. They were just kids, but one look into the leader of the gang's crazy eyes ensured people paid. The town's paper, The Portsmouth and Gosport Gazette, ran a story on the gang of thieves, a story that identified Alfred Mudd, a boy of ten with red hair, as its leader.

"The town was shocked and they quickly set out to catch and punish the young thieves. The huge navy base which dominated the town housed an officer training academy and many houses for officer's families to reside. As a result the town had its fair share of wealthy aristocratic families. Many of the navy officers had young children who would soon be following their father's footsteps into the navy and leaving for their first stints at sea as midshipmen. These wealthy children, who had never felt the pangs of hunger, heard of the thief Alfred Mudd, a name most of the town despised, and like everyone else they quickly grew to hate him. Nobody back then knew how deep that hatred would grow, or that many of these navy children would earn a place on the ruthless pirate's notorious death list.

"When Alfred Mudd was eventually apprehended by the local magistrate, along with the rest of his gang, they were all thrown inside Portsmouth's jail. Most children of his age would have been petrified, but not Alfred Mudd. The boy was far from normal: though to describe him as fearless wouldn't quite be accurate. Mudd thrived inside jail amongst the worst of the scum caught across the south coast of England. At first he watched with those crazy eyes of his, eyes sailors would later claim had the power to burn deep into a man's soul. Within a matter of days the boy had figured out who amongst the other prisoners held power, which of the guards were weakest, and how he could seize control of the prison. Alfred Mudd set his young thieves to work earning favour in the right places with the intention of formulating an escape plan, however it wasn't meant to be, and Alfred never got the opportunity to escape from prison. In many ways his plan worked none the less. The boy had earned the respect of many dangerous men whilst inside the walls of Portsmouth Prison, and some of these same dangerous men were destined to eventually stand by his side.

"After nearly three months rotting in jail, Alfred Mudd's gang were finally sentenced, and due largely to the fact that they'd never actually stabbed anyone with the knives they'd waved in their victim's faces, they managed to get off lightly, in a manner of speaking. Looking back on it now and knowing what the boy would go on to achieve in the art of piracy, it was a huge mistake sending Alfred Mudd away to sea to serve his punishment on board a merchant ship which was due to leave the docks the following week. What made it worse was that Mudd wasn't the only prisoner on that ship as it sailed out of Portsmouth's harbour. Prison offered free labourers: ruthless merchants in particular took advantage of this system and crewed their ships with as many young criminals as they could lay their hands on. Often, the youths were guilty of only petty crimes or vagrancy. Most would grow to become talented and able seamen in the years ahead. After paying their debt to society they frequently spent the rest of their lives working for the same merchants who'd taken them to sea in the first place. Alfred Mudd wasn't one of these men. The boy was as sharp as a razor and incredibly manipulative. He was the type of sailor any captain would fear aboard his ship. Alfred Mudd was a natural born thief and the sort of person who could quickly calculate how to manoeuvre around anyone standing in his way. The boy, even at the tender age of twelve, posed a huge threat to the captain.

"Initially Mudd planned to overthrow the merchant captain as the ship left the English Channel and sailed out into the Atlantic. Working as a deckhand, the youngster joked around with many of the ship's crew over the course of the first few weeks, secretly planning mutiny with his fellow criminals in whispered conversations below decks. Mudd knew he would need many more of the merchant sailors on board to stand at his side if he really did want to lead a mutiny and take control of the ship, so he started to work his silver tongue. Most of the sailors were simple men, nowhere near his league. Alfred Mudd isolated the sailors who were most likely to turn against their merchant captain and began to manipulate these men with stories of treasure and unimaginable wealth. The boy sold these men hope, and fed their dreams and ambitions without them ever realising what he was doing. Within weeks they grew to resent the work they were doing as they slaved away for a pittance to make some rich merchant even richer. Before his arrival, these same sailors had felt content with their lives, and privileged for the opportunities life had given them. Now they dreamed, and, like Mudd himself, they wanted more. The skinny young kid, who was tall for his age, watched with satisfaction as he played his game, a game he'd learned whilst gaining control of a dozen different street gangs in Portsmouth as a child and a game he'd never lost.

"One day whilst on deck he began a conversation with the ship's Captain, a merchant in his early thirties who, much to Mudd's surprise, came from similar stock as most of his crew. Already Alfred Mudd had fallen in love with the idea of a life at sea. The young ruffian considered everything aboard ship to be simple. He'd carefully studied every man he was sailing with, their likes and dislikes, the loyalties they had to each other and, most importantly, how to persuade each man to go along with his plans. To Mudd in many ways it was just the same as life on the streets, but on a ship things were far easier to predict, and therefore control was much easier to obtain. During that first conversation with the ship's Captain, who immediately took a liking to the cheeky young deckhand, Alfred Mudd decided to put his mutinous plans on hold.

"Over the next few weeks Mudd turned his attention away from manipulating the other sailors and concentrated on turning the one person he would definitely need on his side if he wanted to use the ship for his own purposes and try his hand at piracy. Alfred Mudd spent all day long at the Captain's side laughing and joking as he cleverly planted a seed in his mind, a seed the thief knew would grow and grow. Mudd learnt of the man's dreams and aims, and broke them down, slowly convincing the Captain that he would never achieve any of them ferrying goods across the Atlantic to the colonies for pittance. The Captain began to drink more and more, and the young deckhand encouraged him as he hinted that the Captain had nothing to lose. Many sailors on board watched the young deckhand work the Captain, just as he had worked them, and did nothing. For these sailors now wanted more: they wanted the wealth and power the boy had convinced them was out there for the taking, and they wanted Alfred Mudd to succeed. Then the Captain would turn his back on his merchant friends back in England and use the ship to gather large quantities of money in a very different way.

"Finally, after landing on the shores of Jamaica and unloading their cargo, the vessel began its journey back across the Atlantic. Alfred knew that he had achieved his goal. The game he'd been playing for months on end was coming to its inevitable conclusion. The crew were at the point of despair, and Mudd almost feared that he'd left it too late: that the crew would mutiny and take control of the ship without him. The fruit was ripe for the picking and the time to pick it had arrived. One evening in the Captain's small cabin Mudd whispered in the young merchant's ear of the rumours out on the ship's deck that the crew were ready for mutiny. He whispered an idea that the Captain would interpret as his own. The next day the Captain, who was still in a daze from his skinful of grog the night before, ordered all hands on deck and voiced his intention to turn to piracy for a living. The sailors, for the most part, welcomed this news and shouted their support for the Captain as they grinned at the sly young deckhand standing at the Captain's side, the precocious lad that nobody doubted was calling the shots; the street-urchin turned thief that they would follow for many, many years to come.

Suddenly Admiral Saunders paused in recounting Mudd's story as loud bells began to ring out on the deck of his own ship and his crew rushed around changing watch. Benny sat patiently, eager for the man to continue, but the hour was late and he could see the Admiral was exhausted.

"I think that'll have to be enough for today. It's going to be a long voyage. Tomorrow I will tell you some more," Saunders promised. Benny Swift climbed slowly to his feet and wished the Admiral a good night's rest before leaving the cabin. A short time later he lay in bed wondering how a young boy from Portsmouth lacking even a day of education could ever become as infamous as he had. Benjamin Swift was looking forward to hearing the rest of Mudd's story and finding the answer to that conundrum.

Chapter Nineteen

The days that followed the assassination attempt on Admiral Saunders passed quickly for Alfie Bicks, who was lost in his own thoughts. The man who'd worked loyally for years as bodyguard to England's most efficient smuggler was very confused, and as he sat alone and in darkness in the brig of the HMS Romulus reflecting on his actions, the anger he felt towards Admiral Saunders lifted a little, allowing him to think more clearly than he'd been able to since his previous employer's death.

Even before the brig's door finally swung open and he was shackled once again he'd realised the mistake he'd made. In his early years he'd been recruited into the smuggling trade by a man who'd seen potential in him, a man named Billy Bates, who'd turned a young ruffian's anger and used it as a weapon to help build a smuggling empire on the south coast of England. Now as Alfie's anger subsided he realised for the first time that his greatest strength was also his greatest weakness. As he was dragged out of the brig with a blindfold over his straggly red hair Alfred Bicks felt many emotions, but the strongest of them all was shame. He was marched in shackles through a labyrinth of corridors and placed in one of the Romulus' boats, a twenty-five foot cutter. The Romulus, like all ships of the line, was well equipped with smaller boats. Such boats were crucial for operations such as transporting officers, crew and supplies to and from the ship, and landing troops and marines on shore.

The wind had finally eased up for the first time since they'd set sail from England and now, whilst anchored off the coast of West Africa, Admiral Saunders' complete squadron, all six ships, including HMS Brunswick and HMS Mars who had now joined the fleet, came together for the first time. The lack of wind meant they were losing some ground in their race with the French, a race only Saunders and a handful of his most trusted officers were even aware of.

In the absence of wind the Atlantic was fairly flat and offered little swell. The small cutter was rowed by a handful of tough sailors whilst others guarded their prisoner. Alfie offered no resistance. After Blackheath had arrived in his home town, destroyed his livelihood, and killed many of his close friends, Alfred Bicks had accepted that his life was over. He had been caught and had truly believed his neck would feel the pressure of a noose tightening around it. Much to his surprise he'd managed to escape justice, rescued by the very man he'd sworn to punish, and now after attempting to kill that man he was still alive: for the first time in weeks he was glad of that. Alfie hoped that it wasn't too late to make amends. When he arrived on board the deck of the only other frigate in Admiral Saunders' squadron, a ship that would range several hundred miles ahead of the convoy, he was led straight to that ship's brig. In all honesty, he'd expected precisely that.

During the days that followed, Alfred Bicks spent his time in the dark alone, with only his thoughts to keep him company. The scene on the deck of the Romulus when he'd had that dagger pressed against Saunders' throat swam back and forth through his mind, torturing him. He regretted his actions, and realised that it wasn't just Saunders he owed an apology to, if the Admiral would ever be willing to listen. Alfie knew in his heart that he needed to apologise to Benjamin Swift. Whilst lost in his own grief over losing his friend he'd been blind to Benjamin Swift's pain, the man who'd lost so, so much more. Slowly the prisoner came to terms with the situation he was in and vowed to make his peace with Admiral Saunders and seek forgiveness from

Benny. In his dark and cramped solitude, Alfred Bicks sat twisting the end of his ginger beard thinking of the life at sea he faced, and eventually he smiled: a sinister smile, but a smile none the less.

Lying on the brig's hard timber floor Alfie tried to block out the noise from the ship which was relentless, vibrating through the walls in every direction. Conversations and orders alike could be heard in the intervals between heavy boots trudging around on the deck above him as he closed his eyes and tried to sleep. Eventually he drifted off, but after only an hour or so the brig's door swung open, waking him. Opening his eyes and sitting upright he watched as several guards dragged in another prisoner. Alfie wondered what the hour was and how long he'd actually slept as he tried to make out the figures in front of him shuffling around in the dim light.

The guards chained the new prisoner to a railing on the opposite side of the small cell, almost unaware of Alfie's presence in the shadows. Alfie could hear the new prisoner wincing in pain, the guards ignoring his injuries, focussed on their efforts to fasten his chains in place. Alfie watched curiously, pleased with the prospect of some company after many days alone. How many days Alfie wasn't completely sure. Once the guards shuffled out an uncomfortable silence fell over the small room. After a short while Alfie assumed the man had fallen into slumber and decided to pursue a similar path.

Suddenly the man spoke, though his words raised far more questions than they answered.

"We won't be safe in here when the devil comes for his treasure!" the voice said shakily. Alfred Bicks had spent a lifetime putting fear into even the most hardened of men and could tell his new cellmate was absolutely terrified. He thought about the sentence again and wondered how drunk the man was. Surely he hadn't lost his mind already. Alfie didn't think they'd been at sea for nearly long enough, but he didn't rule it out. Instead he offered a vague answer that he thought would please his new cellmate's ears.

"When the devil arrives, nowhere will be safe," he said. In answer the man chuckled, making Alfie conclude that he'd lost his mind after all. Silence fell over the brig once more and eventually Alfred Bicks fell asleep again, wondering about his new cellmate, and exactly where in the Bible it talked of treasure?

Chapter Twenty

The British squadron anchored off the coast of West Africa. The wind had blown itself out and the sea was flat. Signallers stood at various lookout points sending and receiving messages from the other ships using numbered flags.

Admiral Philip Saunders was very aware that he needed to use this time wisely. The boy who'd sat on his father's knee listening to the story of how the great pirate Captain Mudd had shown his father's crew leniency was now a man who knew that the time for secrets was over. At that meeting with his spymaster friend and Sir Robert Burns, Saunders had been advised to keep his orders to himself until he'd left Europe in his squadron's wake, a tactic aimed at minimising the threat posed by any potential French spies within his own ranks. The chances of one of his men relaying a message from ship to shore was low, but a risk all the same. Now, with Europe behind them, it was time to tell the captains sailing under his command what their orders were. The squadron's commanding officers wouldn't get another opportunity to talk at length before they set sail across the Atlantic, and if Saunders left his men in the dark any longer he would lose the respect he'd spent many years earning. Above all else the squadron needed to be fully prepared and ready to deal with any threat in their path, whether treacherous seas or engagement with French cannon.

The horizon was clear in every direction, neither a ship nor a cloud in sight when Admiral Saunders gave the order to arrange the meeting aboard the Romulus. Within an hour the Captains and senior officers from each of his vessels had ferried over to the flagship and were packed into his dining room. The Captains themselves sat, as Saunders did, around the table. Surprisingly, Saunders – who was by far the most senior in rank among them – was also the youngest. The Admiral knew each of the Captains well. Some he rarely saw eye to eye with, but he none the less respected their experience and skill at the helm of a ship. Standing behind their Captains in a circle around the table several rows deep were the Lieutenants and Midshipmen. Outside the cabin door Hendricks, Saunders' most trusted marine Commander, stood on guard, making sure none of the Romulus' crew were in earshot of the meeting. Admiral Philip Saunders was well aware of Mudd's reputation. The pirate had spent a lifetime making his enemies believe he had supernatural powers and even though he was now dead and rotting in the ground, his name still struck fear into sailor's hearts and Philip Saunders wanted to avoid panic amongst his men at all costs. It was of the utmost importance that his officers didn't allow Mudd's reputation to cause fear within their crews. Once all the officers had gathered at the meeting, and all eyes were on the Admiral, Saunders rose to his feet and addressed his men.

"All of you know me well and most have served at my side at some point. Some of you have been privileged to know some details of this mission whilst others have steered their ships thus far knowing very little but the rumours muttered below decks. I stand here today and thank you all," Saunders stated, as his men nodded. The Admiral watched with pride knowing that, if he asked, most of them would say they would sail through the gates of hell and back again if he ordered them to do so. The truth of that statement was about to be sorely tested.

"Some of you have heard rumours that the pirate Alfred Mudd is dead, and that we sail to retrieve his treasure," Saunders said, watching the flare of curiosity on his officer's faces for a moment before finishing, "I can confirm that these rumours are true."

Some of the men failed to hide their shock, some failed to hide their fear, and some their excitement. The officers muttered to each other, before one of them, Captain Spruce, pointed out the obvious, "Mudd's territory was the South Pacific. If he hid his wealth anywhere it would be on one of the thousands of islands that lie there, and that means rounding the Horn!" The table fell silent and everybody waited for Saunders' answer.

"We'll brave the Horn," Saunders stated, as several of his men gasped in surprise, "and through the most dangerous seas on this earth before we reach the island group where Mudd buried his fortune, but we'll reach it none the less."

The small room, which was crammed with men the Admiral had personally selected, descended into silence as every officer present considered the long and dangerous journey ahead. Finally somebody spoke.

"Are we alone in this treasure hunt, Admiral?" Captain Spruce asked, and Saunders simply shook his head confirming what his men already suspected.

"Unfortunately we've been betrayed by one of our own. The French sailed out of Bordeaux two days before us," Saunders said, before recounting to his men the details of Louis Francis' treachery. The officers listened intently, and Saunders watched the anger grow on his men's faces with every word he spoke. Once he'd finished he allowed them a moment to digest the information. There were threatening gestures and several of the men, through gritted teeth, swore vengeance on the Royal Navy man who'd turned his back on his father's homeland for a shot at revenge on his lifelong enemy.

Once the table had finally fallen silent the Admiral continued, "We cannot allow the French to get their hands on the treasure. If they get to it first, our mission is simply to engage them and sink their squadron. The treasure will weigh their ships down and slow them enough to allow us to easily intercept them during the voyage home," Saunders said, before one of his men cut in.

"But that coin spins both ways, Admiral!" one of the captains pointed out: "They may just sink us!"

The men crammed around the table in the captain's quarters voiced their agreement before Saunders silenced them all with one raised hand.

"That is true, gentlemen, but if that treasure ends up at the bottom of the ocean this mission will have succeeded. We only fail if the French get it back to Europe. Once it's in their hands they'll use it to build the largest fleet in existence and the whole of Europe will fall under French control. Our task is to make sure that doesn't happen," the Admiral stated, as the men sat in silence.

"And if we catch the French fleet before we reach our destination?" another captain asked, and Saunders smiled.

"Then we show those frogs what we're made of, and blow them to kingdom come!" he said, at which his men stamped their boots on the timber floor and cheered in support.

"When we get under way we'll sail in formation. Captain Spruce, you'll sail the Sandown ahead of the squadron to act as reconnaissance. Use her speed to our advantage. If you sight the French squadron then prepare for battle, but do not fire upon them unless they engage you first. Understood?" Saunders asked, and Captain Spruce agreed whole-heartedly.

"I'll slow them down and wait for reinforcements, Admiral," he replied. A moment later somebody asked the question they'd all been thinking.

"How much treasure?" one of the captains, a man named Fenwick, asked, leading to complete silence in the room as the men waited eagerly for Philip Saunders' reply.

"Enough to fill the hold of this frigate, and many more like it, and there'll be prize money for us all. If Captain Mudd's haul is half as large as they say we'll all be rich men!" Saunders promised. The officers cheered at hearing this, all but one. Captain Fenwick stared at Admiral Saunders with not even a hint of a smile on the old sailor's weather beaten face.

"That treasure will be just as cursed as Mudd himself, it's a mistake sailing for it in the first place! But, orders are orders and follow them I will," Fenwick said. His warning fell mostly on deaf ears as the gathering rose to their feet, but his warning would come back to haunt Philip Saunders.

Chapter Twenty One

The following morning the wind began to blow north-easterly allowing Admiral Saunders to issue the order for sails to be dropped and the flotilla to get under way. The squadron of British navy ships of the line resumed its journey, one that would lead them through the most dangerous ocean on earth and end in an island group where the largest treasure haul in history was buried. Admiral Saunders' men were brave and they sailed that evening with their heads held high.

Captain Spruce's frigate, the HMS Sandown, led the pack, and due to her design and the fact that she carried fewer cannon than her companion seventy-four gunners, she made good speed, leaving the other five ships in her wake. By nightfall she was a dot on the otherwise clear horizon, having taken up her assigned position as their reconnaissance vessel. Admiral Saunders remained on his frigate, the HMS Romulus, which was the centre of a box formed by the four seventy-four gunners as protection.

Locked away in the HMS Sandown's brig as it made steady progress towards an island group off the coast of Africa known as the Verde Islands, Alfie Bicks was in deep discussion with his fellow prisoner, a man he'd decided was as mad as a hatter. The pair had been talking for most of the day, mainly about a pirate named Mudd. Much to Alfie's frustration the prisoner talked of little else.

"So you say this Mudd fellow was human once, until he met the devil himself on the high seas?" Bicks enquired, finding the prisoner's story ridiculous but appreciating the conversation none the less.

"To be sure. Mudd was nothing more than a common thief before Lucifer gave him his power and the right to control the seven seas in his name," the prisoner replied. Alfred Bicks smiled a wicked grin, but it was wasted on his cellmate who could not make it out in the dark. As crazy as the story was, Alfie had already concluded that the man believed it, and he wondered what had happened to his cellmate to make him lose his mind. Bicks concluded that he'd probably hit his head out on deck, or maybe he'd drunk too much sea-water.

Alfred Bicks wasn't a religious man. As a child he'd lived on the streets amongst the poor and had seen things that couldn't have happened in a world where god existed. He thought the devil was just a made up character in an old book, and nothing more. As the brig fell into silence and Alfie Bicks twisted his ginger beard and listened to the waves crashing against the ship's hull he thought about the forces of good and bad in the world. Alfred Bicks knew that bad people existed. He'd known this for many years, ever since he'd learnt that wielding a dagger had the power to take away the agonising pain of hunger. Alfie had fought his way out of the gutter and had quickly learnt that not all men were the same. Some men were very dangerous and Alfie had realised early on that he was one of those men.

Meanwhile on the HMS Romulus Admiral Saunders was seated alone in his private cabin finishing his evening meal when his servant entered with Benjamin Swift. The old fisherman had taken to life at sea easily, but this didn't surprise the Admiral at all. It had been the old man in front of him with his grey hair and blue eyes that had taught his son to navigate the English Channel and out-manoeuvre any vessel that gave chase. Saunders was still in the middle of this thought when Benjamin Swift sat at the table opposite him, and the Admiral's servant left the cabin and the men in peace. After a moment Saunders poured both of them a brandy.

"So, where were we in Alfred Mudd's tale?" Saunders pondered as he sipped his brandy. Benny Swift, who had thought of little else as he'd worked away at various navigational tasks for most of the day quickly replied: "Mudd had finally convinced his merchant captain to turn pirate," Benjamin prompted. Saunders took another sip of his brandy and began the pirate's story where he'd left off.

Chapter Twenty Two

❝ After the merchant captain's announcement on deck of his intention to turn to piracy, life on the merchant ship changed. As it was, most of the men aboard were serving out a sentence, and few had any good reason to return to the shores of England. The captain promised them they'd all live like kings and they believed him, or, to be more accurate, the boy who stood at his side. The skinny deckhand who was barely even a teenager advised the captain to plunder the first merchant vessel they came across and the weak willed man agreed. Alfred Mudd's plan was simple, but effective, and with a simple plan there was less that could go wrong.

"The ship was now out in the open Atlantic ocean of with a half empty hold that the crew were eager to fill. After delivering their cargo to Jamaica the ship had taken on a sizable cargo of tobacco to sail back to England, but that cargo would never reach Blighty's shores. Following Mudd's advice, the merchant captain gave the order to make sail and waited for a ship to sail into their path. Several days passed slowly before a ship was sighted, but those days weren't wasted. As the sailors drank the young deckhand told stories of the exciting life they now faced, stories of far-away lands, exotic women and, of course, treasure.

"By the time a ship *was* sighted, Alfred Mudd had worked his fellow sailors into a frenzy with that silver tongue of his. He was, of course, just a boy with a big imagination. He had never raided a ship before in his life. Over the course of the next decade he'd hone his skills and eventually become the most powerful of all pirates, but back then he was just a clever little boy with, perhaps, too much courage.

"Whilst the ship sailed closer and closer the merchants concealed their weapons and began to signal distress. The signal was received without even the slightest suspicion. As the target vessel approached many of the merchants-turned-pirates crouched out of sight on the deck giggling excitedly like children.

"Finally the ships were within a few dozen yards of each other. The Captain beginning his piratical career stood on deck looking as scared as a child on his first day at school. Next to him stood a child, but there wasn't an ounce of fear on his gaunt face as he looked over his men.

" 'Don't hurt anyone unless it's absolutely necessary!' Mudd hissed at them. They returned silent nods, and in that moment everyone aboard knew who their leader was: even the Captain – who was trembling in fear beside his deckhand – had no doubts.

"The attack happened so swiftly that the poor merchants who had offered assistance to a fellow ship in distress were completely overcome before they even realised what was happening. The sailors who were trying their hands at piracy for the first time quickly tied the men up and left them on deck with a guard watching over them before they began the slow task of emptying the ship's hold and transporting it to their own vessel. The ship was Portuguese and was carrying a fine selection of goods to the colonies. The hold was loaded with tools, beads, trinkets and half a dozen cases of firearms. The operation of transporting the goods took several hours, but the time passed quickly for the pirates, who were in the best of spirits.

"Before raising the anchor and sailing off into the sunset, Alfred Mudd spoke at length to the Portuguese Captain, who spoke English. The young pirate offered his apologies to the Captain and his crew, as they glared and spat insults in his direction.

"After that first raid the pirates sailed back toward the New World and straight to a notorious island in the Caribbean known as a haven for pirates and thieves alike. It took weeks to reach dry land. The men drank and celebrated their new lives. Many of the crew spoke of their initial doubts about turning to a life of crime, and how their doubts had already been swept away. Alfred Mudd himself was pleased with the success of his first raid, but was very aware of the dangers they now faced. The pirates had stolen their prize, but now they had to sell the goods on the black market. The island of Arraya in the Caribbean Sea was known to be a lawless place where thieves and bandits sold their goods and plotted their crimes. The small harbour town there housed dozens of brothels and drinking dens, and hundreds upon hundreds of men who wouldn't think twice about stabbing their own mothers for a handful of coins. In the years to come the youngster wouldn't have such concerns. His reputation would grow to such a point that when he sailed his pirate fleet into such ports, even the most dangerous of men would bow at his feet, but by then he would be a different man entirely, a damaged soul incapable of mercy or compassion towards anyone who stood in his path Such was to be Mudd's destiny, but those days were a long way off.

"During the journey to Arraya, Alfred Mudd had time to plan the safest way of selling the goods that filled his ship's hold. Initially, Mudd selected the toughest of his crew to venture onto dry land, men he knew held little or no fear. The young pirate had realised many years before whilst living on the streets of Portsmouth that fear was a weakness that dangerous men could smell, and once they'd smelt it on their enemies then they'd already beaten them.

"Once his choices were made, Mudd turned his attention towards his so-called leader. As a candle burned throwing shadows over the small cabin, and the merchant Captain drank himself into a stupor, the young deckhand whispered his intentions in to a drunken ear. The very next day he armed his chosen men with fine weapons from the cases in the ship's hold. The crew waited and waited as the ship navigated cautiously through the mouth of the Caribbean Sea past countless islands that they'd come to know well in future years. Finally the island of Arraya appeared on the horizon nestled amongst a dozen others and drawing closer with every hour that passed. The young pirate whose eyes scared every man aboard the merchant ship gathered the crew for a meeting and spoke of his intentions whilst the ship's Captain yet again slept off his liquor.

" 'When we reach Arraya and dock in Splinters Bay we'll all go ashore. You will carry your firearms and be ready to use them,' the boy warned, as his men sat and listened intently to every word he spoke. To these men he was no longer a mere deckhand. Many knew him well from their shared time locked away in Portsmouth Prison. They all knew he was the smartest and most dangerous amongst them, and had no scruples taking orders from him.

" 'Our Captain,' Mudd continued, receiving sniggers from some of the men, 'will stay aboard this ship for his and our safety. As far as anyone on Arraya is concerned, Digby here will be our Captain's First Mate and the voice amongst us.'

"Every eye around the room fell on Digby the young thief, who was barely eighteen. He stood there smiling with pride, but the smile looked strange on a face that bore a horrific scar that ran down the side of his left cheek. Alfred Mudd had met Digby even before he'd been incarcerated in Portsmouth Prison and trusted him completely. Digby had lived a pauper's life on the same streets as Mudd and the pair had earned each other's respect on many occasions. Digby was fearless and had even fewer scruples than the young deckhand himself who wasn't a violent individual. Where Alfred Mudd used his tactical mind to overcome obstacles in his path, Digby used a knife. Several years earlier Digby had met his match and had received the facial scar to prove it, but Digby had at least survived the knife fight, unlike his opponent who'd been found with his throat cut from ear to ear in one of Portsmouth's dark alleys.

" 'We'll trade our goods and ship out. I want no drinking on shore. If we let our guard slip for a moment these men will steal our cargo and feed us to the sharks. Do you understand?' the young deckhand asked, and his men nodded, bringing the meeting to an end. They marched out on deck and assisted their fellow sailors navigating the ship towards Arraya and Splinters Bay, a place known by all sailors as a den of thieves."

Chapter Twenty Three

Later that night, after Benjamin Swift had left his cabin, the Admiral sat at his table thinking about the pirate who'd sent this mission on an adventure around the world and back, the man who had been a thorn in the Royal Navy's side for decades. Captain Mudd was a name that generated terror in most men and was the main character in most of the dark stories that parents told their children on cold winter nights. Admiral Saunders knew that now the great pirate was just a collection of bones buried in an unmarked grave, and for some strange reason it saddened him. Saunders wondered why and eventually concluded that it was because the pirate had always been a link between him and his father, a link that was now broken. Philip Saunders had always been close to his father and though it was many years since his death he sorely missed the man.

He sat for a while longer before retiring to bed, wondering whether he should include the complete truth of what happened on Antigua in the story he was telling Benny. In the end he decided not to. The fact that Alfred Mudd was now dead made the events on Antigua largely irrelevant, he told himself, but in the pit of his stomach Saunders knew that that wasn't the truth. Deep down Saunders wanted, no, in fact, he *needed* Benjamin Swift on his side and the incident on Antigua would only make the old fishermen question the morality of the British navy. Quite exhausted, Philip Saunders decided he would skip over the events on Antigua and simply tell Benny that the navy attacked Captain Mudd there, but he managed to escape. Having made that decision, he felt a little better and finally retired to bed.

In the early hours of the morning a storm hit the squadron. The wind picked up, whipping the Atlantic into a fury as sailors battened down the hatches, fastened everything on deck down and reefed most of the ship's many sails for fear the storm would tear them like paper. Jim Robson, Carp and the rest of the men who'd once smuggled across the English Channel were below decks feeling sick to their stomachs as the ship was thrown back and forth and lightning lit up the sky, followed by thunder so loud it woke every man from their slumber. Benjamin Swift, on the other hand, had never felt so alive. As the sun appeared on the horizon he was standing on deck clinging on for dear life as waves crashed around him.

The storm eventually died down and the wind dropped: by midday the squadron had dropped all of their sails once again and were cruising at a good speed. During the afternoon the Canary Islands were sighted off the Romulus' port side. Admiral Saunders handed Benjamin his telescope and the old fisherman stared excitedly through its lens. Then Saunders turned to his ship's Purser, a man named Matthew Harriet, who was in charge of the stores on board the ship.

"How do we fare with our provisions?" the Admiral asked. The purser stepped forward without delay.

"Our stores fare well, Admiral, except fresh water. In order to we cross the Atlantic we'll need to land and re-supply before heading towards the Spanish Main."

The Admiral rubbed his chin for a moment before turning to another of his officers. "How many days' sail before we sight the Verde Islands?" Saunders asked Robert Peer, his navigator who was standing at his side, smiling at Benny. The Admiral knew that, like himself, Robert Peer was feeling the effects of Benjamin Swift's contagious excitement. Robert Peer turned to his boss.

"The Verde Islands are still over a thousand miles away, but these trade winds can be relied upon. I would estimate we'll sight those isles within a week, Sir."

Saunders stared out at sea towards the Canary Islands in the distance as he gathered his thoughts. Around him his men kept quiet, waiting for his decision. However it wasn't the Admiral who eventually broke the silence. Benny Swift who had continued staring at the islands through the Admiral's telescope, finally lowered it.

"Why are they so...so mountainous?" he asked nobody in particular, and the Admiral chuckled. Robert Peer, who was gaining great pleasure educating the old fisherman, explained that they were volcanoes, a term Benny Swift – who had never left the flat landscape of Kent – wasn't familiar with. Admiral Saunders listened to the conversation between them, and once it was over he turned back to the Mr. Harriet.

"We'll sail to the Verde Islands and stop there to re-supply fresh water and any other foodstuffs we can get our hands on. We will land a thousand marines, as I want us to heave to, re-supply and resume our voyage without delay. From Cape Verde we'll cross the Atlantic," he ordered. Several of the officers present voiced their agreement with his plan, and Saunders ordered his First Lieutenant to signal the other ships with the instructions. By now it was approaching mid-afternoon and the sun was scorching the men on deck.

Turning to Benjamin Swift, Saunders invited the old fisherman to share a spot of lunch, with the promise of continuing the story. Benny agreed without hesitation. The old fisherman had been thinking of what Saunders had told him before beginning the pirate's tale - *"Once I've finished you'll know why you can help me. If you want to help you can, and for what it's worth I wouldn't blame you if you didn't,"* the Admiral had said. These words had stirred up a storm of curiosity in the old fisherman's mind. A short time later the unlikely pair were seated in the captain's cabin, and Saunders began the story where he'd left off.

Chapter Twenty Four

" "O nce they'd sailed into Splinter's Bay they dropped anchor a few hundred yards off-shore, and the men crowded on deck, taking in the stunning shoreline of the tropical island. Splinter's Bay boasted a white sand beach that ran into the distance in both directions. Beyond the beach lay deep jungle with trees and bushes offering the eye a thousand different shades of green. The merchants turned pirates who had grown up on the filthy streets of Portsmouth and London had never seen such a beautiful landscape.

"Anchored all around their merchant ship were dozens of vessels of various shapes and sizes. Some sported a fine selection of cannon and the newly turned pirates all hoped that on this island they'd find some honour amongst thieves. Whilst they prepared the row boats for launch, Alfred Mudd turned his attention to the lawless town, which sat on Splinter's Bay like a boil on an otherwise flawless face. The island of Arraya was apparently home to some of the most dangerous thieves and pirates to have ever lived, and Mudd was excited to have finally arrived there. Before leaving his small ship he warned the men he was leaving on guard to shoot anyone that came near the vessel. His men nodded their agreement, but the young leader could see they were scared out of their wits at the prospect.

"The trip to shore took only a few minutes and once they hit the beach the men climbed onto dry land for the first time in many, many weeks. However, they didn't have time to savour the moment. Mudd wanted to conduct his business speedily, so the gang quickly marched up the beach and onto the town's main street, where they all stood for a moment in shock at the sight that greeted them. The settlement stretched from the beach edge inland for a mile or so. Both sides of the road consisted of drinking dens and brothels that spilled into the street. Men stood boozing at tables: some arm wrestling or playing card games, whilst scantily clothed wenches wandered to and fro plying their trade. Turning to his right Mudd watched two men begin to argue before a fight broke out. They rolled around on the dusty ground that made up the town's main thoroughfare and nobody stopped them: some cheered but nobody intervened. Alfred Mudd watched eagerly, curious to see if the men would kill each other, but after a few minutes or so the punches stopped flying and the men were cheering and drinking together once more. Alfred Mudd smiled to himself. It was absolute chaos, and he felt at home from the very start.

"Standing by his side surrounded by their men Digby gave the impression that he was the small gang's leader. Alfred Mudd eyed him for a moment with pride. The deckhand was about the same height as Digby, but was years younger. Mudd was confident that nobody on shore would guess that he was actually in charge of their little expedition, thus if they faced hostility from the islanders Digby would be first in the firing line. This prospect didn't bother Digby in the slightest. The man was like a wild dog. In fact Mudd thought Digby enjoyed the possibility of doing battle.

" 'Greetings, friends,' a voice bellowed, and they all turned to face the newcomer. Standing only a stone's throw away was a man with shoulder length grey hair. Mudd admired the man's grey wispy beard which covered a large section of his weather beaten face and dangled down to his chest, a face that had clearly experienced a lifetime of sunshine. At his side were a dozen armed men, and at the sight of these men Mudd's small crew of amateur pirates gripped their own weapons nervously.

" 'Welcome to Arraya!' he continued, 'The name's Leonard, right hand man to Captain Tibb, Governor of our little slice a' paradise here,' he smilingly said as he stared at Digby.

"Alfred Mudd watched Digby return the smile, but even a smile did little to improve Digby's scarred face.

" 'Your arrival has already been reported to the Governor,' Leonard informed them, 'and Tibb wants to parley. Follow me, gentlemen.'

"Digby glanced at the young boy he'd known since his days on Portsmouth's streets with a look of panic on his scarred face, and Alfred Mudd nodded his consent whilst his men stood around nervously. Suddenly Leonard turned on his heels and began marching straight up the small town's main street, along with his guards. A moment later the whole group began to follow and Mudd quickly picked up his pace, in an attempt to catch Leonard and engage the man in conversation. As he marched along Mudd watched as even the drunkest most unsavoury looking characters shuffled out of Leonard's way and offered the man respect. He realised that Arraya wasn't as lawless as he'd first suspected, and that whoever Captain Tibb was, he was held in the highest regard by the islands folk. On reaching Leonard the young deckhand quickly fell in line next to the man, who looked over his shoulder and smiled Mudd's way.

" 'You have a beautiful home, sir,' Mudd offered, and the old man laughed and turned his way.

" 'On this island, boy, being called sir is considered an insult, but I respect your manners all the same. I'm Leonard, nothing more and nothing less,' he stated, pausing for a moment. 'So what brings you boys here?'

"Alfred Mudd took a few steps and gathered his thoughts before replying, 'We come to trade, Leonard, nothing more and nothing less.'

"At this Leonard roared with laughter and patted Mudd on the back. 'Well, you boys have come to the right place,' he said, and the pair walked along in silence for several minutes. The drinking dens on both sides of the road gave way to shacks and Mudd guessed they were where the island's residents rested their heads after a long night of boozing, or before raising anchor to leave for a stint at sea.

" 'So tell me about your Governor, Leonard, is Captain Tibb a fair man?' he asked, and Leonard chuckled to himself as he rubbed the ends of his wispy grey beard. Then suddenly he stopped in his tracks, and every one of his guards followed suit. Leonard stared at the youngster for a moment, before glancing over towards Digby and the rest of the island's latest arrivals. A second later he stared back at Mudd's gaunt face and the unusual eyes that, in the years to come, would terrify thousands upon thousands of sailors.

" 'You're a funny one, boy,' he barked, but Mudd stared back and read the expression on Leonard's face like an open book, concluding he had nothing to fear. 'Over the years this island's had some very bad men at its helm, but trust me Tibb's one of the better ones and believe me I should know. You ask me if he's fair. The man is the leader of our island here, a place which is home to some of the most dangerous men on this earth. Many would call such men scum, but Tibb calls them his brothers. Tibb's a crook, a thief and dare I say it a murdering pirate, but you ask me if I think he's fair and I'll answer that I do,' he said, as he gazed into the youngster's eyes.

"Leonard must have liked what he saw there, as a second later he chuckled and ruffled Mudd's ginger hair, before beginning to walk once more. The rest of the journey was made in silence and eventually the group reached a large and tastefully decorated house which stuck out like driftwood on a sandy beach amongst the small shacks surrounding it. Leonard marched straight through a wide door and into a huge room, and Mudd followed. At the far end of the room was a large chair made of bamboo cane, currently empty.

"As Leonard's soldiers filed into the room they lined up along each side of the room. Digby and the rest of his men entered and approached the empty chair, eventually coming to rest in the centre of the room. Alfred Mudd glanced from left to right eager to get his first glimpse of the lawless island's governor, but no one else entered the large chamber. Turning his attention he watched as Leonard strolled towards the chair and occupied it, and Mudd couldn't help but smile. Leonard Tibb, Governor of Arraya, smiled back at him.

" 'My name is Governor Tibb, boy,' he stated, completely ignoring Digby and the other men and fixing his gaze on the child amongst them.

" 'Why did you pretend to be someone else?' Alfred Mudd asked, but he already knew the answer. The boy who'd grown up on the streets of Portsmouth fine tuning his skills of deception and manipulation knew all the tricks in the book. Leonard Tibb laughed, before he replied.

" 'For the same reason you fell in-line next to me boy. I lied to fool you, gain your trust and learn your motives. Knowledge is power, but I'm certain I don't need to tell you that.' He turned to Digby, who was glaring at Leonard Tibb ready to pounce on the man, regardless of the guards who held firearms pointed at 'his' crew. 'I saw you for what you are as soon as you glanced at this young'un for instructions back near the shore,' Tibb told Digby, 'but it didn't surprise me. I've lived a long and unusual life and have seen things you couldn't even imagine. Now, tell me, I'm curious, would you die for this boy you take orders from?' he asked.

"Digby – who wasn't the smartest of men, but was a man you would want at your side when trouble arose – didn't take long to reply. 'I grew up on the same filthy streets as this boy, and I've seen Mudd here convince grown men to do the most dangerous of things. As far as I'm concerned, his youth aside, he's the savviest little thief I've ever known. I would die at his side with a smile on my face, and I fully expect to one day. I just hope that day isn't today!' Digby finished.

"Arraya's governor roared with laughter, and his guards joined him. A moment later he glanced back at Digby. 'Don't worry, you're thieves, and my sort of people. Consider yourselves well met and well-come on this island from this day until your bones are washed into the ocean,' Tibb promised, then he turned his attention to the skinny young pirate whose reputation would one day eclipse all others.

" 'So, what goods have you got to trade, boy?' he barked, grinning from ear to ear, and Alfred Mudd stepped forward to negotiate the sale of his first looted cargo, an act he'd repeat hundreds of times over the course of his infamous career."

Chapter Twenty Five

The HMS Sandown, the flotilla's reconnaissance ship was nearly fifty nautical miles ahead of her sisters when Captain Spruce spotted the first of the Cape Verde Islands through his telescope. The intrepid Captain had been given strict instructions that the squadron would be dropping anchor and sending marines ashore for supplies on the island of Sao Vicente, landing at Mindelo, a superb natural harbour. Captain Spruce's orders were to heave to offshore and wait for the rest of the squadron. The Captain was doing just that when he spotted something through his telescope that left him temporarily lost for words. It was late in the afternoon, the sun well on it's decent to the horizon when the HMS Sandown passed the small island Sal on her port side. Captain Spruce was standing on deck with his men studying the small island when he caught sight of something that made his skin burst out in gooseflesh and a shiver race down his spine. Turning pale, the Captain lowered his telescope, standing speechless. At his side his First Lieutenant asked what was wrong, and then word came down from the lookout atop the mast: hidden from view behind the island the Sandown had just passed and now sailing towards them, was a French warship, and it was followed by many more.

Captain Spruce and his officers stared in shock for a moment as he counted the masts of nearly a dozen ships of the line in the Sandown's wake, and his mind raced. He surmised that the French hadn't been waiting in ambush but had simply stopped to re-supply their ships unaware of the British, who, thanks to the spymaster Rupert Knightly, were giving chase. The Sandown was a reconnaissance ship, a frigate designed with speed in mind and in any other situation Captain Spruce would have immediately gone about and made a run for it, but unfortunately, the French were between him and the rest of his squadron. Knowing that the rest of his squadron were too far behind to offer support, Captain Spruce realized that he faced an impossible battle if the French decided to attack.

"Of all the rotten luck!" Spruce mumbled, as he watched in horror. Now the French were fully aware of the British ship, seemingly all alone, they piled on all sail and steered an interception course. To his relief Captain Spruce could see that the French were beyond the range of their cannon, but they were closing swiftly. Knowing that escape was impossible, Captain Spruce made the most difficult decision he'd ever faced in his career.

"Prepare to engage!" he ordered his officers, who stared at him in shock for a long moment.

"But, Captain, we're completely out-gunned. The French have ten ships!" his First Lieutenant gasped. Spruce turned and stared at the young man.

"We have the wind, Lieutenant! We'll try to hold them off until support arrives, or we'll sink, but we aren't going to go down without a fight!" he said. "Now get the men to battle stations. Cannoneers are to target masts and sails. If we can't sink their ships we'll at least slow them down!"

With that the HMS Sandown's officers burst into action shouting commands across the deck as the frigate came to arms and sailors and marines alike raced around preparing the ship for imminent attack.

Seated in his dining room and completely unaware of the Sandown's predicament, Admiral Saunders paused in recounting the story of "the notorious pirate Alfred Mudd" and gulped from a beaker of water. Perched on a stool in front of him Benny Swift turned his attention away from the ornate wall clock he'd been staring at and fixed those blue eyes of his on the young Admiral.

"It's quite a story, but I still can't figure out why or how Mudd became so notorious. With all due respect, he doesn't sound like the madman in the stories I've heard…" Benny said, filling the silence. Admiral Saunders sighed, and the fisherman could tell he was troubled. Benny watched as he twisted the tumbler of water around on the table, considering how best to respond. Finally he looked up and across at Benny.

"After selling his first cargo he lived for several years on Arraya, and became an apprentice to Tibb, who had taken a shine to him. It's hard to imagine, but you have to remember he was just a boy of twelve back then, and the person he became was almost a different person entirely. In those days he still had all of the dangerous traits that would one day make him infamous, but they were restrained. At that time Alfred Mudd had a few good traits, too, like a conscience for instance," Saunders said, pausing once more.

"The stories say Mudd traded his soul with the devil for control of the seas, but the truth is that somebody hurt him so badly that he never truly recovered, and he lost what little humanity he ever had," the Admiral said. Benny was staring at Saunders but the man wouldn't meet his eyes, and Benjamin Swift was now very curious.

"So what happened to him? What turned him into the monster he became?" Benny asked, and Saunders glanced up at him. The Admiral's troubled expression deepened, and Benny wondered what exactly that look on his face meant, in the end supposing it was guilt.

"I think you should hear the rest of the story," Saunders said, before beginning the pirate's tale once more.

Chapter Twenty Six

"The boy who'd grown up on the streets of Portsmouth many thousands of miles away made the island of Arraya and Splinter's Bay his home. The young pirate used the profits from his first looted cargo to construct a number of buildings on the island for his small crew. The men, who had always felt like outcasts back in England, soon grew to love Arraya. Every night they would booze in the drinking dens that littered her shore drinking the sweet rum that was made on the island.

"Under Governor Tibb's rule, the island had become much more productive than Mudd's first impression had suggested. The Governor was a smart man, and the young deckhand quickly realised that there was a lot he could learn from him, a realisation that had been the biggest factor in his decision to stay on Arraya and build a home.

"Tibb, who had first arrived on the island's shores three decades earlier, had found Splinter's Bay to be a place of violent chaos, but had seen the potential. For many years he'd dropped anchor in Splinter's Bay and drunk in her many taverns, but back then Arraya had been a place where pirates docked for a few days at most. The island wasn't self-sufficient and nobody could afford to live there long term. Tired of his life looting ships, Leonard Tibb decided he wanted to settle down on Arraya, and become its leader. He didn't waste time executing its previous governor out in the street where everyone could see. Tibb, aided by his own pirate crew, just took over the island and announced himself as Governor. Within a few years he had created a haven for his fellow pirates where crops were harvested, wells were dug and rum was refined out of sugarcane. The island's new Governor also placed restrictions on the inhabitants' piratical activities in the immediate vicinity, a move intended to limit unwanted attention from the powers of Europe who had colonies – and navies – in the area. Governor Tibb was a fair leader and was appreciated for it. The man whose wispy beard dangled down to his chest had been Governor of the island for fifteen years by the time Mudd's arrived.

"As the years passed by, and Alfred Mudd grew from a boy to a man, he didn't waste his time drinking, gambling and fighting in the taverns like the rest of his crew. Instead he spent it at Governor Tibb's side, learning everything the old pirate knew. The Governor taught him well. At the age of twenty Alfred Mudd was six and a half feet tall and with his long ginger beard, gaunt face, and eyes that scared even the toughest of men, he was a force to be reckoned with. Governor Tibb had been generous to his young apprentice, who spent almost half of his time away from Arraya on the open sea, having been awarded command of the best of the island's fleet.

"Mudd sailed the Caribbean, occasionally looting merchant ships, but never hurting anyone in the process. The young thief had honed his skills and was as cunning as a fox when it came to piracy, always leaving ships' holds bare of their cargo. When his small fleet wasn't out at sea they were exploring the islands that littered the near seas. Alfred Mudd was happy and living the life he'd dreamed of. From time to time his fleet would return to Arraya and he would always bring a fine selection of goods for Governor Tibb and Arraya's inhabitants.

"In the summer of 1755 the world changed for Alfred Mudd, whose pirate activities were already earning him a reputation. The daring young thief who had never been a violent man experienced real pain for the first time, and the young thief turned into a monster, a monster with no conscience or remorse who was only interested in one thing… revenge.

"Unknown to him, the raids on British merchant ships had been reported in the newspapers back in England for several years. On the British colony of Antigua, where the Royal Navy had built a dockyard and training academy, his activities had been a hot topic. In the summer of that fateful year the skilled pirate made a disastrous mistake, anchoring one of his ships in a small cove on the far side of Antigua, a fair distance away from the British navy's base. Whilst Alfred Mudd and most of his men re-supplied the ship with fresh drinking water and other necessities, a small group of his men took shore leave and over-indulged in rum.

"Alfred Mudd was completely unaware that his past was about to come back to haunt him. On the other side of Antigua, a few dozen young officers had just completed their training at the academy and were celebrating their success, and they weren't just any officers. The vast majority had been raised in Portsmouth and remembered the thief from his younger days when he'd robbed many of their fathers and their fathers' fellow officers. So after hours of drinking and celebrating, when word finally reached them that the pirate had dropped anchor on the far side of Antigua, they were keen to teach him a lesson, a decision that would haunt the Royal Navy for decades to come.

"Led by an arrogant young officer named Louis Francis, the drunken navy men quickly rode to the far side of the island, thinking they would be hailed as heroes for catching the already notorious pirate. Fortunately for them all they didn't come across Mudd himself and his trusted men like Digby, who would have killed the young navy officers without a second thought. Instead they caught the small group of pirates who had chosen to take leave and drink. Inspired by a gutful of liquor themselves, the twenty or so young officers attacked and killed Alfred Mudd's men before retreating back to the navy base on the other side of Antigua to sleep off their grog. When Mudd returned he collapsed amongst the bodies of the men he'd spent a decade leading, men who he thought of as his family, and he wept like a child. When he finally rose to his feet his soul had been destroyed and a monster had been created. Mudd climbed aboard his ship vowing to wage war against the Royal Navy until every officer that had spilled his crew's blood were no more. After sailing to safety he sent his spies to Antigua, spies who spent a small fortune in gold obtaining the names that would populate Mudd's infamous death list, the list of men who had been training on Antigua on that fateful day. Then Alfred Mudd began attacking Royal Navy ships and wreaking havoc, as he continued to do for many, many years."

Chapter Twenty Seven

The Admiral paused for a moment from telling the pirate's tale and looked over at Benjamin Swift who was staring back at him with those blue eyes of his. Saunders could see the old fisherman's mind was busy, and his face wore a confused expression as if he hadn't quite understood or believed what the Admiral had told him. Deep inside Saunders pushed away a surge of worry. The Admiral hadn't lied, but he had omitted some very important details about the attack on Antigua, the very details that had motivated Alfred Mudd's three decades of relentless attacks on the Royal Navy.

"Did Mudd return to Splinter's Bay? And to Governor Tibb?" Benjamin Swift asked, and Saunders rubbed his chin before replying.

"No, Alfred Mudd never set foot on Arraya again. Once he had left Antigua and acquired his death list he went on a rampage, attacking every British Navy ship he sighted. Within weeks he was the most wanted man on earth with a huge bounty on his head. Mudd knew that as soon as he attacked the Royal Navy he would be welcome on Arraya no more. Leonard Tibb loved him like a son, but the Governor always put the island first and knew that the British navy would sail their warships into Splinter's Bay without hesitation if they offered these particular pirates sanctuary. Tibb couldn't risk it," Admiral Saunders stated, and the dining room lapsed into relative silence once more.

Benny Swift stared out of the portside window at the choppy ocean and listened to the sounds of the ship. The old fisherman had many questions, and still had no idea whatsoever about how the dead pirate's tale affected him, and why the Admiral would need his help in the months ahead. Finally he asked the one question that seemed most obvious.

"Sir, just how could Mudd ever pose a threat to the Royal Navy in the first place? He must have had what, a few dozen men at best?" Benny pointed out, and the Admiral sighed.

"In the beginning, that was true. He had three ships and barely enough men to sail them, let alone man the cannon during battle, but Mudd had the element of surprise, and surprise the navy he did. No pirate before him had tried to attack and commandeer a ship of the line, and nobody expected it. The first ship he attacked was a frigate off the coast of Jamaica. Mudd left all of the crew alive and even though that ship's captain wasn't on his death list Alfred Mudd took the man captive along with his ship," Saunders said, taking a sip of water and checking the time on his pocket-watch before continuing, "Over the next few weeks he interrogated the captain, learning everything the man knew about ship deployment in the area, what ships the men on his list sailed on and planning how to exact his revenge. Several months passed as he sailed great distances to target ships that were sailing alone or in small squadrons. Within a year Alfred Mudd had killed two of the men on his death list and had increased his fleet to half a dozen vessels.

"How did the navy react?" Benny Swift asked, and Saunders actually laughed.

"They were incredibly embarrassed, as you can imagine, but they were also a little shocked. Up until that point they didn't believe it was possible to be outgunned by a pirate, but Mudd would continue to surprise and embarrass them for many years to come," Saunders said, as Benjamin Swift continued to stare out of the portside window at the ocean as the ship lifted and sank on her waves. Finally he turned and focused his attention back on the Admiral.

"One thing doesn't quite make sense, Sir. If he didn't return to Arraya where did he get his men from? Alfred Mudd couldn't sail a fleet with a few dozen men. He would have needed hundreds upon hundreds of men," Benny Swift said, and the Admiral smiled. The old fisherman could see that it wasn't a happy smile, but more of an awkward pained one.

"Well, Benny, Alfred Mudd was always a very clever and calculating man. The pirate did something that nobody expected," the admiral said, and returned to the story once again.

Meanwhile on board the HMS Sandown sailors moved swiftly in the organized chaos that was the preparation for the inevitable battle against the French. On deck Captain Spruce shouted orders at his men as he watched with dread as Louis Francis' ships manoeuvred into attack position. The traitor himself, the man who'd led the drunken gang over to the other side of the island of Antigua many, many years earlier stood on the deck of his squadron's flagship a short distance from the Sandown. The half French, half English navy Admiral had ground his teeth in anger when he'd first sighted the British ship, but his anger soon subsided. Louis Francis' hatred for the English went back decades, and the prospect of commandeering – or sinking – one of her ships surprised all alone in the Atlantic held great appeal.

Below decks on the HMS Sandown in the darkness of the brig Alfie Bicks was still in conversation with his cell mate.

"Captain Mudd leads the devil's army!" the stranger was telling Alfie, "They say he has a thousand demons with painted skin that the devil allowed to flee through the gates of hell," the prisoner warned Alfie, who was struggling to hold back laughter, completely unaware of the HMS Sandown's dreadful predicament, and the efforts being expended just over his head.

Chapter Twenty Eight

"A lfred Mudd came to realise that all of the gold, silver and priceless gems his men were stealing were really of little use to him. The pirate had already acquired a handful of ships and considered them of far greater value than the treasure they had ferried, but ships alone were worthless without loyal and capable crews to sail them. The young pirate, who was still wracked with grief, could have recruited hundreds of crooked sailors from the dangerous ports he sailed into. Port towns on islands that were outside the reach of law, where dangerous criminals drank and lived in safety, and every pirate captain in the seven seas sought sanctuary. Mudd was held in high regard in such places and had already carved out a reputation amongst his own kind. If he managed to sail his growing fleet towards Jamaica or a dozen other Caribbean islands he'd find men in the thousands to fight his cause. Many a sailor would join Captain Mudd's crew and he would easily outfit his ships, but, as usual, Captain Mudd came up with an idea that few could have even imagined.

"The pirate who had once dreamt of becoming the greatest thief in the history of the world now had a different dream in his sights. After the events on Antigua thievery meant little to him. The gaunt pirate who now stood at over six foot six lived solely to enact his revenge and punish the British navy. Mudd realised he needed men at his sides that weren't driven by money. Men who, like him, shared a hatred for the English and had the courage to stand against them and wage war.

"So Alfred Mudd sailed to neither ocean coast. Instead he remained where he was, in the middle of the Atlantic Ocean, promising his men that the English would bring him an army. His small fleet raised their sails and waited. As the days passed his crew were patient, never doubting their young leader's promise.

"The first vessel to get caught in the pirate's trap had sailed out of Guinea days earlier and had left the coast of West Africa far in its wake before running into trouble. The ship's captain was a merchant named Charles Johnson and even when his vessel sailed into thick fog he felt there was little to fear. The man had been sailing the mid-passage to the colonies for decades and knew there wasn't dry land in his ship's path for over a thousand miles, but he still ordered his ship to slow as his lookouts peered into the fog searching for other vessels.

"For a moment Charles Johnson glanced over at his merchandise, checking on the condition of his goods before turning and staring back out to sea. Charles never looked for long at their grubby faces and dark skin. It left a bad taste in his mouth and was apt to put him off his evening meal. The three dozen slaves that littered the deck were still cowering in fear, but that didn't bother Johnson. The merchant only really cared for the physical condition of his cargo and felt he took generous steps to maintain their well-being. Captain Johnson rotated his slaves regularly from the cramped hold below decks where another four hundred and seventy black faces that he owned were currently stored, making sure that every one of them received fresh air and the sun on their faces for at least thirty minutes each day. Johnson knew other merchants that weren't so generous, but Charles Johnson had been in the game for many years, and knew that a little bit of daylight made all the difference when it came to negotiating their sale with the plantation owners. Out in the New World they required the very best of workers. Slaving cutting sugarcane was back breaking labour. Even the toughest of men didn't last long, for which Charles Johnson was thankful. The merchant had earned a small fortune over the years keeping up with the demand. As far as Johnson was concerned he could never cross the mid-passage fast enough, because when the plantation owners had bought every prisoner in his hold, even the weakest of the women and children, they still wanted more.

"Suddenly a bell started ringing on deck, much to the Captain's surprise. Aloft in the crow's nest the lookout reported sighting several ships lying directly in the slave ship's path. Leaping into action Charles Johnson adjusted his course as he shouted commands to his lookouts. A few moments passed anxiously for the Captain, but once he was certain that collision had been avoided he left the wheel to his First Mate and reached for his telescope. Barely lifting the tube to his eye, one of his men informed him that there were three ships out there, all Royal Navy and signalling them to heave to. The fog was thick, but Charles Johnson managed to glimpse the Union Jack dangling from one of the warship's masts, and that was enough for him. The merchant had many friends in the navy and wasted no time ordering his men to strike the sails. While the sailors set to their tasks with alacrity, the slaves watched through eyes filled with terror.

"Charles Johnson had no concerns as he stood proudly on the deck of his ship watching as several rowing boats approached. Due to the fog, visibility was far from clear, and the merchant failed to notice that the men aboard the boats were not wearing navy uniforms. The next thing Charles Johnson knew they were pouring onto his ship's deck from every direction, dozens of them. Charles stood speechless as they quickly took control of his vessel with the muskets they gripped in their hands. The merchant's crew didn't put up any resistance either. They had been caught by surprise and it was all over before they even knew it. Finally the merchant Captain found his voice. 'You can't do this! You're Royal Navy!' he screeched at them, still confused by the British navy warships now visible in the fog. An icy voice behind him offered his only reply.

" 'I've been called some insults in my time, but Royal Navy tops them all!' the voice warned. Charles Johnson slowly turned and with one glance things suddenly made more sense to him. Alfred Mudd was admiring the scene unfolding on the ship's deck. Few people knew what Alfred Mudd looked like: over the years the British navy had worked very hard to squash the stories about the pirate. Nowadays few would be able to recognise him, but on that day many years ago Charles Johnson recognised the pirate immediately. One of Johnson's friends had once joked that Alfred Mudd looked like a man who'd been buried then dug up a few weeks later, and Charles Johnson could now see why.

"For a moment I imagine that the merchant wondered why, with all Mudd's wealth, he couldn't afford a hot meal once in a while, but then the merchant must have realised it was much more than that. Alfred Mudd looked haunted: like a man who'd lost his soul. Many of the merchant's crew believed the tall tales that Alfred Mudd had traded his soul with the devil, and Johnson must have wondered if there could be any truth to that particular story. Suddenly, anger pulled him from his thoughts, and he confronted the pirate who was staring at the slaves on deck with a sad expression on his gaunt face.

" 'How dare you!' Charles Johnson shouted at Mudd, who paid absolutely no attention to his outburst. 'You think you're invincible, that you can just attack and steal from whoever you like!' the merchant continued, 'But let me tell you, boy! The Royal Navy will have your head on a spike when they catch up with you. You have a few ships and a few dozen men. The navy will bring an armada to fight you!'

"Charles Johnson watched infuriated as Alfred Mudd continued to gaze at the slaves, but now a hint of a smile had appeared at the corners of the pirate's mouth. Suddenly the anger that had brought Johnson courage was replaced by absolute terror. Alfred Mudd pointed to one of the slaves, a thin man with jet black skin and eyes full of hatred that blazed in the direction of the wealthy merchant Captain, telling a painful story. Alfred Mudd of course understood hatred and pain more than most and could spot them both easily.

" 'Unchain him and bring him to me,' he ordered. One of his men unshackled the slave and marched him to where Mudd and Charles Johnson stood. The slave didn't even glance at the pirate. Instead he continued to glare at the merchant who had destroyed his life and the lives of all the others in the ship's hold. Alfred Mudd watched the slave, his expression an unhealthy mix of fascination and pity before finally turning his attention to the merchant Captain.

" 'You speak true on many counts, Captain. I have the ships, but you're right: I don't have nearly enough tough men who share my hatred for my fellow Englishmen,' he stated, pausing as he glanced at the slave and produced an eerie smile that sent shivers down the merchant's spine. When he turned back to Charles Johnson the smile had gone. 'I can easily out-manoeuvre the British navy and pick off their small flotillas in open water, but I agree with you: I'd struggle fighting a war, that's if they ever risked sailing a large enough fleet out of Europe. What I need is a few thousand men who'd fight at my side,' Captain Mudd said, turning and glancing again at the slave whose own eyes continued to burn into the merchant's. 'Any idea where I could find them?' Alfred Mudd asked, and his pirate comrades laughed at Charles Johnson's expression. Then Mudd turned his attention to his own men. 'Who speaks this man's tongue?' he ordered, and one of his pirate crew stepped forward. The man was just as black as the slaves on deck, but his eyes told a different story. The black pirate issued terror, he hadn't been stolen, enslaved and forced to receive it.

"Alfred Mudd then ordered the man to translate a message. He offered the slaves a life of freedom, a life where they would fear nothing and live in paradise. The message was quickly translated as the slaves began to stir and mutter amongst themselves, talking for the first time to each other without fear of punishment from their slave masters. Finally the slave's eyes turned for the first time away from the wealthy merchant, and settled on the scarily thin pirate whose red hair was blowing in the wind around his shoulders. Alfred Mudd stared into the slave's eyes, haunted eyes that in many ways matched his own.

" 'Tell this man I'm a man of my word,' Mudd ordered as he pulled a pistol from his waistband and offered it to the slave. "Tell him this pistol only has one shot, and if he doubts my word he can kill me now.' Some of the pirates on deck were surprised by their leader's offer, but they'd come to learn that Captain Mudd always knew what the outcome would be before he offered anyone anything. As the message was translated the slave continued to gaze into Mudd's crazy eyes, but his facial expression offered nothing but the terror and pain he'd experienced. The slave's soul had been destroyed, but Mudd already knew he would one day help the man rebuild it.

"Once the message had been translated the slave continued his gaze for several moments, and then he gripped the handle of the pistol the pirate held out for him, pointed it straight at Charles Johnson's forehead and pulled the trigger. The explosion was loud, and in the relative silence that followed the merchant's body fell to the deck with a thud, missing a considerable amount of the man's head. The remaining crew of the slave ship, many of whom earned their living by wielding the whips in their hands, were now cowering on the deck in fear. The slaves however were on their feet, many were crying and hugging each other.

"A short while later the rest of the slave ship's crew were loaded onto row boats with enough rations to last several weeks. They would have all died at the hands of the slaves if it hadn't have been for their new leader, Captain Mudd, who only really had a taste for killing men of the Royal Navy. Then Alfred Mudd sailed his small fleet out of the mid-passage's main shipping path with nearly five hundred new comrades whose loyalty to him was unquestionable, men he'd train to be expert sailors in the years that followed. The crew of the slave ship were picked up a few days later by another merchant vessel. Eventually they reached England and reported the loss of the ship, its crew and cargo to the Royal African Company, and then to the Royal Navy who swore them all to silence. A good friend of mine, Rupert Knightly, one of the very few men who know the extent of Captain Mudd's achievements, recounted this tale to me only recently."

Chapter Twenty Nine

Suddenly the distant sound of a single cannon shot was heard, pulling Saunders from his story. The Admiral leapt to his feet as a loud bell began to ring out from the crow's-nest far above their heads.

Admiral Saunders moved swiftly to his place on the quarter-deck, where he turned to his First Lieutenant who was staring into the mist ahead as more cannon fire was heard, echoing like thunder.

"Battle-stations, Sir?" the First Lieutenant asked turning to Saunders who shook his head in response.

"Not yet, Lieutenant. The Sandown is still several hours ahead, even at full sail," the Admiral replied, "Signal the other vessels to come to battle readiness but maintain present course, and order all hands on deck."

The First Lieutenant acknowledged his orders with a salute before relaying the command which was picked up and repeated by other officers. Deep down in the heart of the ship sailors scrambled out of their hammocks, whilst others swiftly stored the tools they held and clambered up to the Romulus' main deck, while the signallers raised the flags instructing the other ships.

Within minutes hundreds of men covered the decks as Admiral Philip Saunders stepped towards the quarter-deck railing and looked over them all. Saunders could see they were a tough bunch, from the eager expressions they wore, and even the smugglers seemed angry and ready for battle. Picking them out in the crowd was harder than he'd imagined. The likes of Carp and Jim Robson who'd smuggled many cargoes under the cover of darkness onto British shores, had earned their places amongst his men over the last few weeks. As he caught Jim's eyes for the briefest of moments the wide-shouldered young smuggler's gaze directed an accusing expression towards Saunders, and the Admiral glanced away. The look seemed to shout "Alfred Bicks is on the HMS Sandown!" a fact Saunders was all too aware of.

"Men! The HMS Sandown appears to have come under attack by the French!" Saunders bellowed at the crowd, watching the anger grow within them. "Unfortunately she is still a distance ahead, but when we reach her, we'll engage the French and sink them all!" At this the crew stamped their feet and several men cheered, "Let's show those cowards why we're the most powerful navy on earth! God grant us the victory!" Saunders shouted over the noise of the wind and the occasional echo of cannon fire from up ahead: "To battle stations!"

All the men cheered and began the intricate dance that prepared the ship and her cannon for fire. Admiral Saunders stared ahead into the distance hoping and praying that Captain Spruce would hold his own, that the HMS Sandown would survive the attack, and that Alfred Bicks would live... Saunders needed Alfred Bicks alive.

Standing on the quarterdeck of HMS Sandown, Captain Spruce watched as the French squadron's intercept course closed the gap on their quarry. The wind was fair and the French were using all its strength. Spruce watched in frustration as the French squadron sailed into two parallel battle lines, each consisting of four ships. Two of the enemy vessels dropped off, and Spruce knew Francis would be aboard one of those ships. The traitor had always been a coward. Spruce also knew that once the battle lines closed up the French vessels would sail past the Sandown firing their cannon individually at the target, in a devastating manoeuvre known as a rolling broadside. The French wouldn't be intending to sink Sandown: they would have assumed it was alone. Spruce had known Louis Francis for many years and knew the traitor wasn't stupid. He would most likely try to clear the decks and board her. Remembering the conversation he'd had in confidence with Admiral Saunders only a few days earlier, Captain Spruce clenched his teeth in anger. If the French boarded the Sandown and Louis Francis discovered Alfred Bicks, Spruce didn't even want to think of what the cowardly French man would do to him. This thought helped Captain Spruce make up his mind. Stepping forward, he bellowed orders.

"Turn to starboard and prepare to fire a full broadside across the French squadron's course!" To his First Lieutenant he said "We can at least *try* to hit their ships where they're weak."

His officers relayed his orders, and the mighty HMS Sandown began to turn below his feet. The Captain wholeheartedly believed that the enemy had no inkling any other British ships were in the area, and if the Sandown could slow the French down her sisters could well catch them up. The French would still outnumber them ten ships to six, but Spruce believed Englishmen made better sailors which would make a huge difference. Either way Captain Spruce was ready to sacrifice his life, his men and his ship for king and country. Peering through his telescope and watching as the French gained on his vessel, Spruce waited and hoped their ships wouldn't emulate him and turn. Spruce prayed his ship would manage to turn in time to get a broadside off as the Sandown slowly manoeuvred into an attack position.

"Prepare to fire a full salvo. I want those cannon swabbed out and reloaded double quick!" Spruce shouted, but before his order could be obeyed the French were turning out of the HMS Sandown's cannon range. Spruce felt a mixture of emotions, part frustration and part relief, but the latter was short lived. The tough old Captain knew he'd bought himself some time, but nowhere near enough. The French were now sailing back into position as the wind pushed them to within range. Captain Spruce knew he had the wind to position his gunners to fire on the French vessels, but with eight ships against the Sandown he was massively overmatched. Turning to one of his officers he grabbed hold of the man by his lapels and pulled him close.

"Get below decks and get that red-haired prisoner up on deck now!" he shouted into the man's face, before the officer scrambled out of sight. Watching the French ships inch closer and closer he waited for the first roar of cannon fire that would tear his ship apart, and Captain Spruce prayed.

Chapter Thirty

Meanwhile on the Romulus Admiral Philip Saunders stared towards the horizon listening for cannon fire, whilst his officers stood around him in silence. Eventually he glanced to his side where Benjamin Swift stood staring at him with a look of anger on his face. Saunders noted the look and exhaled a lungful of air in frustration. The Admiral hadn't wanted to end his story under these circumstances, but with the HMS Sandown under attack and Alfie Bicks' life at risk, time had finally run out.

Turning to his officers the Admiral ordered them to leave the quarter-deck, an order that was received with looks of surprise but wasn't questioned. Finally Saunders turned to Benjamin Swift and stared into the old fisherman's bright blue eyes.

"You look like you have something to say, Benny?" Saunders asked, and Benjamin gritted his teeth in anger.

"I've known Alfred Bicks for many years, and the man's as crazy as they come. But when all's said and done he saved my boy's life and risked his own on a dozen different occasions," Benny raged, before pointing out towards the horizon. "Now he's on the front line in war and you put him there! He hasn't a clue how to protect himself out on the ocean and didn't stand a chance from the beginning."

Admiral Saunders listened to Benny's rant and smiled at his choice of words, a smile he struggled to conceal before finally responding.

"Enough is enough, Benny! You want to know why I thought I may have needed your help?" Saunders said, returning Benny's glare.

"I think you owe me that much," the old fisherman replied, and Saunders stared out at sea for a long moment before replying.

"Alfred Mudd continued his campaign against the British navy for many years and as his fleet grew the names on his death list were removed one by one. In the end Mudd had only one name left on his list, and his fleet was a force to be reckoned with. The pirate had raided ship after ship and had an armada dozens of vessels strong. His private army of freed slaves numbered tens of thousands and were loyal to a man. To be honest, it got to the point around a decade ago that it wasn't just Louis Francis that was scared to go to sea. Most of the Royal Navy were scared to sail into the South Pacific, or 'the devil's land' as many sailors called it. But Captain Mudd, on the other hand, wasn't scared of sailing any sea, and even landed on our shores. Over the years his men visited England on several occasions, and the British Government worked very hard to cover the fearless pirate's tracks," Saunders said, pausing and glancing over at Benny whose expression of anger had been replaced by one of curiosity.

"My friend and informant Rupert Knightly monitored Mudd's activity closely. Of course he never knew of Mudd's presence until after the pirate had set sail, but Knightly always discovered Mudd's reasons for visiting our shores."

"Why would he risk returning to England?" Benny interjected, and Saunders rubbed his chin as he thought how best to reply.

"Good question, and the answer is simple: to spend some of his immense fortune. Rupert Knightly discovered that Mudd and his men were spending a fortune on purchasing weaponry on the black market. Mudd's ships would sail in and sail out loaded to the gunnels with the finest cannon, shot and powder that money could buy. Gold that had been plundered on Mudd's raids began showing up all over England." Saunders stated, before pausing and gazing out to sea as the old fisherman tried to absorb this revelation. After a moment he continued. "And it wasn't just weaponry Mudd was acquiring. The pirate was stock piling seeds, tools and all sorts of equipment."

"But why?" Benny asked, and Saunders smiled.

"Simply to help build his own colony. Nobody lives on ships forever. My friend Rupert Knightly, who is never wrong, believed for years that Alfred Mudd, just like Tibb before him on Arraya, built a home for his men, a place where they'd be safe and secure for the rest of their days." Suddenly several pieces of the puzzle fell into place in Benny's mind.

"An island in the South Pacific: and that's where we're headed," the old fisherman mumbled. Admiral Saunders let out a lungful of air and fiddled with the buttons on his jacket for a moment.

"Mudd's dead, but that doesn't mean his men are gone. What if we reach this island and meet a huge force?" Benny asked, and the Admiral wasted no time replying.

"We're confident most of his men fled after his death, but up until a few hours ago we did have one ace card up our sleeves," Saunders said, turning from the horizon and fixing Benny Swift in the eye. "In the summer of 1761 Alfred Mudd sailed into a port town on the south coast of England where he drank and celebrated with his crew for the best part of a week. During the celebrations and after a gutful of rum he frolicked with a local girl. Before sailing out and disappearing over the horizon the girl had been sworn to silence by Mudd's second in command, told that if she ever mentioned Alfred Mudd's name to anyone his crew would return and silence her forever. She was just a peasant girl who'd entertained a sailor to earn some coin. As you can imagine she was terrified and never uttered a word, but that wasn't enough to stop Rupert Knightly finding out, and that man is exceptional at storing away information until it is of use to him. Nine months later that peasant girl gave birth to a baby boy, and as that boy grew Knightly watched and waited for his moment," the Admiral finished as he stared at Benny.

"So Mudd has a son, what difference does that make?" Benny asked, and Saunders laughed to himself as he rummaged in his jacket and produced a scroll of paper which he handed to Benny. Unravelling the scroll and staring at the image in front of him Benjamin Swift froze and the colour drained out of his face. Saunders watched, but the old fisherman's reaction didn't surprise him.

"That's a portrait of Alfred Mudd. His face looks familiar to you, I'm sure," the Admiral stated. Benny Swift's mind was racing. He found himself muttering that it couldn't be true as the final pieces of the puzzle fell together. Suddenly it all made sense and he knew that Saunders was telling the truth. Staring at the image of the pirate's gaunt face, the deep sunk eyes that were terrifying even on paper, and the red beard and hair that framed his face, Benny Swift remembered the first time that he'd seen that face: many years earlier when the son of the world's most notorious pirate was living like a pauper on the streets of his home town, Deal.

Remembering the story of Mudd's own childhood living on the streets of Portsmouth Benny muttered, "Like father like son."

Saunders smiled, "Very true. It certainly explains Alfie's nature." Benjamin Swift was silent for a long time.

"Alfie fell out with his mother and ran away from home because she would never tell him the identity of his father. All she would ever tell him was that his father was a sailor and his name was Alfred," Benny said, feeling pity for both Alfie and his mother who had only been trying to protect her son.

"If it had ever reached further than the ears of Rupert Knightly, then the Royal Navy would have killed her and Alfie, and anyone else who knew of Mudd's visits to our shores. Thankfully Rupert Knightly kept that information to himself, storing it away just in case he ever needed it. The man is incredibly good at keeping secrets, even against his own friends," Saunders said bitterly, "So now you know why I need you, Benny. You're the only person Alfie Bicks listens to, and if we'd sailed into the South Pacific and met resistance from any survivors of Mudd's colony I'm sure they would have listened to Alfie Bicks. One glance at him and it's clear that he's his father's son, but now… " the Admiral's voice trailed into silence as he stared at the horizon and another volley of cannon fire echoed across the sea.

Chapter Thirty One

L ouis Francis watched with delight from his safe distance as eight of his squadron's ships surrounded the British frigate. Spotting the lone British vessel as they sailed out from the Verde Islands, he'd ordered his men not to sink the vessel, but to attempt to take the ship.

"Why would they be sailing out here alone, Captain?" one of his officers asked, and Francis turned to the man.

"A routine mission to the colonies, I would surmise. Don't you worry: the English pose no threat. Have the men clear the decks and prepare to board her," Louis ordered with his usual air of arrogance.

Meanwhile below decks on the Sandown in the dark and stuffy confines of the brig, Alfie Bicks was trying to block out his fellow prisoner's crazy ramblings as he struggled to hear the commands being shouted on deck. Alfie had a gut feeling that something terrible was going on, a feeling that had been confirmed when he'd heard the cannon fire. Since that initial explosion the prisoner across from him had become even more animated with his mutterings about the devil sailing the earth, mutterings that Alfie didn't want to admit were starting to put him on edge. When the ship began to turn sharply Alfie shouted questions at the prisoner in an attempt to discover if the man had any real answers, but all he got in return was crazy babble. Then suddenly the brig's door swung open, shining light into the small room for the first time in many hours. Alfie squinted as his eyes adjusted to the light, barely making out the officer as he rushed into the room. Alfie Bicks glanced over at his fellow prisoner hoping to finally get a good look at the man, but as their eyes met for the first time the prisoner let out a gasp and clambered backwards as far from Alfie as he could get. The deranged ramblings ceased now that fear had rendered him speechless. He cowered, terrified of Alfie as he avoided the gaze from Alfie's crazy looking eyes. Alfie tried to make sense of the prisoner's behaviour, but suddenly the officer was unchaining him and dragging him out of the brig into a narrow corridor.

"Listen, we're being attacked!" the officer shouted, but then the first barrage of cannon exploded from the decks above them and Alfie staggered to his knees as his ears rang from the explosion. The officer was pulling him now and Alfie scrambled along a few paces more before the Sandown was hit by a broadside of cannon fire that smashed through her starboard gunports, killing a few dozen men and disabling most of her cannon. Alfie was flung against the wall with such force that it knocked the wind from his lungs, and he lay gasping for air as the ship was battered from multiple directions.

Above him on Sandown's decks sailors were attempting in vain to fight off the attackers. The French marines were now targeting the English with musket fire, attempting to clear the decks. Captain Spruce was still shouting orders from his elevated position on the Sandown's quarter deck, but his orders were lost amongst the explosions and general chaos and his prayers had been far from answered. Within minutes, one of the French ships had pulled close enough to the Sandown's starboard side for gangplanks to be lowered, and as dozens of French marines poured onto the Sandown's main deck all hope for Captain Spruce and his crew fled. The marines quickly overpowered the remaining sailors, moving efficiently across the ship and killing anyone in their path. Climbing up onto the quarter-deck they cut down all of the ship's officers except Captain Spruce himself with musket fire. The marines were under orders from Louis Francis to leave the Captain alive. The man who had been awarded full control of the French squadron had waited years to reap his revenge on the Royal Navy, who he collectively despised. Francis wanted to look the Captain in the eyes as he took the man's life himself.

Below decks Alfie finally struggled to his feet and pulled the officer up with him. Both men stood and caught their breath for a moment before proceeding. The corridor was slowly filling with smoke as the officer led them up to the main deck. Alfie was in pain, but he feared drowning in the 'tween decks of the ship and wasn't willing to go down with her, so he quickly followed the man. After climbing a staircase and passing through a maze of corridors the pair reached a door and the officer burst through it closely followed by Alfie who was unarmed but, as always, ready for battle. The officer took two steps before a pistol vomited a shot that hit him in the chest knocking him backwards into Alfie, who collapsed to the deck with the man on top of him.

At the far side of the HMS Sandown Louis Francis strolled over the gangplank and onto her deck having been informed that the ship was secure. Captain Spruce was on his knees surrounded by French marines who held muskets levelled in his direction. Reaching the small group Louis Francis pulled his own pistol from his waistband and smiled broadly.

"Spruce, it's been too long," he said, enjoying every moment of his one-time colleague's misfortune. Captain Spruce stared up at the man who'd betrayed his country and summoned the last of his courage.

"I wish I could say the same, but sharing the deck of my ship with a coward and traitor like you brings me nothing but shame," Spruce stated. The French marines surrounding him sniggered, and Louis Francis smiled.

"Well, let's not drag it out then, sailor," Louis Francis spat as he shot Spruce in the chest and the lifeless body of the Sandown's Captain collapsed to the deck with a thud. A moment later a flicker of movement caught a marine's attention as Alfie threw the officer's body off and climbed to his feet, towering over the French marines. Instantly half a dozen weapons were pointed in his direction, but no-one fired, instead opting to look to their leader for instruction. Francis was frozen solid with fear as he stared closely at Alfie Bicks, taking in his every feature. The traitor wondered if Mudd himself had returned from the grave, and if the rumours of his super-natural powers were true after all. Aware that he was standing speechless and his men were staring at him he forced himself to remember that the great pirate was dead. He made himself step forward and approach the tall red headed man in front of him, but the arrogance and swagger he normally possessed were gone.

The marines were wondering what was going on. Louis Francis looked terrified, which was a strange look from someone who currently held a pistol in his hands aimed in the direction of an unarmed man. Finally the relative silence was broken as a bell began to ring out above them. One of the lookouts shouted across the decks warning of British warships in the distance, which was enough to bring Francis out of his trance.

"A further five ships, Captain Francis. Would you like us to prepare to attack?" his First Mate, Pierre Gerrard, asked in English.

Louis Francis wasn't interested in anything but reaching his nemesis' treasure and claiming revenge on the man who'd spent a lifetime humiliating him, and had no intention of risking his own life in battle. Francis wanted to punish the English, but he knew that day would come sooner if he had Mudd's plunder in his ship's holds.

"Clap this man in irons and lock him away in the brig," Francis ordered his First Lieutenant, "and light this ship up. Let's sail now. We'll build a hundred ships like this once we've got the gold! And then England will be ours for the taking."

The First Lieutenant barked the command and suddenly the deck of the Sandown burst into action as men dumped paraffin into the ship's hold and returned to the French vessel. A short time later, whilst the English ships were still just dots on the horizon, the HMS Sandown was lit and fire raced over her decks and down into her innards. As the French squadron sailed away from the fiery carcase, flames finally reached her powder stores and the ship exploded in a fireball that tore her to splinters.

Chapter Thirty Two

The HMS Romulus was at full sail and making good progress alongside the rest of the British squadron, but Admiral Saunders' hopes were diminishing with every roll of cannon fire that echoed across the ocean towards them. Standing by his side and all across the deck were the ship's crew who were holding their heads high despite the fact that every sailor present knew in their hearts that the fate of the Sandown had already been decided. When the Sandown's powder store finally ignited, the explosion that followed was far greater than any previous cannon fire, and the men cursed the French in anger for the loss of their fellow sailors. Within minutes a thick plume of smoke could be seen in the distance drifting high into the blue sky. Saunders himself gripped his telescope, watching in anger as the French squadron sailed away leaving a fiery blaze as the remains of the mighty frigate sank down to Davy Jones' locker where it would rest for eternity.

The Admiral had been dealt the first of many harsh blows that he'd experience before the long and treacherous journey were complete, but in the years to come he considered the sinking of the HMS Sandown the worst. It also marked the moment Admiral Saunders realised that the French squadron outnumbered his ships two to one, a fact that would weigh heavily on his mind. Standing on the quarterdeck he looked around the faces of his men and felt their pain. Philip Saunders hid his emotions well. The time for grieving the lives lost in the taking of the Sandown would come, but Saunders knew his men were looking at him for strength, and strength was what he would give them. Turning to his side he measured the look on Benjamin Swift's face. The old fisherman expressed anger but no grief, and Saunders wondered if Benny would ever fully recover from the loss of his son. Losing Alfie Bicks, as much as Benny had liked the man, was insignificant in comparison. Snapping out of his thoughts the Admiral shouted an order across decks.

"Prepare to rescue men from the water!" Saunders roared. "If any of our men are still alive I want them safe aboard our ships."

Romulus' sailors and marines answered "Yes, SIR!" in unison, but, like the Admiral, they knew they'd find few survivors. Saunders knew that each and every man he had selected had fought countless battles, and had witnessed death first hand many times. For the small band of smugglers, men like Carp and Jim Robson were about to get their first experience of wholesale slaughter, and it would leave a foul and bitter taste in their mouths.

Several hours later the British squadron finally reached the HMS Sandown's final position, but the frigate itself was nowhere to be seen. Surrounding the British squadron, on the choppy ocean surface bodies and debris bobbed around in silence. The ships dispatched rowing boats and men worked tirelessly for hours retrieving the bodies from the water hoping against hope for survivors.

The Admiral eventually went below and sought sanctuary in his cabin having already decided to give up on chasing the French squadron who would soon be clear of the Verde Islands and making their way across the Atlantic. Saunders opted to stick to his original plan: heave to for the night and land his marines on San Vicente. The hundreds of bodies that had been pulled out of the water were taken ashore. The Admiral knew that storing them in his ship's holds was impossible, as they'd soon decompose, spreading disease amongst his crew.

By nightfall a thousand marines had landed on the small island off the West Coast of Africa and had buried the bodies of the Sandown's crew in a shallow communal grave before beginning the task of re-supplying the squadron with fresh water, fruit, wood for fires and sundry other items. Admiral Saunders gathered with his captains and fellow officers in a sombre meeting to announce his intentions to sail from the islands across the Atlantic, making for the Spanish Main at the earliest opportunity.

"We have lost the first battle and our squadron is one ship down, but I promise you, men, we will win the war and by the time we're finished Louis Francis will pay the ultimate price for his treachery," Saunders informed his men. After the meeting had adjourned the Admiral tried to sleep, but as he lay there all he could think of was the face of his one-time friend Alfred Bicks and he cursed himself for being so stupid as to lock him away on the HMS Sandown after the smuggler had tried to kill him. Eventually his mind drifted to Louis Francis, and Saunders wished that the dead pirate had been able to scratch that name from his infamous death list. In the end Philip Saunders muttered "I'll do it for you, Mudd," to himself, and endured another sleepless night staring at the ceiling of his cabin.

Early the next day the marines began to return from San Vicente hauling barrels upon barrels of fresh water and supplies. Saunders wasted no time in meeting with his senior and most trusted marine, Hendricks.

"You examined every single body yourself?" he demanded, and the tough marine nodded.

"And Alfred Bicks wasn't amongst them?" Saunders continued, and Hendricks shook his head.

"But, Captain, that means nothing. Bicks was locked away in the brig: he would've gone down with her," the grizzled marine suggested, and Saunders nodded and rubbed his chin.

"Thank you," the Admiral said before dismissing the man.

An hour later the remaining smugglers who had become part of the Romulus' working crew were rounded up and led to the Captain's cabin. They all stood facing Saunders who was seated behind his desk.

"I'm sorry," the Admiral began, but much to his surprise Jim Robson stepped forward.

"Don't be, Captain. You saved our lives more than once. Alfie was born and bred for conflict. He died doing what he loved. Just promise us all on Alfred Bicks name that the French will pay, and pay in blood for what they've done," Jim said.

"I promise that we'll sail to the ends of the earth and the French will pay ten times over," Saunders replied. Jim Robson, Carp, Benjamin Swift and the rest of the ragtag band of smugglers saluted him, and Saunders felt incredibly proud of each and every one of them. A few hours later the five ships of the line set their canvas and sailed away from the Verde Islands on the next leg of their journey, which would take the squadron across the Atlantic Ocean.

Chapter Thirty Three

The passage across the Atlantic Ocean passed very slowly for Admiral Saunders and was one of the most depressing stints at sea the young admiral had ever faced. After the sinking of the HMS Sandown morale was very low, and the excitement of the adventure into far-away lands – not to mention prize money – had seeped away. Those officers aboard the Romulus who knew the secret mission's destination had far more to be depressed about than the common men below decks, but they tried to project optimism for the benefit of the rest of the crew. During the weeks that followed every sailor tried to get on with the task at hand, whilst they mulled over the events surrounding the attack on the HMS Sandown, the comrades they'd lost and the likelihood of sharing a similar fate. The men still gulped their grog until they were merry, but few had anything to smile about. The musicians that had played various songs such as 'Rule Britannia' and 'Britons Strike Home' to encourage the sailors and keep their spirits high had fallen silent.

The crossing was far from plain sailing. The British squadron were ravaged by several storms, each of which threatened to smash the ships to pieces. The sailors that the Admiral had chosen were experienced in such seas, but for Benjamin Swift and the ex-smugglers the journey was tough and they suffered huge swells that up until that point they couldn't have even imagined. The old fisherman spent much of his time in the company of the Romulus' navigator, Robert Peer, who'd become a good friend. The pair spent many evenings huddled in conversation whilst Robert poured out a lifetime of knowledge and Benny listened intently to every word. Some evenings Benny sat alone in his cabin clinging onto his bed as the ship battled its way through the ocean, not willing to step out onto deck for fear of getting swept into the sea.

Admiral Saunders manned the quarter-deck during even the most severe of storms, often alone, contemplating the loss of life that was his responsibility. For the best part of a week Benjamin Swift kept out of the Admiral's way, observing at a distance the weight of despair that responsibility brought. Finally, when the storm subsided and the wind died out completely, delaying their progress, Saunders seemed to snap out of his grief. Normally during times the fleet was becalmed, Admiral Saunders worried the most, knowing from experience that men needed to be kept busy, and having too much time to reflect and think was never a good thing, but this time things were different. Knowing that all the men had had a tough stint at sea due to the storms, and were struggling through lack of sleep and physical exhaustion, he allowed them a day's rest from duties.

Under normal conditions he would not have done so, but the lack of any wind and the fact that the horizon was clear of vessels in every direction meant the squadron had nothing to fear. Admiral Philip Saunders also knew that the ships' crews needed it. The young admiral had risen swiftly through the ranks, due in great part to the respect that he earned from each of his crews along the way. Morale aboard the ships needed a boost. So for a whole day, whilst the officers and captains were ferried to and fro from the Romulus for meetings with their Commander in Chief, the rest of the crews drank their rations of grog along with an extra bonus and toasted farewell to the men who'd fought and died in battle aboard the HMS Sandown less than two weeks earlier. Some of the squadron's remaining captains urged

Saunders against such generosity as they sat in his dining room over lunch, arguing from fear of mutiny aboard the ships, but the Admiral wouldn't listen. Philip Saunders had been chosen to lead the most important mission in the history of the Royal Navy for a reason, and a few days later, once the chaos on decks had returned to normal and the sailors were working efficiently with smiles on their faces once more, those captains agreed the Admiral's judgement was sound.

The wind however had not returned, and Saunders tried to keep the men busy to avoid despair creeping in once more. Every practice and drill imaginable was ordered to be carried out, and as the days slowly crept by and the surface of the Atlantic remained as flat as a mill-pond Admiral Saunders secretly began to pray for wind.

The following day when Saunders awoke to a sharp knock on his cabin door, he arose listening for the sounds that would have meant the ship was underway again. His ears disappointed him. Clambering out of bed and opening his cabin's door he was greeted by his First Lieutenant, whose dour news couldn't have displeased him more.

"I'm sorry to disturb you, Captain," the younger officer said, saluting, "But I have troubling news. I've heard word that the sailors have been speculating amongst themselves regarding where this squadron's headed. Mutterings of sailing the dreaded Horn are being whispered below decks. Some are even saying that we've been sent to fight Mudd's army. You know how superstitious some of these uneducated men are, Admiral. I think the time to inform them of prize money has arrived. Forgive me if I speak out of line," the First Lieutenant stated. Philip Saunders exhaled a lungful of air in frustration and rubbed his chin for a moment.

"Don't worry, Lieutenant, you're doing your job, and doing it well. Thank you for bringing this news to my attention," Saunders said, pausing as he tried to think how best to proceed. The timing was terrible given the recent lack of progress across the Atlantic, but the Admiral had always known that he would have to come clean to the crews at some point. Both Sir Robert Burns and Rupert Knightly had warned that the mission would be the most difficult he'd ever been given, and Saunders was in absolute agreement.

As a Royal Navy Captain, Saunders expected his crew to sail into battle even when outgunned, and to face whatever seas the ocean could throw at them, but where Alfred Mudd was concerned things were a little different to say the least. The pirate was considered a monster, but unlike most horror stories, he'd actually existed – and still did as far as the crew were concerned. Captain Mudd had used terror as a weapon for decades, and even after his death Admiral Saunders would have to deal with the fallout of that terror, and handle his crew delicately to avoid panic. Looking at his First Lieutenant once again, standing nervously in his cabin doorway, he ordered the man to arrange an announcement on deck within the hour. It was time to inform his crew exactly what the dangerous mission involved. Admiral Saunders just hoped that when he mentioned Alfred Mudd's name, his crew wouldn't go berserk and attempt a mutiny.

Chapter Thirty Four

Eanwhile, Alfie Bicks was struggling to control his anger. The man who'd spent his entire life in a small town on the south coast of England smuggling brandy and tobacco for a living, had found himself in shock after his capture and the sinking of the HMS Sandown, but that shock had soon morphed into fury. Locked in the brig of the French squadron's flagship, the Severe, time passed slowly: how much time Alfie had no real idea. Occasionally the brig's door would open and the French guards would curse at him in their foreign tongue, often spitting at him and kicking him pulling him from his thoughts.

Alfie Bicks would grit his teeth during these moments and struggle against his chains, wishing that he wasn't restrained and that he had a knife in his hands. Instead he would suffer the agonising pain of their blows. Eventually the guards would throw him some food, which was barely edible, before slamming the door and leaving him alone in the dark once more. During these moments Alfie would often find himself thinking of Admiral Saunders, reflecting on how fair the Admiral had been and how well the Royal Navy had treated him considering what he'd done. Alfie Bicks was truly sorry for the way he'd treated Saunders, but he knew now he'd never get the chance to make amends to the Admiral.

As more time passed Alfie found himself questioning his own sanity as he found different ways of passing the time, such as scratching his nails on the timber floor until his fingers bled and he nearly passed out from the pain, hoping that unconsciousness would offer a brief period of escape. At other times he found himself appreciating bad weather, as while the ship was thrown around in the ocean and he was tossed around in the small cell whilst his restraints cut into his ankles and wrists, he had a break from the monotony of being alone in the dark.

Fearing that his mind was on the brink of a wave that would destroy him if it broke, like the strange man he'd shared his cell with on a ship that now lay on the bottom of the ocean, Alfie began to give up hope and face the inevitable: that his predicament couldn't deteriorate any further, and he was going to die alone in the dark. Alfie Bicks was wrong and his situation was about to get much, much worse.

The next day he was awoken with a kick to his bony chest that knocked the wind out of him and left him fighting for breath. The French guards had no sympathy for their prisoner as they dragged him to his feet and out of the cell. Suddenly, after the best part of a week in the pitch black, Alfie Bicks found himself out on deck where he was forced along, blinded by the dazzling sunlight, whilst dozens of sailors hurled abuse his way. Eventually he was chained up once more, this time by each wrist leaving him on his back staring up at a bright blue sky. Initially he was pleased, glad that at least he'd die in the fresh air. Little did Alfie know that it would be months before he'd leave the deck, and that he'd face the agonies that only the elements of nature could throw at him, that his skin would burn and blister in the sun that would beat down relentlessly or in colder seas and at night he'd nearly die of frostbite as waves crashed over the deck turning his lips a shade of blue.

During that first day though a smile crossed his gaunt face as he listened to the calm sea and breathed in lungsful of fresh salty air. Hours passed and that smile soon vanished. Days passed, and much to Alfie Bicks' surprise he eventually found himself wishing that he was back alone and in the dark of the brig, where he could have a break from the constant noise and commotion on deck, the heat and the cold, and the wind and rain that felt no remorse as they punished him all day and all night.

The only benefit Alfred Bicks found from being outside on deck was that he could pass the time watching the French. He observed how the men ran the ship, and even though he'd spent just a few days on the HMS Romulus amongst the crew he could see there was a distinct difference in management between the two navies. When the Captain came out on deck the behaviour of the French sailors always changed. Their easygoing demeanours switched to expressions of fear and concentration as they abruptly ended their conversations and focused on the tasks at hand.

A long time ago a wise old crook had taught Alfie Bicks the difference between fear and respect, and the ex-smuggler sensed that the French Captain controlled his vessel through fear. Thinking back to the time he lay in a hammock plotting his revenge on Admiral Saunders he remembered the way the sailors had spoken of their Captain with respect, and Bicks was sure the French wouldn't share the same sentiment for the older looking French Captain who seemed to eye every one of his crew with contempt. The Captain, who Alfie had heard being referred to as Francis, never ventured near the end of the ship where Alfie Bicks was chained. The ex-smuggler often caught Francis staring down at him out of the corner of his eye, but for weeks the Captain did not venture near his captive.

Alfie observed that the French crew were usually in good spirits due to their victory over the English, but when in the presence of their Captain those good spirits vanished as if a terrible storm had appeared on the horizon. Captain Francis clearly ran his ship with a tyrant's power, far removed from Admiral Saunders. Not a day passed aboard the Severe without a flogging on deck, and the punishment was always issued at the changing of watch so most of the crew would witness the horrific spectacle. The French Navy rarely flogged their men, so the sight was even more brutal for the sailors who would flinch and grimace as the cat o' nine tails found its mark on the victim's back, and the Captain grinned sadistically as the man broke and collapsed to the deck in agony. Even Alfie, who'd grown to hate the entire crew, struggled to watch from his vantage point and always pitied the poor sailor who'd more often than not done very little wrong. And he took satisfaction from the looks the French officers would flash their Captain's way in those moments of madness knowing they didn't share their leader's love of punishment and pain.

Alfie often wondered, if that was the way Captain Francis treated his own men, what abuse would be coming his way. Sometimes he hoped that that punishment would come sooner rather than later, but above all else he wondered why the French Captain had taken him prisoner in the first place, and why he was still alive when hundreds of others had perished.

Chapter Thirty Five

Meanwhile on board the HMS Romulus word soon spread through the ranks of the Admiral's intention to reveal their orders, and from the crow's nest to the bilges men whispered and speculated. Some sailors who were coming off their watch were eager to hear confirmation of the rumours they'd heard before slipping below decks and into their hammocks for some much needed rest. Others had just awoken to the news, but were equally keen.

Within an hour of that knock on Admiral Saunders' cabin door the Romulus' decks were crowded with sailors. The hatches were opened and men who were unable to reach the open air packed out the lower tiers ready to hear news of the mission from the decks above. Even the masts were crowded as dozens of men had climbed the ratlines in order to watch the announcement. They held on for dear life and stared out at the flat lifeless sea, and waited patiently for Saunders, the Captain who they considered one of their own, to confirm or deny their worst fears.

Saunders himself stood on the quarter-deck overlooking his crew, and surrounded by his officers who were already well aware of the dangerous mission's objective. Finally Admiral Saunders stepped forward towards the railing, eager to put his crew's minds at ease or at least attempt to.

"Men, from the days preceding our swift exit from London you've all known in your hearts that this isn't a normal tour of duty. Many of you were summoned at the last moment, barely having time to say farewell to your families. For that I have no apologies to make: you are sailors of the Royal Navy, the most powerful navy on this earth. I stand

159

here now as your Captain and offer these words, not because I am duty bound to, but because I respect each and every one of you enough to honour you with an explanation, from my First Lieutenant Lucas here to the kitchen boy, and the few landsmen we have aboard this ship," the Admiral bellowed, finding a few smugglers faces amongst the hundreds of faces on deck. The crew, as on every ship he'd captained since his early twenties, were staring up at Saunders with admiration. Any fear generated by rumours below deck wasn't visible now.

"Some of you may have noticed that the crew aboard this ship is a mismatched bunch, made up of sailors and marines who over the years have proven their worth by my side. As a crew you have a wealth of experience amongst you, far greater than a standard vessel and the Romulus isn't alone. This squadron of ours is made up of the best of the best in order to succeed in the most important naval mission in our country's history!" Saunders shouted down at the men who stood in silence and awe.

"You're some of the best sailors our country boasts, and as such should stand privileged and proud to man these decks," the Admiral stated, as he paced up and down to allow his compliment enough time to sink in, and prepare them for the difficult news to come.

"Some of you say this squadron is headed for the Horn, and headed there it is!" he roared. The massed men gasped in shock, but the Admiral continued regardless, "The great pirate who some say couldn't die is finally dead! Captain Mudd is no more! We sail into the South Pacific, and when we return, our holds will be filled with the greatest hoard of treasure ever accumulated."

The crowd stood in complete silence, stunned, as the Admiral's words penetrated their consciousness. Saunders stared down at them whilst his officers stood at his side with their heads held high. The Admiral's Marine Commander

Hendricks and dozens of his men stood overlooking the main deck ready to deal with any outburst from the crew, but none came. As the Admiral had stated, this wasn't a normal crew. The sailors were a tough bunch and each man had at some stage in their career at sea faced up to their fears and confronted their foes. Finally the silence was broken, but not by Saunders himself. A skilled carpenter – who the Admiral called Sidney, having known him for a long time – asked the question that they all wanted to be answered.

"How do you know he's dead? Captain Mudd has skills far greater than any mortal being. The man can move his fleet and intercept his enemies, knowing where they'll be before they've even arrived there! Men like that can't die!" the carpenter shouted, earning both mutters of support from his comrades and glares of disapproval from many of the marines standing guard. Hendricks looked the Admiral's way for permission to silence the man, but Admiral Saunders shook his head, dismissing the marine's request. Instead Saunders addressed the carpenter's question. Philip Saunders knew in his heart that Mudd was no more, but the Admiral was privy to a wealth of information that his crew were not. The most important thing Saunders wanted to achieve was convincing his crew that the notorious Captain Mudd was gone, and the biggest threat they faced wasn't a supernatural pirate but attack from the French.

"I'm absolutely certain Alfred Mudd is long dead now, and the pirate was only human after all. He was incredibly skilled at navigating and naval warfare, having spent a life battling at sea. That I don't doubt. Alfred Mudd's bones were found with a handful of his men by a merchant ship over six months ago. The bones belonged to a man over six and a half feet tall, much taller than any native from the South Pacific. The body was also found alongside many possessions that were known to belong to the pirate, including a silver ring that was inscribed with a message. Mudd wore that ring on a chain around his neck, refusing to ever take it off. Trust me, men, there can be no doubt." The Admiral finished, as he stared at the crowd once more. The sailors seemed to weigh the information up for a moment and Saunders let them.

"I don't fear the Horn, Captain. If finding treasure is our mission then so be it!" a sailor eventually roared from somewhere at the back of the crowd, and others began to cheer. Finally someone else shouted the question Saunders had been hoping for.

"So, Captain, if we succeed can we expect prize money given the treasure and all?"

Philip Saunders smiled, knowing that the seed of hope, a powerful emotion that had the power to make men face the toughest of challenges, was about to be planted.

"Not *if* we succeed, sailor, but *when*, and there'll be a share for you all. If the hoard is the size they say then you'll all have enough money to grow old on dry land with smiles on your faces!" the Admiral bellowed, as each and every sailor whooped with joy and cheered.

Saunders let the men have their moment as they stamped on the deck and rejoiced at the news of potential wealth. A few minutes later the Admiral stepped forward once more.

"Now, let's get back to work and get this ship moving once more," he ordered, and the men began to clear the decks. When he turned to his officers many of them congratulated him on the success of his speech, but out of the corner of his eye Saunders could see Benjamin Swift standing next to Robert Peer. The old fisherman was as sharp as they came, and from the expression on his weather beaten face he was wondering where the silver ring Mudd wore around his neck fitted into the story he'd been told. Philip Saunders hoped that he'd never have to explain as he walked back towards his cabin.

Later that day the wind finally returned and the various crews, all of whom had now learned of the squadron's destination and purpose from their captains, busily dropped their sails. Within hours the previously flat water had stirred up and waves crashed against the ship's hulls as the squadron pushed on towards the Spanish Main.

Chapter Thirty Six

Lying on his back on the deck of the Severe whilst the
sun beat down relentlessly, Alfie Bicks stared up at the
cloudless sky and dreamed of nothing but quenching
his thirst. Days earlier the French squadron had finally
sighted the Spanish Main, and now they were cruising south
towards the infamous Cape Horn, the most dangerous stretch
of ocean on earth.

The English prisoner, whose fair skin had blistered
and burnt, was unaware of the squadron's treacherous course,
and was beyond caring. Hope had slowly evaporated with
every peak and trough the Severe had sailed through, and now
Alfie hoped only that the end would come soon for him and
put him out of his misery. He had considered suicide, but
much to his frustration even taking his own life wasn't
possible whilst shackled to the deck as he was. Occasionally
when the French brought him food he threatened and
insulted them with taunts about their mothers and sisters, in
the hope they'd retaliate angrily and end his pain.
Unfortunately they were under strict orders from Louis
Francis, their vicious Captain who they feared above all else,
not to injure him further.

Time passed by in a daze for Alfie who drifted in and
out of consciousness due to the lack of food and water. The
man who'd once made a living smuggling the best brandy and
wine was severely dehydrated, suffering from malnutrition,
and as skinny as a rag doll. Through his scary eyes, now
sunken into a gaunt face, he saw the sailors on deck wrapping
up in thick jackets as the nights slowly became colder. During
the midnight hours under a night sky of countless stars he'd

often find himself shivering and breathing white plumes, and desperately hoped that the cold would have the strength to kill him. As more time passed by and the squadron sailed even further south the ocean became more violent and the days themselves became chilly and cold.

It had been a long, long time since Alfie had shared a conversation with a fellow human and that man had been as mad as a March hare. At times Alfie would regain consciousness to discover that he was still shackled and had been muttering to himself. On occasion he'd listen to sailors on deck conversing in their foreign tongue, but he was barely able to make out a word. When he'd first been taken captive he'd assumed it was so that the French could interrogate him for information regarding the British fleet, but much to his surprise no such effort was made. Throughout those first few weeks of bitter cold whilst he was exposed on deck, Alfie Bicks prayed for such an interrogation. He knew nothing of Admiral Saunders' plans and was certain the French would quickly realise he could offer no assistance, and then perhaps they would end his pain.

One particularly cold night he awoke as a gust of wind raced across the Severe's deck and as he looked around he realised he wasn't alone. Only a dozen feet away was a man much older than the rest of the crew, and Bicks recognised him instantly from the distinctive uniform he wore. Captain Francis had dark hair that was greying in places and olive skin that made him appear Mediterranean in the dim moonlight. He was sitting a dozen feet away staring at Alfie through dark eyes speckled with red from the gut-full of brandy he'd consumed to bolster his courage.

Months earlier, when Louis Francis had first heard of Captain Mudd's death, he'd stood tall for the first time in decades. The great pirate had been his lifelong nemesis and had cast a dark shadow of fear that had sunk deep into Louis Francis' very core. The stories of Mudd's almost supernatural abilities hadn't helped! Francis was a superstitious man by nature and some of the tales he'd heard, tales the Royal Navy considered to be true, defied belief. Like many others Louis Francis considered the possibility that the bizarre stories were true and the pirate had actually brokered a deal with the Dark Lord himself. Occasionally on cold winter nights, hidden away in Paris where he hoped that Mudd's tentacles couldn't reach him, he'd think back over what he'd done on Antigua, and for a moment he'd regret his actions, but then the moment would pass and anger would return, anger driven by his deep rooted fear that one day Mudd would succeed in crossing his name off the infamous death list.

On hearing of Mudd's death that fear had finally vanished, after a lifetime of living in hiding and constantly scheming to guarantee his safety. Louis Francis had quickly decided the time for his own revenge had arrived. After briefing the French on the British discovery of Mudd's body, he'd taken advantage of the situation, using all his skills of treachery, and set out as Commander in Chief of the French squadron. Francis believed the time had arrived to counter his cowardice, and his reputation would greatly improve if he was the one to retrieve Mudd's treasure. As he'd sailed from France with over four thousand men under his command he'd felt more confident and powerful than ever before, finally living the life he believed he'd been raised for. Then during his moment of triumph, as he'd marched across the deck of the Sandown feeling completely invincible, he'd seen a sight that shook him to his very core and all the fear he thought he'd overcome had flooded back a thousand fold. Louis Francis had stood petrified with a gun in his hand and a thousand or so men at his back staring at the mirror image of Alfred Mudd in his prime, desperately hoping the men under his command wouldn't see his terror. Wondering if the rumours were true and Captain Mudd had in fact been blessed with invincible power by the devil himself, Louis Francis had been too scared to act. Instead, he'd panicked, and ordered his men to lock the apparition away, half expecting the unarmed man to attack and defeat his entire crew.

In the weeks that had followed the traitorous Captain had sat in his private cabin struggling with his fears and questioning his ability to lead the French on this treasure hunt. The fear had brought on the return of his anger, and everyday he'd punish some poor soul in a manner they didn't deserve. During those moments on deck Francis would feel powerful once more, and as he removed the skin off sailor's backs with the whip in his hands he managed to forget all about the red headed prisoner chained up only a stone's throw away.

The fear, though, always returned as Louis Francis sat alone in his cabin. The traitor had never served alongside his French colleagues, and with his arrogance, coupled with a life of hiding, he lacked the social and leadership skills to earn their respect. Instead of dining with his officers and getting to know his crew, he ate alone and compounded his fears. Now, though, enough was enough. Having drunk over half a bottle of brandy he was facing his enemy. Alfred Bicks stared back at him through eyes that had a way of intimidating even the most hardened of men, hoping that the moment had arrived when the French would begin their interrogation and finally end his pain and suffering.

"Who are you?" Francis demanded, mustering all of his courage. Alfie stared for a moment: unlike the French crew the red headed ex-smuggler immediately saw the Captain's fear, which intrigued him. He was also surprised by the Captain's ability to speak English, but he didn't dwell on this strange fact for too long.

"My name is Alfie Bicks. I was a bad'un back in England before the Royal Navy forced me onto one of their ships," he replied, hoping that once the captain knew he was a worthless criminal he'd order his execution and end his pain.

Instead, however, Louis Francis stared at him for a long time like he was a new species of insect.

"And this is your first stint at sea?" the Captain enquired, and Alfie nodded.

"I killed a soldier back in England, so they took me prisoner to serve out my sentence at sea," Alfie stated. Louis Francis was slowly finding his heartbeat returning to normal and his confidence returning as he eyed the common thief chained up in front of him. The prisoner clearly had no idea who he truly was. Suddenly Francis was beginning to realise that the prisoner wasn't the reincarnation of his lifelong nemesis, but in fact that man's son, and a clueless bastard at that.

"So you know nothing of Captain Mudd and his treasure?" Francis finally asked in an attempt to confirm his suspicions, and Alfie Bicks laughed like a madman.

"Not you as well. My god you're all as crazy as jackrabbits you sailors!" he told Francis, who suddenly stared at him with even more interest.

"Why do you say that?" the Captain demanded, but for a long time Alfie laughed uncontrollably, and Francis was happy to see that the punishment the prisoner was experiencing was taking its toll.

"I shared a cell with a lunatic who didn't stop going on about some crazy pirate who traded his soul for control of the sea. Its absolute nonsense," Alfie finally stated, "I guess you're as crazy as he was, but I didn't expect anything less from a filthy Frenchman like you!"

Looking into the French Captain's eyes Alfie hoped that his death would be quick and merciful, but instead of rising to the insulting bait Captain Francis smiled broadly.

"You have no idea, do you?" Francis barked at him, laughing himself now. Feeling confused Alfie lay there speechless for a long moment listening to the Captain's strange drunken laughter.

"What's going on? You froggy son of a whore! Why don't you just kill me now and end this?" he shouted. Suddenly Captain Francis stopped laughing and stared down at him.

"Oh, don't worry, my friend, you'll die eventually, but for the moment I'll keep you alive. The English thought you were of value after all. And from this day forth I'm going to get even more pleasure from seeing you suffer," was the Captain's parting shot, as he staggered off in the dark towards his cabin feeling fearless once more and confident of the success of his mission.

Chapter Thirty Seven

One hundred nautical miles in the French squadron's wake Benjamin Swift was in the navigator Robert Peer's cabin. The hour was late, but neither men were good sleepers and Benny had found great comfort in sharing a nightcap or two with the man Admiral Saunders described as the greatest navigator on earth. In truth, as much as the old fisherman appreciated Robert Peer's company, he loved to pick the man's brain. Benjamin Swift had spent most of his life steering fishing luggers on the English Channel, and had always loved the sea, but until a few months ago he'd had no idea how vast the oceans were.

The pair were currently examining a chart of the infamous Cape Horn, the stretch of water below the tip of the southern Americas connecting the Atlantic to the South Pacific, the sea-lane that would lead the British squadron into an area that was once known by many a scared sailor as Captain Mudd's territory.

Studying the chart, which showed a group of islands, Benny was struggling to see what all the fuss was about. Over the last week since Saunders' announcement on deck he'd heard the crew muttering horror stories about the dreaded Cape Horn, but from a navigational point of view it appeared completely straight-forward. The Horn offered several different routes. Some, Benny guessed, were riskier than others. Many courses circumnavigated chains of islands, whilst one led through straight water known as Drake's Passage. Recognising the name, the old fisherman turned to Robert, who was lost in his own thoughts.

"Drake's Passage, is that named after Sir Francis Drake?" Benny asked, and Peer turned his way and beamed a tipsy smile.

"The one and only. I'm sure you grew up hearing stories of Drake, and his victory over the Spanish and their armada in 1588, but it was a decade before that when he sailed around the world that he sailed through that passage. He was actually aiming for the Strait of Magellan, but he got caught by a storm and was blown south into this stretch of open water," The navigator said, pointing at the chart. Benny nodded and sipped at his brandy, as he thought about the long journey that still lay ahead.

"Robert, what's south of Drakes Passage at the bottom of the world?" the old fisherman asked, and Robert Peer smiled.

"Nobody knows that, Benny. Any ship that's sailed that far south has never returned," he said, and a long silence fell over the small cabin.

"So would I be right in saying the Strait of Magellan here is the safest route?" Benny eventually asked, and Robert Peer scratched at his chin and pondered the question for a long moment.

"The problem with the Horn is the blasted wind. You see, as soon as you pass below forty degrees south the wind has no land blocking its path and it tears around the earth like a banshee! And the further south you go the worst it gets," Peer explained, as Benny stared at the map of the world on the cabin wall and studied the land masses, completely fixated. Suddenly he understood why the tip of the Southern Americas, the dreaded Cape Horn, was so treacherous.

"And Cape Horn is at a southern latitude of fifty-six degrees…" Benny observed, and Robert Peer chuckled, sending shivers down Benjamin Swift's spine.

"That it is, my friend, and as you well know by now with wind comes waves," Peer stated, before pointing at the map, "You see, these routes through the islands offer some shelter from the wind and waves, but if you get blown off course you'll be wrecked on the jagged rocks that lie there in wait like they've been put there by the devil himself. On the other hand if you sail through Drake's Passage, which is open water, you avoid the treacherous rocks, but you face waves like you couldn't even imagine."

Benjamin stared at the chart in front of him thunderstruck, as the dreadful stories he'd heard below decks rushed through his mind.

"And then there is the risk of icebergs the size of town-houses drifting around under the surface that'll smash a ship's hull like matchwood!" the navigator continued, and Benjamin Swift took another gulp of brandy to steady his nerves.

Chapter Thirty Eight

The French ploughed further and further south and as the degree of southern latitude grew higher and higher, the ocean grew rougher and rougher. The French sailors struggled on deck trying to ride the wild ocean and harness the wild wind nature provided. They worked tirelessly in fear of reprisals from their vicious Captain. At their feet Alfred Bicks lay shackled and suffering. The ocean swells had grown in height and the Severe was tossed around like a piece of flotsam as she climbed up the wave and plunged into troughs over eighty feet deep. The Severe's terrified crew held on for dear life whilst they prayed to God and thought of their loved ones back home.

Alfred Bicks was less fortunate. The only thing keeping him on the deck of the French ship as waves crashed over her decks were the chains fastening his arms and legs. The shackles bit into his skin and agonising pain rushed through his body. The freezing water kept him conscious, for the most part, but physically in a state somewhere between alive and dead. Sleep only came during the moments when it all became too much and exhaustion took its toll. Like the rest of the sailors Alfie prayed, but not in the hope that the ship would make it and he'd survive. Instead Alfie prayed that the ship would strike rocks and would sink into the ocean, ending his pain and drowning his cruel captor Louis Francis in the process.

Occasionally Alfie would hear the Captain's sickening laughter from up on the quarterdeck, and he'd glare at him between the waves of both water and pain that washed remorselessly over him. Captain Louis Francis spent much of that treacherous stretch of ocean locked away in the comfort of his cabin drinking brandy and feasting on food the rest of his crew could only fantasise about. Out on deck the Severe's First Lieutenant, Pierre Gerrard, navigated the Severe and experienced hell on earth. During one of those terrible nights as a full moon shone down Alfie came to the conclusion that the end must be close and that his body surely couldn't survive much more. He started to feel hopeful that death was near. By the time the sun finally clambered over the horizon, the ocean had calmed slightly and the wind had dropped. Staring to port Alfie Bicks spotted land in the distance. It was the first time the ex-smuggler had seen a coastline in weeks and it brought on mixed feelings. As he stared closer at the jagged landscape he spotted the rotting corpses of multiple wrecked ships stranded on the rocks. Gaunt masts stripped of their sails poked forlornly up into the morning sky. The sight of land stirred up memories of days gone by and the cobbled streets of a town he knew he'd never return to, whilst the wrecks – much to his surprise – made him feel thankful. The Severe was still afloat, and he was still alive, but for how much longer he had no idea.

Unknown to Alfie as he lay there shivering, the Severe was passing through the Strait of Magellan between the mainland of the southern Americas and an island group known as Tierra del Fuego. The French squadron had been fortunate to avoid the full wrath of the notorious williwaw winds that often appeared from nowhere and blew ships off course and onto sharp rocks. Alfie lay on deck lost in thought. The man had believed that he'd lost all hope, but he now knew that deep down a little still remained.

Chapter Thirty Nine

The British reached the infamous Horn a few days behind their enemies. Admiral Philip Saunders stood on the deck of his frigate, the HMS Romulus, cheerful and in good spirits, inspiring confidence amongst his men. Secretly he harboured dark concerns: worries that the French had too big a lead and would reach the location of the treasure, load up and sail away before his squadron could fire a single cannon. The fact that the French squadron outnumbered his mattered not a bit to the experienced admiral. Saunders had fought a number of battles at sea and had never been bested. Since losing the HMS Sandown he'd evaluated the difference it would make when facing the enemy, and concluded that his men would still fight fearlessly. The Admiral knew that confidence was often the key to success, especially at sea.

The time to ponder such concerns wasn't upon him though, a fact the Admiral was all too aware of. Sailing around the treacherous Cape Horn would take all of his concentration and attention. The Admiral who had once sat on his father's knee and listened to a story about a pirate who had shown leniency vowed to make sure his squadron made the most out of the wind and caught the French in the South Pacific. It was the best he could do.

So, as the Romulus lifted and dropped on every wave Saunders shouted commands for sails to be tightened whilst Benjamin Swift and Robert Peer worked around the clock taking a hundred different measurements to guarantee the Romulus stayed on course. The frigate was now sailing slightly ahead of the rest of the squadron, leading the way.

Admiral Saunders trusted Robert Peer above anyone else to navigate the Horn and lead the little fleet to safety.

When they finally reached the tip of the mainland of the Southern Americas the wind was still raging and the ocean swells were enormous. Admiral Saunders summoned his chief navigator and his officers to his cabin. The men huddled around the Captain's table as the Romulus was thrown around and the vessel creaked as powerful waves battered her, threatening to tear her to pieces.

"What course do you suggest, Lieutenant Peer? You've sailed the Horn a handful of times," the Admiral asked, and the navigator scratched his chin in thought.

"Each route presents different risks, Captain, as I'm sure you know," Robert Peer replied, as the ship dropped suddenly into a trough and the men gripped the table for support. "In these conditions I'd recommend sailing through Drake's Passage. It's the widest route and presents less of a risk of hitting any of the rocks that the Strait of Magellan offers." Many of the officers present muttered their agreement as Admiral Saunders pondered this advice.

"Then we'll sail through Drake's Passage, but I want this squadron sailing north-easterly at the first opportunity. We need to get out of the southern latitudes and up into warmer waters without delay," Saunders ordered, pausing as a loud creak rumbled through the ship. "Remember, men we're in a race to get to that treasure, and it's a race we're losing."

The men nodded, all well aware of the importance of the mission's success. If they failed the future of their homeland was in jeopardy, and within a decade invasion from the continent would be inevitable. Before departing the cabin they saluted the Admiral who remained below, deep in thought.

Later that day the British squadron finally rounded the last of the islands that littered the vicious Horn and entered the wide open passage of water that their ancestor and fellow sailor Sir Francis Drake had navigated centuries before them. The wind had settled somewhat and the HMS Romulus was now cruising with all sail and making good progress, much to the Admiral's relief.

The sun was just setting, but there was no need to heave to and wait out the night. Drake's Passage presented no islands or obstacles for the squadron to navigate. The risk of icebergs existed, but at this time of year it was incredibly unlikely they'd face anything large enough to pierce the ships' hulls. As the sun vanished from the sky and darkness descended the Admiral remained on deck. At his side stood a handful of his officers, joined by Benjamin Swift. The old fisherman had been looking for an opportunity to question the Captain further regarding the story of the pirate Alfred Mudd ever since Saunders had mentioned the ring the man had worn around his neck, but the opportunity for such a discussion hadn't arisen. Following the sinking of the HMS Sandown and the conversation when Saunders had revealed that Benny's friend Alfie Bicks had been the notorious pirate's son, the Admiral seemed to have little to say to him. The old fisherman's curiosity was nagging him, and he hoped that at some stage he'd finally get a few answers to his questions.

That night Benny Swift remained on deck by Saunders' side, but the old fisherman would receive no answers. The Romulus continued to make good pace well into the early hours. Benny spent much of his time taking sights using a sextant. It was of the utmost importance that the Romulus remained on course so that they knew exactly where they were located on Robert Peer's nautical charts. Every thirty minutes the old fisherman would take a measurement by lining up a celestial body, in this case a particular star, and the horizon – which, due to a near full moon, they could just make out. Using a calculation Robert Peer had taught him Benny could then make a mark on the nautical chart mapping their progress through Drake's

Passage. At other times the old fisherman would simply gaze up into the sky staring at the countless stars and constellations, many of which Robert Peer had taught him.

When trouble arrived it arrived so quickly and it hit the HMS Romulus with such force that few were prepared. It was a sudden roaring noise that first caught Benny Swift's attention, causing him to look down from the heavens and towards the decks. The sound was like the screams of dead sailors whistling through the night and it made Benny shiver to his very core. Before he could even think about its source a gust of wind hit the Romulus: it was so strong that it swept a handful of men from its decks into the water. The British squadron were experiencing the williwaw winds, a terrifying force of nature so unpredictable that it kept sailors awake at night, and gave many nightmares. Benjamin Swift gripped the railing around the quarter deck and managed to wrap one of his legs around it for support, as screams echoed around him and were lost in the night.

The Romulus' mains'l tore free and was whisked away as sailors staggered around struggling to lower the remaining sails. Benny Swift continued to cling on, believing that life was over for all of them. The ocean suddenly swelled to epic proportions and waves battered the Romulus from all angles, as the old fisherman gripped tightly and listened to the horrific noises the ship made as she was smashed around. Looking around at the violence of the ocean, a force that he'd never believed possible, the colour drained from Benny's face and he closed his eyes. The old fisherman lay there remembering all of the things he'd loved and lost as waves crashed over the Romulus' decks and seawater soaked into his very bones. Benny believed that if the ocean didn't kill him, his chest certainly would.

How many hours passed Benny had no idea as he held on for dear life, but suddenly the wind died out, as if God himself had flicked a switch on Mother Nature's control panel. Within ten minutes the swells began to die down and Admiral Saunders was out on deck ordering his crew to bring the spare mains'l from the sail locker. Benny watched, semi-delirious, as the sailors jumped to carry out his orders seemingly unaffected by a night of absolute terror. Benny thought about their bravery and felt proud of them, wondering if it would be the last thought he ever had. It was Hendricks, the Admiral's Marine Commander, who pulled the old fisherman free and carried him gently to the ship's doctor.

Chapter Forty

That morning the Romulus' doctor had his hands full. The fearsome williwaw winds had wreaked havoc on deck: tearing sails from masts and ripping countless objects free of their fixings where they'd careered across deck striking sailors. Over two dozen men were injured, and a handful required wounds to be stitched, but as soon as Doctor Jones saw Hendricks carrying Benjamin Swift – who looked like a drowned rat – he knew that the old fisherman required his immediate attention.

The doctor, whose private cabin was only spitting distance from Benny's, had come to know the man well. The old man who'd spent a lifetime fishing out on the English Channel had confided early on that he suffered from the long lasting effects of a bad case of pneumonia. Sometimes, during bad weather, the pair would sit up in their bunks leaving their cabin doors open, and talk for hours. Months earlier, shortly after the pair had first met, Jones had produced some medicine that had cured Benny's shortness of breath, which resulted from even slight exertion, and had aided him considerably in assisting the Admiral's chief navigator Robert Peer. The doctor really liked the old man, and was well aware that the Admiral felt he owed the fisherman a debt.

As Hendricks laid Benny down in front of him Jones wasted no time, removing Benny's sodden clothes as, incongruously, his long grey moustache bounced up and down, though his spectacles remained perched on the end of his nose. A few of the other casualties tried to claim his attention for themselves, but one glance from Saunders' tough marine silenced them. Hendricks remained by Benjamin

Swift's side, assisting the doctor by drying Benny off and wrapping him in a number of blankets as the doctor poured some concoction of liquids down the man's throat. That administered, Jones instructed the marine to carry Benny to his cabin, and as Hendricks strolled along the Romulus' narrow passageways with Benny in his arms like a baby, the old fisherman mumbled deliriously, apparently in conversation with a lady he called Anna.

Stowing Benny carefully in his bunk, the marine watched for several hours as Benny slept. When the old fisherman finally awoke he was fully conscious and thanked the marine for his ministrations.

"What *was* that, Hendricks?" Benny asked as he looked over at the giant of a man perched on a stool and taking up much of the remaining space in his small cabin.

"That wind, my friend, was God's wrath, but it's over now." The marine answered, before saying his goodbyes and firmly instructing Benny Swift to rest.

On deck the carpenters and sail makers were busily repairing the damage done, and the Romulus was soon sailing once more. Admiral Saunders was standing on the quarter deck in deep discussion with his officers. The ships in the squadron had been exchanging messages for several hours and none of the other vessels reported serious damage.

"How many men were lost?" he asked his First Lieutenant, dreading the man's reply.

"We've taken a head count, and eight men were swept off our deck, Captain, and a further twenty-six across the squadron," the man replied: the officers present shook their heads and stared at their feet thinking of each man's terrible death.

"We'll say some words on deck for the lives lost once we're out of this dreadful passage and into safer water," the Admiral grimly said.

The next few days passed slowly for the crews as the ships sailed out of the passage and steered north-easterly. As they climbed into higher latitudes the seas eventually began to calm and the days grew warmer. Saunders' excitement began to grow with the knowledge that, within weeks, they'd enter the huge stretch of ocean littered with islands which had been the pirate's domain: an area the Royal Navy hadn't dared to sail for decades.

Chapter Forty One

As the French squadron sailed away from the feared Cape Horn they passed from the furious fifties into the roaring forties. Long weeks drifted by as Alfred Bicks lay on deck, delirious and experiencing hallucinations of days gone past and friends lost. Occasionally he'd be pulled out of these fantasies by wild laughter and would glance up, squinting from the sunlight, to see the cruel Francis standing over him, taking pleasure from his suffering.

The French soon sailed into the South Pacific and the days and nights grew warmer, and kept on into ocean once regarded as Captain Mudd's territory, seas that no ship had dared navigate in several decades. Below decks the men were scared, fearing that trespassing into the barbarous pirate's stretch of sea would provoke harsh consequences, but nobody was willing to show their fear for risk of punishment from Francis.

The ocean gradually calmed as the wind that had blown relentlessly for weeks fell to a gentle breeze. Most commanders would have taken the opportunity to give the crew a well-earned rest, but not Captain Francis. The man was driven by revenge and greed, and completely obsessed with getting his hands on his nemesis' hoard. He ran his ship like a slave master, creating fear and terror amongst the sailors. Even the ship's officers had grown to despise their Captain. When the suggestion of heaving to was raised by his First Lieutenant, an experienced sailor named Pierre Gerrard, the Captain scoffed at the idea: Gerrard angrily turned his head away, hiding his opinion of the man giving him orders. The squadron pressed on. The seas had been gentle for several days when the lookout in the crow's nest informed the Captain he could see land. The news was quickly repeated across the decks, causing a commotion.

"Atterrir avant, une île!" Alfie heard the words clearly, but the only survivor of the HMS Sandown had no idea of its meaning. Scanning the deck he watched as the sailors clambered the ratlines attempting to get a better view of the ocean ahead. He tried to follow their line of sight and stared into the distance, but all he could see was clear blue sea stretching all the way to the horizon. Standing on the quarter-deck, Louis Francis extended his brass telescope and examined the horizon, spotting a small stream of smoke rising high into the blue sky. Focusing his attention on the trail of smoke's origin he noticed a tiny speck of land.

"So it's inhabited," he muttered to himself, letting the brass telescope fall to his side. Stationed only a few feet away, Lieutenant Gerrard asked what course of action he'd like to take, and he quickly ordered the man to prepare a small landing party. The First Lieutenant saluted and gave the necessary orders to the sailors and marines. Pierre Gerrard had grown to dislike his Captain and despise the way he treated the sailors under his command, but he obeyed orders none the less. Francis remained on deck watching the small island grow larger and larger as the ship approached, and speculating what or who he'd find there. The half-breed wondered if the island's inhabitants knew of the late Captain Mudd. The pirate had supposedly controlled this entire stretch of the South Pacific: it was possible that the island's inhabitants had met the pirate or possessed information that could prove to be of use to Francis. In either case he was looking forward to torturing them.

The crew took soundings to ensure the ship didn't run aground, and got to within two hundred yards of the island. Louis Francis ordered the crew to heave to and drop the anchor.

The island was a jagged outcrop of rocks that jutted out of the Pacific Ocean creating an ugly blotch on an otherwise barren and lifeless stretch of sea. It was tiny, barely a dozen or so acres and from where Louis Francis stood on the Severe's quarter-deck he wondered how it was that such a small space could support life. The smoke that had initially caught their attention had gone, and Francis guessed that the fire that had created it had been smothered as the French warships approached. Peering through his telescope he discovered that a small area of land appeared to be pasture, and as he looked closer he noticed rows of crops. Suddenly he caught a flicker of movement and looking closer he saw something which really caught his attention. Near the middle of the small island stood a wooden tower, crudely constructed, that appeared to serve as a lookout. Louis Francis wondered for a moment if he had in fact glimpsed a figure atop of the tower staring back at him through a telescope, before quickly pushing the absurd thought from his mind.

The island was small but his marines and crew were still eager to explore, looking forward to the prospect of setting foot on dry land for the first time in many, many weeks. Those off watch quickly climbed down into half a dozen small boats and began to row the short distance to shore. On the Severe's quarter-deck Pierre Gerrard turned to his Commander in Chief.

"Will you stay aboard, Captain?" he enquired, and Louis Francis – who was as excited as a small child on Christmas Eve – turned his way.

"Have the men secure the island, and once that's achieved I'll land. I'm curious to see who inhabits such an ugly piece of rock," he ordered, turning his attention back to the small island that must have been known to the pirate, sitting as it did well within the seas he was known to control.

Meanwhile the boats crowded with marines armed with cutlasses and muskets reached the island and examined the sharp rock face. It showed no signs of a path to access the cleared area, so they rowed around her looking for the way up and soon found a small beach. Within moments dozens of marines were climbing towards the centre of the island where the crops were located and the lookout tower stood. One of the marines saw something move. He raised his rifle and aimed at a black man who stood staring boldly at the countless marines invading his home.

"Ne bougez pas!" [Stand still!] the marines shouted, the tone of voice conveying their instruction to the island's inhabitant to stand still and not attempt to reach for a weapon. The man stared at them fearlessly as a squad of uniformed men levelled muskets in his direction. A short distance away stood a small group of shacks, and as the marines approached cautiously some birds fled, startling them. The marines stared at the birds flying into the distance, wondering whether they were edible as they clutched their weapons. A door swung open and they focused their attention – and aim – on several more natives, who came outside with their hands held high.

"Ne bougez pas!" the marines continued to shout: it mattered not whether the men understood French. They clearly recognised the weapons the marines carried and understood the consequences of resistance. Following the small group was a man whose appearance was vastly different to that of his fellow inhabitants. Like the rest of the islanders he stood and glared at the marines fearlessly, but unlike them, he was genuinely intimidating. The man had white skin and clearly came from European shores. His wrinkled skin suggested that he was at least sixty years of age, and had lived a lifetime in the burning sun, but what caught the marine's attention was the savage scar that ran the entire length of his face and across his cheek. The men all stood in silence for a moment, a silence that was eventually broken by Louis Francis himself who had marched up from the shoreline and was now standing, surrounded by another squad of marines, a short distance from the shack.

"Well, well, well, if it isn't the man they call Digby!" he roared, with a deep grin splitting his face. The marines continued to hold their weapons aimed at the small cluster of men standing in front of the shacks, unable to understand a word their Captain spoke, as he used the tongue of the country he'd betrayed. Much to many of the soldier's surprise, though, the white man who bore the horrific scar smiled in return, a smile that only accentuated his injury, giving him the appearance of an ancient savage.

"So this is the great pirate paradise of the world famous Alfred Mudd! An ugly rock and a few measly acres," Louis Francis stated smugly, before laughing like a madman. "You know, you once robbed a relative of mine back in Portsmouth, and, believe me: now you'll pay for it."

Turning his attention away from Digby, the late Captain Mudd's loyal friend and First Mate, Louis Francis ordered his marines to shoot the black men, but warned them that any man that harmed a hair on the white man's head would be hung. The marines listened to the commands issuing from the lips of the most ruthless Captain they'd ever sailed under. A moment later dozens of muskets spat fire and each of the natives was hit by countless shots. While the bodies of his comrades fell to the dirt in bloody heaps that stained the soil, Digby continued to stare at the man who had once topped his best friend's infamous death list, but the smile had disappeared from Digby's scarred and wrinkled face.

A short time later he was shackled, dragged to the beach, and thrown aboard one of the rowing boats before being ferried the short distance to the Severe. As he was dragged onto her main deck he caught sight of another prisoner, a man whose months of punishment had taken their toll. Alfie Bicks lay there as thin as a skeleton, covered in burns and blisters from the sun, but the long red beard and hair framing his gaunt face had held its hue. Suddenly Digby's jaw dropped in surprise and recognition.

"What's wrong, pirate? You look like you've seen a ghost!" Louis Francis shouted at him, before the first of many clubs hit his back knocking him to the deck.

Chapter Forty Two

Saunders slept very little after the squadron he was commanding sailed north away from the treacherous Cape Horn. On reaching calmer waters sails were dropped, and the remaining five ships huddled together, alone in the vast ocean that surrounded them. Messages were relayed from ship to ship and a small service was performed for the brave sailors whose lives had been lost. The decks of the Romulus were crowded when the ship's priest stepped forward and delivered a short sermon. Philip Saunders stood surrounded by the squadron's remaining captains and many of its officers as the morning sun beat down and the ship's musicians played a selection of sombre songs that drifted out into the empty ocean. Eventually the Admiral stepped forward and addressed the sailors present.

"Men. Today we say our farewells to some of the bravest sailors ever to stand on the deck of a ship! Men who stood up fearlessly in the face of Britain's enemies!" Saunders projected his voice out over the crowds, making eye contact with dozens of his comrades who all stared back courageously. "And for them I ask you all to stand strong, and to make sure they died for good reason. We sail with the odds stacked firmly against us, but we will succeed, we will succeed."

The crowd gathered clapped and stamped on the timber deck, whilst the officers looked at him, demonstrating their admiration of his leadership. Most of the officers had realised many months ago that they'd been recruited to a suicide mission, and that the chances of survival were slim. Ever since the Sandown had been captured and destroyed near the Cape Verde Islands and they'd discovered the true strength of Louis Francis' squadron they'd all known that success was by no means certain. The officers knew that Philip Saunders was fully aware of this, but the Admiral possessed the courage to lead his men on this mission, and the skills needed to snatch victory from the enemy. His orders were, if capture proved impossible, to sink Mudd's treasure, where it could no longer be used by any of Great Britain's enemies. That would still be a victory. The officers knew what they faced, but their loyalty and respect were such that they would all follow Saunders' orders to death or glory.

Following the sombre ceremony, the squadron made sail and began the journey once again. During the following weeks the temperature rose as they sailed further into the tropics. They were now sailing in a section of the ocean that had barely been navigated in nearly three decades and was littered with thousands of small islands. The maps Robert Peer possessed were old and inaccurate, so sailing through the night was no longer an option for the British, much to the Admiral's frustration. During those tough weeks Saunders stood on deck all day and most of the night, often only retiring once the sun had appeared again illuminating a bright blue ocean, and his hope steadily dwindled as they caught not even a glimpse of a French mast on the horizon.

Robert Peer was navigating a perfect course towards the co-ordinates where the dead pirate's treasure haul had been buried, and the squadron had been cruising at full sail for every moment of daylight for weeks. Philip Saunders' concerns were turning into nightmares at the thought of missing the French completely. One evening he stood on deck under a sky full of stars as his officers talked of their lives back in England. Saunders more often than not instigated such conversations, always keeping hope in his men's hearts and morale high. He stood staring out to sea lost in his own thoughts when suddenly First Lieutenant Lucas asked him a question that pulled him back to reality.

"Captain, are we to intercept and attack the French targeting only the treasure ship? Is any hope of retrieving the treasure ourselves lost now?" Lucas asked, and Saunders turned to him. The Admiral had been thinking of nothing else for weeks. The original objective, sailing up the Thames and delivering Mudd's riches to his spymaster friend Rupert Knightly was now impossible to achieve, sinking with the HMS Sandown and its entire crew.

"If all goes to plan the French will load the hoard on to one or more ships. I imagine one of those vessels will be their flagship, which will then be avoiding battle at all costs. Louis Francis is a coward and has no taste for conflict and I'd bet any money on the fact that he'll want to be close to that treasure," the Admiral replied.

"All that gold and silver," one of his officers muttered dreamily, and Saunders smiled.

"It'll weigh her down so we'll easily be able to tell which are the treasure ships: but don't think for a moment that the French won't try to protect them. We'll have to attempt to ram and sink the flagship and any of her sisters showing reduced freeboard, regardless of the lives that'll be lost in the process," Saunders said. The quarter-deck fell silent and the officers listened to the wind whistling through the rigging. For the remainder of that evening few words were spoken other than the necessary commands to run the ship. The British squadron were now well within the dead pirate's territory and if Robert Peer's calculations were correct and the wind held, they'd reach their destination within a day or two.

The squadron soon fell in to the routine of heaving to when the light failed, and awakening to make sail as soon as the navigator could see well enough. After several weeks the officers and crew were well used to the daily round, so many men were taken by surprise when the lookout eventually reported, "Sail Ho!". "Where away?" shouted the Officer of the Watch. "Ahead! Directly forrard!" came the answer from the crow's nest. Within the hour the French squadron could be seen anchored off a small rocky island. Admiral Saunders turned to Robert Peer.

"How far are we from our destination? Have the French reached it first, Robert?" he demanded. The navigator stared at his charts for a long moment before glancing up at his Captain.

"According to my estimation they can't be far off it. It is quite possible that they are at the coordinates we were given, Captain." he replied. The Admiral considered how to proceed.

"Let's press forward," he finally ordered, "We'll put pressure on them, but from a sensible distance. Once we're close enough to read their signal flags we'll heave to and attempt reconnaissance."

The HMS Romulus continued at full sail, but as the squadron approached the French, Saunders watched as his enemy's ships raised anchor and sailed away from the island. This piqued the Admiral's curiosity, but could not stop to have any questions answered: the squadron piled on all sail and for the remainder of that day the British continued their pursuit. Peel had taken new sightings with his sextant and informed the Admiral that the destination was in fact still ahead. Eventually the French hove to for the night, and the evening and night passed agonizingly slowly for the British as they followed suit and maintained battle readiness as a precaution against a potential attack. Few slept at all and when the sun rose the next day Admiral Saunders breathed a sigh of relief as he watched the French squadron hoist sails and hasten away. The British squadron followed in their wake. That morning they sailed past dozens of islands and then in the early afternoon the French dropped anchor off an island situated at the exact co-ordinates Rupert Knightly had given Saunders months earlier.

"She's volcanic, and has a rocky formation that has two peaks of an equal height on either side and a shorter peak in the middle resembling the letter W," the spymaster had said, and as the Admiral stared at the island and the distinctive skyline he was certain they'd finally arrived at the location of the pirate's amassed treasure. Looking away from the French warships and at his First Lieutenant, Saunders ordered him to signal the ships to take up battle positions.

"It's time to end this," the Admiral muttered as he put his telescope to his eye once again, while his officers, despite their natural trepidation, gave the orders that brought the ships to battle stations.

Chapter Forty Three

Afer capturing Captain Mudd's right hand man, Digby, the French sailed away from the small island. Lookouts soon spotted the British squadron far behind and wasted no time in warning Louis Francis, but the Captain cared not for the British who, he was sure, posed no real threat. Instead he spent the remainder of the day torturing his latest captive on the Severe's main deck, in front of the crew who struggled with their work manning the sails and watched the British squadron's progress. The sailors who, up until that point had considered their Captain to be a man who used cruelty as a way of controlling his crew, now knew that he was an evil and sadistic man who took great pleasure in causing pain.

On the Severe's quarter deck First Lieutenant Pierre Gerrard stood watching with disapproval at the way his Captain was treating their elderly captive. On several occasions during the course of the day whilst Francis employed different torture techniques to punish the man he referred to as Digby, Gerrard had overheard his fellow officers mutter curses relating to Francis and his unprofessional behaviour. Lieutenant Gerrard, who was highly respected by his brother officers, warned them against voicing such opinions, threatening them with disciplinary action if they persisted, but secretly he agreed with every word they spoke.

After hours of pain the elderly pirate finally confirmed the exact co-ordinates of his dead friend's treasure – the coordinates that Captain Francis already possessed. Satisfied, Francis finally took a break from torturing Digby and retired to his cabin where his dinner would be served, in the knowledge the Severe would reach the treasure the very next day.

Pierre Gerrard, on the other hand, could not remove his gaze from the two prisoners who lay shackled to the deck suffering different but equally painful fates. The exceptionally tall red headed one was literally dying a slow death of hunger and thirst in front of Pierre's very eyes, whilst the older man had experienced a lifetime of pain during the few hours since he'd arrived on the Severe's deck. He lay alongside the HMS Sandown's lone survivor covered in wounds from stab marks to burns. Pierre Gerrard was navy born and bred. Over his long career he'd fought many battles and taken countless enemy prisoners, none of whom he'd ever allowed to be treated in such a way. Suddenly feeling pity for the men he decided to risk Captain Francis' wrath and at least offer some sustenance to the prisoners.

"Fetch me a pitcher of water and some food, and do it quietly, you understand?" he ordered one of the cabin boys, a lad barely in his teens. The boy looked away from the prisoners, a sickening sight that nonetheless drew the eye, and towards the Severe's First Lieutenant.

"I understand," he replied, showing maturity and wisdom way beyond his years. A short while later Pierre Gerrard crept along the deck under the gaze of the night watch, whose silence showed their tacit approval of his action. Leaning down he slowly poured water between the red headed prisoner's blistered lips into his mouth. Instinctively the man tried to gulp, having drunk very little over the course of many months, but Pierre Gerrard implored him to sip. The First Lieutenant had studied the English language and spoke it well. Aware of the time passing and the risk of being caught, Pierre quickly fed the tall prisoner a plate of salted beef which the man ate in huge gulps which he barely chewed. Eventually as the prisoner began to regain some composure he stared up and into the Lieutenant's eyes.

"Thank you," he said, as Pierre Gerrard stared at his gaunt face and wondered why on earth the sailor was of such interest to his Captain, and what the prisoner could ever have done to earn such harsh punishment. Turning to the old man who lay there grimacing from the agonising pain his wounds delivered, Pierre considered for a moment what he could possibly do for the man. Due to his old age the First Lieutenant believed the prisoner couldn't possibly survive much more, and that it was unlikely he'd last the night. Pierre Gerrard was deliberating what to do when he heard bootheels on deck and, to his horror, Louis Francis' voice. Attempting to flee, Gerrard managed a few steps before realising he'd left it too late. The cruel Captain was marching back towards his captives, refreshed after a hot meal and eager to continue his maltreatment of the old pirate. In the nick of time Pierre managed to duck out of sight behind one of the Severe's rowing boats, but he was trapped there, only a dozen or so feet from where Louis Francis now stood gloating over his captives. Having no other option Pierre crouched down out of sight hoping that Francis would at least end the old pirate's life quickly. Meanwhile Digby lay glaring at the man who'd been the focus of his buccaneering life, since he'd vowed to follow his closest friend to the ends of the earth to exact revenge for the events on the island of Antigua nearly three decades earlier.

"Not so tough now as you were back in Portsmouth robbing decent folk of the money they earned fair and square!" Louis Francis crowed, before pulling out a dagger and holding it against Digby's throat. The man who was regarded as one of the most dangerous men on earth by all the seafarers in all the seven seas stared up into Louis Francis' eyes, with not a trace of fear on his face.

"I was just a boy living on the streets and trying to put food in my belly! I wasn't lucky enough to live your privileged life and have the best of this world from the beginning," he managed through gritted teeth.

"And that gives you the right to steal from men like my godfather?" Francis replied, pricking the pirate's throat, drawing a drop of blood.

"I never hurt a hair on your precious godfather's head. I asked for some money, and he gave it like all the rest," Digby riposted, causing Louis Francis to grind his teeth in anger.

"And the knife you waved around had nothing to do with it, huh? He was a navy hero and worth a hundred men like you or that lunatic Mudd!" Francis spat, and much to his annoyance Digby grinned at him.

"He scared you, didn't he? My old friend and Captain," Digby said, pausing as he struggled to draw breath, "but remember you brought on Mudd's wrath. The men you killed back on Antigua we would have forgiven you for. We were thieves and knew about the risks we faced, but for what you did to Andrea there can never be forgiveness, and one day you'll pay."

"She was just a thief's whore who got what she deserved!" Francis shouted, but the fear he felt was obvious by the way the knife shook in his hands. Tears ran down Digby's face as he stared up at Louis Francis.

"She was my best friend's wife, and the most innocent person I've ever had the pleasure of meeting. You and the rest of your officers raped and hung her, and you may think you've managed to escape justice by hiding out in France whilst the rest of them burnt for their crimes, but believe me, one day you'll pay!" the old pirate promised. In return Louis Francis smiled.

"I don't think so. You and Alfred Mudd had your day, but it's over now. It's time you met your maker," he hissed, as he removed the blade from Digby's throat and stabbed him in the stomach. The blow was a mortal wound, but was placed cruelly as was the Captain's nature and death would be long, slow, and very painful. Standing up and kicking Digby in the chest, which made the old pirate squeal in further agony, Louis Francis laughed before strolling away towards his cabin for a brandy to toast victory over his enemy.

Alfie Bicks who, thanks to the food and drink offered by Lieutenant Gerrard had witnessed the entire incident, tried to offer support from where he was chained at Digby's side, but for many long moments Digby writhed in pain trying to escape from the shackles binding him whilst muttering sentences Alfie could make little sense of. Eventually he fell still and Alfie thought he'd finally died and 'met his maker' as Louis Francis had put it, but suddenly the old man turned and stared at Alfie, sending shivers down the ex-smugglers spine.

"When you meet your maker you tell him we won in the end!" Digby managed, as blood poured from his mouth. A moment later his body stopped moving and fell back to the deck. Digby was dead. Lying alone, or so he thought, Alfie Bicks shivered once more as he replayed the old man's last words. They made no sense whatsoever to him, and he quickly concluded that the man had been delusional from pain in his last moments on this earth. Alfie Bicks couldn't have been more wrong.

Only a dozen feet away, First Lieutenant Pierre Gerrard sat in silence and shock, as he thought over and over about what he'd just learnt. The Lieutenant could forgive most things, but he knew he'd struggle to live with the idea of taking orders from a man who'd raped and killed an innocent woman. He sat in silence for a long time before finally creeping back towards the ship's quarter deck.

Chapter Forty Four

Gliding high in the clear blue sky a bird gazed down at the boundless ocean and finally, spotting an island, it began its descent. The brown storm petrel flapped its relatively large wings directing its flight to a very particular place on that island. Within a few moments it was flying over the masts of dozens of ships anchored in the island's natural harbour which was shielded by forested arms that nearly met, the narrow gap providing an interesting problem for navigators. The bird then crossed fields where some of the dark skinned workers stared up at the sky smiling and taking a well-earned rest from their toil. Suddenly the petrel turned and dived, finally coming to rest on a balcony and completing a journey it had flown hundreds of times over the course of its life. On the balcony the petrel wasn't alone. An old man sat staring out to sea lost in his dark thoughts, but as the bird crept closer he turned and smiled at the newcomer. Reaching into his pocket the man removed a small portion of dried food and, as soon as the petrel clapped its small beady eyes on the scrap, it strolled closer, eventually climbing onto the man's arm. The petrel began devouring the food without a care in the world, but the bird had nothing to fear. It knew and trusted the man more than any other, because it had been hand reared by the man a decade earlier. Whilst the petrel finished off its meal the man removed a small item that was fastened to the petrel's leg, before unravelling the small scrap of fabric and revealing a message that appeared to have been scrawled in a hurry.

"As always, your plan worked, however our enemy sails with the French. I witnessed the animal with my own eyes. My capture is imminent. Sailing at your side was an honour. Forever your friend, Digby," the man read aloud, as he stared at the note with eyes that had terrified tens of thousands of sailors.

"Digby. We lived long, old friend. I'll join you soon enough," Alfred Mudd muttered as he climbed to his feet. Now at a ripe old age, having passed his sixtieth birthday, he struggled to manoeuvre his six and a half foot frame, disdaining the aid of a cane. The old man who, the world believed, had traded his soul with the devil for control of the seas, stood and stared at his domain for a long moment as his tactical mind sought out the most efficient way of achieving his goals.

Over the past few decades, the island that the pirate had made home for the slaves he'd freed, had prospered and turned into a kingdom where men, women and children who had once faced misery and agony working on the sugarcane now enjoyed long and happy lives. The island nation had been built on some of the pirate's mentor, Leonard Tibb's principles but unlike Arraya, Alfred Mudd's colony was much more than a den of thieves, it was paradise. Over the years Mudd had spent much of the fortune he'd accumulated on building materials, tools and every commodity his people needed. The islanders had learned skills and worked co-operatively to help their fellow neighbours. They produced their own food and lived in fine houses. The young ruffian who had once lived on the streets of Portsmouth had always believed that knowledge was power. The island's school that taught every child a dozen or more subjects was testament to that belief.

Placing his hand on a brass bell attached to the wall of his balcony Captain Mudd rang it with all his might creating a noise that reverberated through the town he'd created. Men and women immediately stopped their work and stared towards the home of the man they thought of as both their leader, and in many ways their father, and the children paused the games they were playing in the street. Within minutes, some dozen or so tough looking men were gathered in front of Mudd's balcony, where they all saluted and awaited their orders. The men were a mere handful of the captains who had once sailed Mudd's mighty fleet. The old man whose gaunt face was still framed by his red hair had ceased piratical raids years earlier. His fleet still controlled the South Pacific with an iron fist, but for years had only sailed to supply provisions to the lookouts they had positioned on islands stretching across nearly a thousand miles.

The ruthless pirate who over the years had stood and watched the several men on his infamous death list burn alive, had only one target left in his sights. Exacting revenge on the man who had led a group of drunken young navy officers to the other side of Antigua where they'd raped and killed the woman he loved was the only thing Alfred Mudd lived for. The pirate wasn't interested in looting ships and stealing cargoes. His colony had everything they could ever wish for, and so much more.

"Many years ago most of you were mere cargo in the hands of tyrants! I saved you all, housed you, educated you and fed you. I love you all like the children I never had the fortune of bearing!" the old pirate boomed at the small band, "And, as you all know I've only ever wanted one thing in return, to take the life of the man who killed my true love." Captain Mudd paused as memories of a beautiful and innocent girl named Andrea came flooding back, tearing at his heart again, and the pain he rarely admitted manifested, as it seldom did, and he looked what he was: an old man devastated by the loss of his beloved wife. A huge man stepped forward in the ensuing moment of silence.

"My Captain and friend, like you we have waited many, many years for this moment!" he shouted up at his leader, pulling the pirate from his painful thoughts, "Handing

Louis Francis to you would be the greatest of honours that each and every one of us could hope for, but would never repay the debt we all owe you. As always, we are yours: command and we will obey!" the man continued, bringing words of agreement from his comrades.

Alfred Mudd stared down at the man who, nearly two decades earlier, he'd released from a slave ship's hold. Back then he'd been a boy of five and had been scared out of his wits. That little boy had grown into a strong and trustworthy man, and that man had never felt fear.

"My enemy has taken the bait that we offered. As you all know, several of our kin risked their lives to sow the seeds of this plan. Those men stuck to the story we created and now the man I've dreamed of capturing for most of my life has finally sailed into our territory!" Mudd replied, and the crowd cheered and smiled, believing that, at last, their leader would get the opportunity they knew he deserved and complete his revenge.

"Prepare the entire fleet! We sail on the next tide. It's time to complete my life's work," Mudd finished as the group, which now numbered well over three dozen, dispersed to gather their crews. Within hours warships of all shapes and sizes were navigating out of the island's dog-leg harbour. Spanish, Dutch, and French ships of the line were present, but the majority were British. Regardless of the flags they'd once flown all of them had one thing in common: they had all been captured by the notorious Captain Mudd back in his heyday.

Chapter Forty Five

As the sun rose Pierre Gerrard stood on the quarter deck of the French squadron's flagship the Severe observing the British fleet who were still hove to in the far distance. On the main deck forrard the body of the old pirate Digby lay in a small puddle of blood, covered in wounds from the horrific treatment he'd endured the day before. Some of the common sailors spat insults at the corpse, believing he'd finally received the punishment he'd deserved after a lifetime spent in the despicable trade of piracy, but the ship's First Lieutenant looked with pity on the old seaman who'd died so painfully only hours earlier. He had eventually been able to emerge from his hiding place, and had retired to his cabin and tried to sleep. But he'd tossed and turned in his bunk as he tried to force the unwelcome knowledge that he was sailing under the command of a man who'd raped and killed an innocent woman from his mind. He also puzzled over the gaunt and starving red headed prisoner who still had some vestige of life left in him, wondering who the man was, and what he'd done to warrant such enmity from the cruel Captain. These thoughts had kept Pierre Gerrard awake for the rest of the night, and as he ordered the squadron to hoist sails and continue its journey, he felt both physically and mentally exhausted. The Lieutenant came from a proud navy family and had lived his life under the guide of a strong moral compass. Now that compass was steering in a different direction than the path Louis Francis was on and Pierre Gerrard felt disgusted with himself.

Whilst Gerrard manned the decks and consulted charts of the area that had been drawn up many decades earlier, Captain Louis Francis slept off the brandy he'd consumed the night before. Over the course of that morning the French sailed passed countless islands as their squadron edged closer towards the longitude and latitude where the pirate's treasure lay. Finally, early that afternoon they reached their destination, after months of sailing on a journey that had cost the French hundreds of lives. Most had died of illness and disease, but scores of sailors had died on deck at the hands of the squadron's cruel Commander in Chief.

When the island finally rose over the horizon Pierre Gerrard checked and then re-checked the island against the description he'd been given and only after he was completely sure it was the right one did he instruct one of the cabin boys to rouse the Severe's Captain. Within minutes Louis Francis was on deck grinning like an idiot as he watched his nemesis' treasure island grow larger and larger.

The ten French warships sailed to within a long bowshot of the shore, and Captain Francis then ordered eight of his squadron to turn and face the British fleet, who had heaved to out of cannon range at the edge of the island's deep water drop off.

Louis Francis stood staring at the island completely transfixed as he licked his lips and fantasised about the bounty of wealth that awaited them all, but more importantly the revenge he'd finally get on his lifelong enemy before the day was out. Pierre Gerrard had other things on his mind: he was concerned with the battle that he was absolutely sure was coming. The British had sailed for many months to reach the island and they knew all about Alfred Mudd's treasure, and the consequences of a huge cash injection to the French war chest. Outnumbered though the British were, the First Lieutenant knew battle was a strong possibility.

"Captain, how would you like us to deal with the British?" Pierre finally asked, pulling the Captain out of his fantasies and back to reality. Louis Francis stared at him for a moment, still grinning like he'd lost his mind.

"Order a full attack by eight warships, specifically targeting their masts. I want those five British ships rendered unseaworthy. Once their squadron is in tatters they will no longer pose any risk. Severe and Redoutable will load up the treasure, hoist all sail and be gone," the Captain replied, before turning and staring at the rocky island once more. Pierre Gerrard had sailed for decades and fought a dozen or so battles at sea. The First Lieutenant knew that his Captain's plan could well work, but at a huge cost in both ships and lives.

"Forgive me, Captain, but surely we should wait for the British to attack us. If we attack them we risk losing our ships unnecessarily. They may not even attack us in the first place!" Gerrard responded. Louis Francis' head snapped around as he tore his attention away from the island and stared at his First Lieutenant with eyes full of arrogance and anger.

"I don't care how many of our ships we sacrifice, Lieutenant!" he shouted, loudly enough to be heard by his fellow officers who promptly tried to look very busy to cover their embarrassment. "As long as the British don't sink this ship once its hold is loaded with gold. When we reach France and bring this treasure home we'll build dozens of ships and finance a full invasion of England. If you *ever* question me again your punishment will be far worse than that meted out to this old pirate!" he finished, nodding towards the body of Digby who still lay there on deck. Gritting his teeth in anger the First Lieutenant tried not to think of how many of his fellow Frenchmen would pay with their lives for the captain's greed.

"Yes, Captain," Pierre replied. He saluted, Louis Francis smiled that arrogant smile of his, and Gerrard turned away to give the signallers their orders. He knew he had to stay out of the Captain's way until he had his own anger under control. Louis Francis, on the other hand, climbed down to the Severe's main deck and marched forrard, happier than he'd felt in more than three decades. He strutted along the deck to where the prisoners were shackled. He looked down at the body of Digby, which lay in a mess on the deck, before turning to the nearest deckhands, who, as usual, were avoiding eye contact with their Captain for fear he'd have them hung.

"Throw this body into the ocean," he barked at them, and they swiftly picked up the sad remains of Digby and tossed him over the starboard side. Louis Francis stared down at Alfred Bicks who lay there – conscious for a change – and stared back. The man hadn't been fed properly in weeks and the Captain wondered where he'd suddenly found the strength, deciding in the end that Digby's murder must have shaken the man a little.

"I'm glad you're awake, it's going to be a busy day and I wouldn't want you to miss it. First you get to see the remainder of that joke of a squadron destroyed," Francis said, pointing towards the horizon. Alfie looked up and saw the British ships at anchor in the distance and his heart leapt in hope, but then as he stared over and saw eight French ships closing on the flotilla his heart sank once more. Louis Francis watched this reaction closely, and cackled like a lunatic. "Don't worry, by the time this day is over I will have your father's treasure! And I'm going to celebrate my success by tearing the flesh from your bones," the Captain gloated. The threat meant little to Alfie Bicks, who'd been dreaming of death for many weeks, but the mention of his father left him completely confused.

"My father?" he mumbled to himself as Louis Francis stared down at him with a look of satisfaction on his face.

"Yes. You're the bastard child of the world's most infamous pirate, but daddy is long dead now and soon I'll give you the chance to finally meet him!" Francis imparted, before turning and marching aft along the deck, laughing and screaming orders at the sailors. A short distance away the Severe's First Lieutenant stood, shocked but now less confused. A few minutes earlier Pierre Gerrard had caught sight of his Captain down on the main deck, and had ventured down himself in the hope of getting some answers to some of the questions that had kept him up all night, and he wasn't disappointed.

"So you're Captain Mudd's son, and you didn't even know it!" Pierre Gerrard muttered, as he began to make his way back towards the Severe's quarter deck to watch his countrymen destroy the British, hoping that the casualties on his side would be minimal.

Chapter Forty Six

Admiral Philip Saunders watched the French ships turning about and sailing back towards his squadron through his telescope, and in that moment he realised that he would not get the opportunity to ram the French treasure ship. The already slim chance of success had just vanished completely. The Admiral had tried his hardest to succeed against all odds, but the mission he'd agreed to command by his spy-master friend had been risky from the very start.

"Prepare to engage!" he barked across his ship. Every British sailor's face showed that they knew this was a battle they couldn't possibly win, and their determination to fight nevertheless. The Romulus erupted into the controlled chaos that was battle readiness as gun ports swung open and cannon were loaded and run into firing positions, gunners prepared their rammers and matches and the ship manoeuvred into battle position. The wind was blowing from behind them, which gave the French the upper hand. Philip Saunders considered the few options open to him, which only made his heart sink further. He could order his squadron to sail away from the island and abandon the mission, but he would never be able to live with the consequences to his countrymen in the years ahead. He breathed deeply and accepted the inevitable: in an hour or so the squadrons would come together, battle would be joined, and the two forces would exchange cannon fire until they all foundered.

"This is going to be a bad one, Captain," Lucas stated; Saunders' eyes remained fixed on the French ships slowly approaching.

"Too true, old friend. I never thought they would attack like this, it's suicidal on their part. But Francis always was a coward, and this tactic offers the least risk to his own safety. The best we can do is try to take their ships out and hope one of ours survives," Saunders replied, and Lieutenant Lucas grinned at his commander.

"It's been an honour sailing with you, Philip. You've done your father proud, don't ever forget that," he said, and Saunders turned, stared at him and returned his smile before shaking his hand.

"It's been an honour having you at my side as my First Lieutenant. We sailed some rough seas, didn't we?" the Admiral asked, and his First Mate nodded. Then Philip Saunders stepped forward and made a speech which he made sure would be heard by all the crew, thanking them. His words brought a tear to many eyes but stoked the fire of determination to win the battle in their hearts. As he stepped away from the quarter-deck railing and approached his officers, the Admiral shook each one's hand. The men were daunted, but much to Saunders' pride they hid their fear well and exchanged a smile with their Commander as if the danger was negligible. The eight French warships had sailed closer and the Admiral didn't need to use his telescope to see the ships clearly.

"We don't stand a chance, do we, Captain?" Lucas asked, and Saunders turned to the man he'd sailed with for the best part of two decades.

"I'm afraid not, old friend. This is the end for us," he honestly admitted, and they both turned back to stare at the approaching fleet.

Suddenly the bell high up in the Romulus' crow's nest rang, catching the Admiral by surprise. Saunders knew exactly what that bell meant and he crossed to the other side of the quarter-deck and stared out across the ocean and the countless islands that broke her surface. In the far distance but getting clearer with every second that passed was a blip near the horizon, and that blip was moving: it seemed to be sailing around an island and became more and more recognizable as it came further into view.

"Ships sighted, Captain!" the lookout shouted from high up in the Romulus' rigging, and once again Philip Saunders reached for his telescope and peered through it. In the distance he could now see a mass of sails and masts, but as he continued to watch, searching for the colours they flew, and the ships grew closer and more details were visible… he dropped the telescope to his side, and the colour drained from his face. His officers were watching with fascination as the newcomers separated out from line astern in to the line abreast battle formation, and the vessels slowly spread out along the horizon.

"Captain, whose fleet is that? The Spanish possibly, but what would they be doing this far from the southern Americas?" his First Lieutenant was asking, but it was a moment before Philip Saunders was able to communicate once more, and he chose to ignore the question.

"Signal our ships to make all speed towards them immediately, Lieutenant!" he ordered Lucas, pointing at the ever growing number of ships that were converging on them like a storm cloud, but was far more deadly. Lucas wasted no time in transmitting this order to the signallers, who began hoisting the requisite flags. The crew on watch wasted no time, trimming sails and getting under way. The ship answered the helm and turned as swiftly as possible, using every scrap of wind and sailing away from the French and the treasure island. Benjamin Swift was on deck feeling both terrified and incredibly excited. He watched as the First Lieutenant approached Saunders, who was stock still staring at the mysterious ships spread across the horizon.

"Philip, whose fleet is that?" the Lieutenant quietly demanded, snapping Saunders out of his trance. The Admiral turned to him and smiled.

"That isn't a fleet, old friend, it's an armada!" the Admiral replied, and a look of confusion crossed the Lieutenant's weathered face.

"*Whose* armada, then, Captain?" he demanded once more, and Saunders turned to face him with a smile.

"It once belonged to Alfred Mudd," Saunders quietly replied, and the First Lieutenant's jaw dropped and a look of panic crossed his face.

"Are you absolutely insane, Captain? You're sailing us directly into the remains of Mudd's pirate fleet. You've just thrown us out of the frying pan and into the fire!" Lucas growled, but as Saunders looked him in the eye the man calmed slightly.

"Alfred Mudd and his men once offered leniency to my father and his entire crew. Mudd himself might be dead, but his crews loved him like a father. The only thing Mudd ever wanted was to kill the man who now commands that French squadron," Saunders said, as he stared back at the French ships giving chase. "Trust me, old friend, and allow me to talk with whoever now commands Mudd's ships. I believe our odds of survival are greater with them than they would be if we battle the French alone." Lucas rubbed his chin and inhaled a lungful of salty air.

"If this goes wrong it's going to be a slow painful death for us all. We sail under the Union Jack, Captain," was all the First Lieutenant had to say. Admiral Saunders continued to gaze out at the huge fleet in the Romulus' path.

"As did my father" he muttered to himself.

Chapter Forty Seven

S ailing into battle for the first time in many years, Alfred Mudd surveyed the scene ahead with an amused expression on his gaunt face. During the three decades that he'd rained terror on the Royal Navy and in the dozens of engagements he'd fought, the pirate had never sailed with so many ships at his side.

"Vengeance will finally be mine," he muttered to himself, as he stood at his flagship's bow ready to fight the last battle of his life. Surrounding his flagship dozens of other ships of the line were cruising into battle, carrying thousands upon thousands of men who were ready to sacrifice their lives to wipe the last name from their leader's notorious death list.

Gripping his telescope the world's most feared pirate stared at the ships ahead and grinned, causing his gaunt, almost skeletal, face to appear even more terrifying than it usually did. Alfred Mudd's fleet consisted of thirty-eight ships of the line, all cruising with full sail. Ships that the pirate had spent a lifetime acquiring. Watching the flag of the country he'd once thought of as home blowing in the wind atop the masts of the vessels sailing towards him, he chuckled at the irony. Digby hadn't mentioned the British navy in the message he'd sent, but their presence didn't surprise Captain Mudd. The pirate was a born tactician and had considered all of the possible outcomes of his plan, before he'd instigated it over a year earlier.

"The ships coming at us are British, Captain, do you think they've allied with the French?" a sailor with jet black skin asked. The sailor had been trained since he was a child to serve as First Lieutenant in anticipation of this particular encounter. Captain Mudd roared with laughter at the man's suggestion as his red hair blew wildly in the wind.

"Allied with the French indeed!" Mudd said, "You clearly don't know my fellow countrymen that well. The British think I'm dead and they thought that my fleet was no more. Like the French, they've come here for the treasure."

"Do we attack them, Captain?" the man asked, as Mudd continued to stare at the British squadron approaching. A long moment passed before he replied.

"Have our gunners ready. If they don't surrender then blow them out of the water and take no prisoners," he ordered, and the First Lieutenant smiled before shouting commands to the crew, preparing his comrades for a battle to the death: no quarter to be given and no prisoners to be taken.

Chapter Forty Eight

As the huge pirate fleet sailed into view, the men aboard the British ships were frightened as never before. Facing the French would undoubtedly have led to certain death, but many of the sailors, and not just the uneducated men below decks, thought that dealing with the remainder of Alfred Mudd's men would lead to a fate far worse. The infamous pirate had supposedly worked as a servant to Satan himself, and many of the crew were religious men. Below decks the gunners knelt in position ready to snap into action and fire their cannon when the order was given, but as they approached the pirate's fleet many prayed, whilst others babbled like men who'd already lost their minds. On deck, Admiral Saunders watched as the veritable armada that had belonged to the dead pirate converged on his squadron. The Admiral counted over three dozen warships.

"Raise the white flag and signal the other ships to sail no further. The Romulus will approach alone from this point!" Saunders barked at his men, who for the most part stood petrified. The officers aboard the HMS Romulus carried out their Captain's orders, but it was clear from their silence and manner that they didn't agree with them. Saunders was oblivious to this, being completely focused on the ships ahead. It was Benjamin Swift, the old fisherman, who approached the Captain, now standing near the quarter-deck railings. Saunders glanced briefly at him before returning his gaze to the huge fleet once more. The pair had barely spoken a word to each other since the sinking of the Sandown months earlier.

"Captain, if we're to face death at the hands of pirates, I'd like to know one last thing before I die," Benjamin said. The Admiral turned to him and, to Benny's surprise, he smiled.

"Like father, like son, eh? You were always a thinking man, Benny. And your son was brighter than many of his contemporaries. You want to know the truth about the attack on Mudd's men on Antigua all those years ago, right? I knew that as soon as I mentioned the ring that had proved that the body belonged to Captain Mudd you'd figured out that I'd omitted some details from the story I'd told you," Saunders replied, looking at Benny for confirmation, and the fisherman-turned-navigator nodded. The Romulus was now sailing alone towards the pirate fleet. The other British ships had heaved to and, at least for the time being, they had nothing to fear. The eight French ships had halted their pursuit in the realisation that they were no longer the dominant force in the area. Philip Saunders rubbed his temples for a moment.

"Well, what difference can it possibly make now? I want you to know, Benny, that I didn't lie to you. I just chose to leave out some details and I only did that because Louis Francis and his cronies brought shame on the Royal Navy all those years ago. For what it's worth, you've earned my respect over the last few months. I didn't want you to think that Louis Francis' actions represent how the Royal Navy behaves, because believe me, they don't," the Admiral said, as he looked Benjamin Swift in the eye. Then Saunders removed a cord from around his neck, unhooked a gold wedding band and handed it to Benny. The fisherman examined it and read the small inscription - *Andrea, forever yours, Alfred*, before handing it back to the Admiral.

"What makes you so certain it was Mudd's?" Benny asked, and the Admiral considered his answer for a moment.

"Because every report that survivors of Mudd's raids ever wrote mentioned the pirate wearing a gold ring around his neck, and over the years a handful of the pirate's crew were caught. My friend in London, Rupert Knightly, interrogated them all thoroughly and every one of them mentioned this ring. Mudd would often sit on deck for hours just staring at it, apparently," the Admiral replied, before pausing and placing it back on the chain for safe keeping. "Truth be told, Alfred Mudd had already decided to give up the life of a pirate before he set foot on Antigua all those years ago. He visited the island with his crew, accompanied by a young lady who, when they arrived on the island was already named Andrea Mudd. They went there to celebrate their marriage," Saunders said. "The young pirate was soon to take over as Governor of Arraya and fill Leonard Tibb's shoes. Tibb was growing old and he thought his apprentice was more than ready. Mudd had fallen head over heels in love with a local girl, and had been hit with feelings he couldn't have imagined. For the first time in his life he didn't feel alone and the idea of risking what he now had no longer appealed to him, and when he discovered that she was pregnant it only fortified those feelings."

Benjamin Swift nodded as he thought back to his own youth and to his son's mother, the love of his life who, much like Alfred Mudd's true love, had been taken from him leaving a wound that had never healed.

"Alfred Mudd only left her side for a few hours in the evening on the day that changed the course of history. He went out to get some supplies after days of celebration. Mudd and his crew planned on sailing from Antigua early the next day. He took most of his men with him to get supplies, including Digby. When Louis Francis and his drunken friends crossed Antigua, much to their good fortune they found only a small band of the pirate's men, and they killed them all," Saunders said, pausing and staring out at the ships once more. Benny watched the Admiral closely and could see he was struggling to recount the events that had created the terrible pirate and led directly to their dangerous mission.

"They didn't kill Andrea immediately, Benny. Francis and the rest of the young officers who would comprise Mudd's infamous death list took turns raping her. Eventually they hanged her from a tree before riding their horses back to the navy base and promising each other they'd never speak of what they'd done. When Mudd returned and found her body he collapsed and cried for hours, eventually falling silent. Some say he didn't utter a word for days, but when he finally did he was a different person completely. They'd punished a thief and created a monster. He acquired the names of the men who'd killed his wife and child, and stolen his future. Within months he began to attack navy ships, which back then was completely unheard of. Many people initially wondered why anyone would commit such a suicidal act, but once he started handing out his death list the story became generally known, and though the Royal Navy tried to cover up the events on Antigua for fear of the embarrassment it would bring them, they did not entirely succeed." Saunders finished and the incongruous pair stood silently watching the armada approach.

"What now?" Benny finally asked, and Saunders forced a smile.

"We hand this ring back to Mudd's crew, promise to help bring them Louis Francis' head and hope that they let us live," the Admiral replied. A moment later Lieutenant Lucas arrived at the pair's side with a handful of other officers.

"Captain, we've heaved to and are awaiting orders," he reported, as they all stared at the pirate's flagship which towered over the HMS Romulus like an albatross peering down at its prey.

"How many cannon does that vessel carry? I count four gun decks. I've never seen anything like it!" an officer muttered, "If they fire on us we're done for."

Admiral Saunders stared at the officer who froze, as did most of the other men. Only the First Lieutenant and, to his surprise, Benjamin Swift, showed no fear.

"It has one hundred and twenty at least, but don't worry: if they wanted to attack us we would be dead already. Prepare a row boat, it's time to try and negotiate. Lucas, you're coming with me," Saunders said, and his First Lieutenant nodded.

"And you, Benny, if you would be so kind?"

A few of the officers looked shocked at their Captain's request, but most were quietly relieved. They had all heard the horror stories and didn't fancy the prospect of negotiating with men who'd spent their lives burning officers of the Royal Navy alive. Benjamin Swift nodded his agreement as he looked over at the gigantic pirate ship without a vestige of fear on his face.

Chapter Forty Nine

Meanwhile, closer to the shores of the strange looking island where Alfred Mudd had supposedly buried his wealth, Captain Louis Francis stood on the deck of the French flagship Severe. Like the French officers and sailors at his side, the cowardly traitor had lapsed into silence once the huge armada had appeared on the horizon. The ship's First Lieutenant, Pierre Gerrard looked at his Captain for orders, a man he'd come to despise. Since hearing of the brutal rape and murder Louis Francis had committed in his youth, Pierre had struggled with the idea of being on the same side as the man. Now Gerrard noted that Louis Francis had failed to issue any commands to his crew, and was still staring at the ships in the distance looking terrified. Lying on his back and looking towards the horizon like everybody else, the prisoner Alfred Bicks smiled for the first time in many, many weeks and the smile looked menacing on his gaunt face.

Eventually the silence on deck was broken as Alfie turned and stared at Louis Francis before breaking into manic laughter. The Captain's face flushed red with anger as he grabbed a whip and stormed over to the prisoner. Raising the whip Francis screamed at Alfie Bicks, "Your time has come to an end!" but the prisoner continued to laugh. Alfred Bicks was now completely unafraid of death.

"At least I'll die with a smile on my face, knowing that soon you'll join me!" the prisoner shouted back at him. Louis Francis had heard enough. Dropping the whip he pulled a bayonet from the sheath at his waist and stepped forward, ready to end the prisoner's life.

Suddenly a huge explosion echoed off the deck of the Severe and Louis Francis cowered in fear as he turned to face the barrel of a musket that was smoking and aimed directly at his head. The Captain was still taking the scene in as his First Lieutenant cocked the musket's second barrel. Pierre Gerrard stared defiantly at him: "I'm assuming command of this squadron with immediate effect," he informed Louis Francis whose confusion was quickly being replaced by anger.

"Our superiors will hang you for this insubordination!" he raged, "Do you have any idea of the connections I have in Paris?" Much to his surprise Pierre Gerrard chuckled at this statement.

"Connections in Paris! My fellow Frenchmen only tolerated you because of the information on the British you were able to provide. Now, I have a strong feeling that you no longer have access to such information, and as a result you're worthless to our superiors." Pierre Gerrard stated. Louis Francis looked baffled for a moment before the reality of the position he was in dawned on him.

"How dare you!" he spat before turning to his officers who were stood watching the scene unfold, "clap this man in irons! I want him hung!" Francis screamed. Much to his surprise, instead of carrying out his orders, the officers under his command all raised weapons and aimed them in his direction. Over the course of the long voyage the Captain had tortured many innocent sailors for no other reason than satisfying his own sadistic needs, and as a result he had made many enemies aboard the Severe. Pierre Gerrard was an officer held in high regard by his crew, a man that had earned a reputation for fairness over several decades. Above all else Pierre Gerrard was a blue blooded Frenchman, unlike Louis Francis.

"Clap this man in irons!" Gerrard ordered his men, who wasted no time shackling the half French half English traitor. Finally Pierre Gerrard strolled over to Alfie Bicks, who stared up at him in admiration.

"I'm sorry for the way you've been treated. I hope you won't hold that against us. My men were only ever carrying out orders," Pierre stated, as several officers undid the shackles binding the prisoner's hands and feet. Alfie stared up at the man who had crept along the deck to succour him a few days earlier.

"Why would you care if I held it against you or your men?" Alfie asked, and Pierre Gerrard stared out at the dozens of pirate ships on the horizon.

"Because out there are thousands upon thousands of men who were once loyal to Captain Mudd. They loved him like he was their father and not just their leader. I and my crew will only be able to sail out of these seas with our lives intact if I can make a deal with them, and I'm sure that if you choose to exact revenge on my countrymen your father's old fleet will destroy our ships without a second thought," Pierre stated baldly as Alfie touched his blistered face and winced in pain. Suddenly a handful of officers appeared beside the pair.

"Nous attendons les ordres du Capitaine Gerrard," said one of the officers, informing Pierre that they awaited his orders. Pierre Gerrard stared over at Louis Francis who was now shackled and lying on the deck. The man looked scared out of his wits, and was clearly terrified at the fate that awaited him. Glancing over at Alfie Bicks who had climbed to his feet and was towering over the men beside him, the Severe's new Captain made his tough decision.

Pierre Gerrard ordered his men to hoist the white flag and make sail. The men listened to their Captain's orders, and when he instructed them to sail the Severe towards the pirate fleet to negotiate for their lives they looked scared, but they carried out his orders all the same. "We have both Alfred Mudd's only son and the pirate's worst enemy to trade," he informed them. The French sailors, still full of trepidation, sprang to their duties and the Severe began to close the distance between them and the huge fleet of ships on the horizon.

"I just hope they show us mercy. By God we don't deserve it," Pierre Gerrard muttered to himself, as he tried to prepare himself for the most challenging meeting of his life.

Chapter Fifty

Admiral Philip Saunders, First Lieutenant Lucas and Benjamin Swift climbed into a small row boat that was quickly lowered into the water. During the journey to the pirate fleet's flagship none of the men spoke a word. Instead they stared down at their boots and prepared themselves as best they could for what was to come. Eventually they pulled up alongside the huge pirate flagship that had once belonged to the Spanish Navy, as was evidenced by her name, Santisima Trinidad.

The Admiral took a deep breath and looked over at his men, "Are you ready?" he asked as he caught the rope ladder that had been thrown over the ship's starboard railing. His First Lieutenant nodded but the man's expression was stiff, "As ready as I'll ever be, Captain" the Lieutenant replied. Turning to Benny Swift, Saunders watched the old fisherman as he stared up at the huge ship with fascination. A moment later Benny Swift glanced over his way.

"I'm ready, Admiral," he replied, before Philip Saunders began the climb towards the most important – and personally dangerous – meeting of his career.

On the crowded deck of the ship over a hundred men stood clutching an assortment of weapons, and they were obviously very keen to use them. Most of the men had been raised on the island of Andrea, having been freed from slave masters long years before. The men had waited many, many years to pay back the debt they owed to the red headed pirate that had saved them all.

When the trio of Englishmen reached the top of the ladder and scrambled over the ship's railing they were met with hostility. Over a hundred pairs of eyes stared their way, eyes that belonged to the toughest looking men imaginable. Admiral Saunders looked over the faces that bore expressions of hatred and he feared the worst, wondering if he would still be alive to see the remains of Alfred Mudd's fleet when it started to fire on his own ships and hoping that he wasn't.

Summoning some courage from deep within himself Saunders stepped forward: "I would like to parley with your leader," he stated, the sound of his words echoing across the silent deck. The pirates continued to glare at him, noting the British navy uniform he wore, and for a moment the Admiral believed that his life was about to come to an extremely violent end. Suddenly the fearsome looking men stepped aside as a huge figure made his way through the crowd. Philip Saunders felt the breath leave his lungs and the colour drain from his face as that man stepped into view. "It cannot be!" he found himself muttering as the pirate Alfred Mudd stood staring at the trio with a smile on his gaunt face. While the Admiral stared, dumbstruck, at the pirate's red hair and bushy red beard, a multitude of scenarios rushed through his mind. Stories the Admiral had heard repeated countless times over the course of his life, rendering the old man in front of him a living legend.

Several moments passed before Alfred Mudd limped forward, and both Philip Saunders and Lieutenant Lucas dropped to one knee and lowered their heads in both fear and respect. Mudd himself finally stopped only a yard or so in front of them. Saunders was still struggling with shock: that the infamous pirate *wasn't* dead, as he pulled the wedding band from around his neck, slipped it from the string and held it out in front of him. The Admiral dared not look up and into the pirate's crazy eyes. The smile had now left Mudd's face. As soon as he'd seen the ring painful memories had flooded back. Stepping forward he picked it up with his bony fingers and for the first time in many years he read the message.

Benjamin Swift watched the pain those four words caused travel across the pirate's face and felt true pity. The fisherman had himself lost the only woman he'd ever loved, and knew that it was a pain that was never truly assuaged. Slipping the ring onto one of his bony fingers, Mudd stared over at Benny and into the fisherman's bright blue eyes, and in those eyes he saw no fear, just a reflection of his pain. Then he turned to the two men who served in the Royal Navy.

"Rise," he ordered, and they climbed to their feet. Summoning his courage Philip Saunders finally looked up and into the pirate's eyes, and it was clear Captain Mudd recognised his face instantly. Alfred Mudd was a great tactician and even in his old age still had a memory far more acute than most.

"I know your face," Mudd stated, and the Admiral nodded.

"Many years ago you met my father..." he replied, but the pirate cut in before he finished the sentence.

"Alexander Saunders, I remember him well. He is that rare being: a British Navy officer who is an honourable man," the pirate stated, "He even offered his own life in exchange for those of his crew. He was the type of Captain men dreamed of sailing under."

Admiral Philip Saunders found a lone tear running down his cheek at the pirate's words, and quickly rubbed it away. Captain Mudd watched curiously, whilst his crew continued to glare at the trio.

"I thank you for returning this ring to me, Admiral Saunders. Now, what brings your ships into the South Pacific?" Mudd finally asked, and Saunders wasted no time explaining that Louis Francis had betrayed England and sailed for the treasure with the French.

"So you've come to steal my riches?" Mudd suddenly barked at him causing him to look back down at his feet in fear of punishment. In the silence that followed the pirate sniggered, and suddenly Saunders realised that there never were any riches buried on the island a few miles off the ship's starboard side. It had all been an elaborate trap to entice Louis Francis out of hiding. Philip Saunders couldn't help but look up and smile with this realisation, and the ruthless pirate smiled back.

"We sailed after the French to catch Francis. Initially we had no intention of making a bid for your treasure, but as I'm sure you're aware we couldn't risk letting that amount of gold fall into our enemies' hands. People say you're one of the best military strategists that has ever lived, so I have no doubt that you understand," Admiral Saunders said.

"And when you say people, you mean Rupert Knightly?" the pirate asked, causing Admiral Saunders' jaw to drop: he stared up at the pirate in absolute shock. Captain Mudd's sinister smile would have terrified most men. "Oh I know all about Mr Knightly. When I was learning my trade I was taught that knowledge is power and it's a lesson I've never forgotten. I knew that if I could fool Knightly then I could fool England. Now, what do you want?" the pirate asked, and Saunders quickly explained that all he wanted was to sail his squadron back to Europe. The pirate thought for a long moment as he stared out to sea. Finally he turned to face the young Admiral.

"If I could trust you, I'd watch you sail away with a smile on my face, but if your countrymen have taught me one thing it's that they're not to be trusted. If I let you live today in the years ahead you'll return with more men and more ships!" He grimaced. "I'm sorry but many years ago I swore to protect my people at all costs, and protect them I will."

Admiral Saunders face dropped with the realisation that his squadron would never leave the South Pacific. The ruthless pirate would imprison or slay them all, adding yet more ships to his fleet and guaranteeing that word would never reach England that he still lived. This dark thought was taking possession of the Admiral's mind when a huge man appeared at Mudd's side.

"Captain, the French approach, and, like the English, they offer surrender," the man advised, and Alfred Mudd's gaunt face lit up. Saunders let out a sigh and prepared himself for the fate that awaited him and his fellow Englishmen. The mission had finally come to an end, but that end wasn't a complete disaster. The French would fail to get their hands on the war-chest they needed to rebuild their fleet and conquer Europe, but Philip Saunders and his men would never set foot on English soil ever again. Looking at the infamous pirate Saunders observed the gleeful look on his gaunt face as the French row boat approached. The pirate had waited a very long time to get his revenge on the man that had ruined his life, and that wait was nearly over.

"You out-smarted them all, even Knightly himself," Saunders thought, as he waited patiently to see the traitor Louis Francis finally receive the justice he deserved.

Chapter Fifty One

L ike the English before him, Pierre Gerrard climbed the rungs of the rope ladder slung over the pirate ship's starboard rail under the scrutiny of many nasty looking men. The French squadron's new Captain was alone, opting to leave his prisoners chained up in the rowboat, in the belief it would aid negotiations. However, as soon as Gerrard climbed up and onto the huge Spanish warship's main deck he regretted his decision.

Looking over the faces of the pirates who stood staring his way Gerrard tried to suppress the shivers of fear that raced through his body, but as he looked back at the Severe he thought of his men, a thought that forced him to summon enough courage to move forward. After taking half a dozen steps Pierre spotted his English counterpart Admiral Saunders on his knees alongside his First Lieutenant and the French Captain wondered for a fraction of a second why they appeared so scared, but then he caught a glimpse of the infamous pirate's menacing face and suddenly it dawned on him what was happening.

Alfred Mudd stood towering over his men with his red hair blowing in the wind and a baleful grin on his gaunt face. Pierre Gerrard gasped out loud and as a myriad of different thoughts raced through his mind he fell to his knees. Captain Mudd watched and continued to smile as he strolled over to where the Frenchman knelt, staring down at him with those ghastly eyes. Pierre Gerrard looked down at the deck in terror.

"Where is Louis Francis?" Mudd demanded, and summoning courage from the pit of his stomach the French Captain stared up and into the pirate's eyes.

"Louis Francis is tied and gagged in the rowboat that brought me to this parlay. I offer him in exchange for the lives of my men. Personally, I despise the fool and believe he is deserving of the punishment he'll receive, but my men are just sailors carrying out orders. Most weren't even born when Louis Francis' despicable actions set this all in motion," Pierre stated, and when he finished silence fell over the deck as Alfred Mudd twisted the ends of his ginger beard, deep in thought. Only a few yards away Benjamin Swift stared at the pirate, still amazed at the resemblance Mudd shared with the smuggler who had once protected his own son. It was Alfred Mudd's second in command who shattered the silence.

"He speaks true, Alfred, but that coward isn't alone. There are two prisoners," the huge black man who served as Mudd's First Lieutenant stated, and suddenly Alfred Mudd turned on the Frenchman.

"Who else do you bring?" he demanded, and Pierre Gerrard froze in terror as he regretted covering his prisoner's faces and he struggled to form words. In that moment, the French Captain stared over at Admiral Saunders and the English Captain's expression changed from one of fear to relief. Alfred Mudd, as always, never missed a thing, and noted the change in Saunders' mood with a curious look on his face. It was Philip Saunders who answered the question on behalf of Pierre Gerrard.

"The other prisoner is a man who was raised on the south coast of England. He was a smuggler who worked for this man's son," Saunders said, as he glanced and nodded towards Benjamin Swift who stood smiling in confident hope that their odds of survival had just increased. "I took him aboard my ship under the instruction of Rupert Knightly," the Admiral continued, and with the mention of the spymaster

Alfred Mudd's look of curiosity increased dramatically. "The other prisoner aboard that row boat is Alfred Bicks. He is your son," Saunders said, as he continued to watch the sequence of emotions cross the pirate's face. After a moment, the look of curiosity disappeared and was replaced by anger. The pirate stared at Saunders and then Pierre Gerrard.

"Is this true?" he asked the Frenchman who simply nodded in return. Alfred Mudd twisted his beard for the briefest of moments as his tactical mind tried to comprehend this new information, and then he turned to the men who knelt at his feet.

"If you lie, then I'll kill you all and sink every one of those ships," he warned, as he pointed a long bony finger at the British and French Squadrons trapped in front of the strange shaped island. Turning to his First Lieutenant he ordered the man to fetch the prisoners before turning and staring out to sea.

Several long minutes later the two men were hoisted on deck. Both had been relieved of the shackles binding them, but they still had sacks over their heads. They were led to where Alfred Mudd stood. The pirate himself continued to gaze out to sea. The man had dreamed of nothing other than facing the man who had destroyed his soul for so many years, yet now the moment had arrived he was conscious of a strange feeling of reluctance. Finally he turned and stared at the two men in front of him, noting the difference in their heights. The shorter of the two was physically shaking. Alfred Mudd hadn't expected anything less. Stepping forward he pulled the sack from Louis Francis' head and gripped his shoulders, grinning maniacally at the man as he took in the man's features and compared them to all the descriptions he'd been given from the mouths of petrified captains over the years. Louis Francis' nerve suddenly broke: he soiled himself and collapsed to the timber deck weeping like a child. The pirate's eyes continued to burn into the traitor's.

"For what you did to her I will punish you day in and day out for the rest of your life, and trust me, it'll last a lot longer than you think," Mudd promised through gritted teeth, before turning to the other prisoner. When he finally pulled the sack from Alfie Bicks' head revealing his gaunt face, red beard, matching hair and of course those crazy looking eyes of his the pirates all gasped in total shock.

Alfie Bicks stared at the man in front of him, a man who was famous the world over, and he recognised himself in that man's face. Suddenly Digby's last words came flooding back with fresh meaning, "When you meet your maker, you tell him we won in the end," the old pirate with the scar on his face had said, and now Alfie Bicks understood that Digby had sacrificed his own life to complete his best friend's life's work, and wipe the final name off the infamous death list.

Whilst Alfie Bicks pondered these thoughts his astonished father stared at him in amazement. He had spent a lifetime outsmarting people, and was surprised for the first time in many years. In the silence Alfie smiled at him, before walking painfully over to Benny Swift and hugging the man. Admiral Saunders stared up at Alfie Bicks from where he knelt on deck, wondering whether the red headed ex-smuggler was about to finish the job he'd set out to do on deck of the HMS Romulus all those weeks ago, and whether he was about to feel the blade of that dagger once and for all. Much to his surprise Alfie extended a hand and pulled him to his feet.

"I'm sorry for what I did. I know now that you tried to help me. I would be dead several times over if it hadn't been for you, but back then I couldn't see things clearly. That day on deck when I tried to kill you I wasn't thinking straight, and I now realise that grief had clouded my mind," Alfie said, glancing over at Benjamin Swift who had tears running down his cheeks. "Over the last few weeks I've done lots of thinking. I never thought I would get this opportunity to set things right, but here we are."

"I forgive you, Alfie. I had forgiven you by the end of the day that it happened," Saunders said, and then Alfie Bicks walked over to Captain Mudd and for the first time stood at his side.

"What now?" he asked, as Mudd grinned at him, fascinated.

"You tell me?" the pirate offered, and Alfie Bicks stepped towards Pierre Gerrard, the man who had crept on deck to feed and water him.

"You will surrender six of your ships to us and sail back to Europe with your lives," Bicks stated, before turning towards his father who nodded his agreement. Alfred Mudd was deep in thought, still twisting the ends of his ginger beard and Alfie Bicks smiled at the sight of this familiar habit.

"And what happens if they return?" a voice asked and Alfie Bicks turned to his father's First Lieutenant.

"Trust me, they'll never return. I witnessed the reaction on their flagship's deck when they saw the size of your fleet. The French and British alike will not risk sailing so many vessels out of Europe again. We all know that, and if they ever do return then my friend here, Admiral Saunders, will assist us in wiping them out," Bicks replied, and the men nodded in agreement with his logic. Alfred Mudd finally stepped forward.

"Do you trust this man?" the pirate asked, pointing towards Saunders: Alfred Bicks confirmed that he did. Mudd seemed satisfied as he addressed Pierre Gerrard for the last time, "Go now, but understand this: we have no treasure and nothing of any value, and we live on an island nearly a thousand nautical miles from here, nestled amongst a thousand others. You could sail these seas for two lifetimes and never find us."

Pierre Gerrard nodded and offered his thanks, before he made his way to the starboard rail and climbed down to the rowboat, never to be seen again. It would take the French the remainder of that day to remove all the men and supplies from the ships they were to surrender. At sundown the depleted French squadron began the long journey home, leaving six empty vessels hove to.

Chapter Fifty Two

After the French had disappeared over the horizon, Philip Saunders spent several hours negotiating with the man who had once spared his father's life. As the night wore on, Mudd and Saunders hammered out a deal and the Admiral was finally escorted back to the HMS Romulus together with his First Lieutenant and Benjamin Swift.

Alfie Bicks, having killed a soldier many months before, could never return to England. So he chose to stay at his father's side, and when he said his goodbyes to Benny Swift the pair both had tears in their eyes.

As soon as the trio stepped back onto the main deck of the Romulus a thousand questions were asked, but Admiral Saunders simply marched up onto her quarter deck so he could address the crowd.

"Men, we have succeeded!" he shouted at the top of his voice, and the crew cheered. "We will sail back to England having added six ships to our squadron and will receive a hero's welcome!"

That night the decks of the British squadron's ships were alive with celebration as the men drank their grog and toasted their success under a sky full of stars. The handful of smugglers who had entered their naval service in chains were rounded up for a meeting in Admiral Saunders' dining room. Jim Robson, Carp and the others were curious to know what Saunders could want from them, but were joyously overwhelmed to hear that their friend Alfie Bicks had survived after all.

"You each have a choice: you can either return to England where you'll receive full pardons, or you can join

Alfie and settle out here," the Admiral said, and the small group of men huddled together to discuss the options before them. After a few minutes Jim Robson turned to Saunders, and spoke on behalf of his men.

"Most of us will stay with Alfie. We're smugglers, it's all we know, and with the trade wiped out on the Kent coast we have nothing to return to," he said, and the Admiral rose from his chair.

"Men, for what it's worth, during this journey each and every one of you has earned my respect. It has made me proud to serve alongside you," he said. Benjamin Swift stood watching the scene unfold through his remarkably clear blue eyes.

"And you, Benny, will you stay?" the Admiral asked, at which the old fisherman shook his head.

"I was raised on the cobbled streets of Deal, and I have every intention of dying there," he said, and with that the group of men who had once worked for his son began saying their farewells.

The next morning the smugglers were rowed over to Alfred Mudd's gigantic flagship where they were greeted warmly by the pirates. The moment that Alfie Bicks limped onto the main deck was an emotional one to say the least, and it was quite some time before the smugglers could truly believe that their friend had survived.

Under instructions from Captain Mudd, Admiral Saunders remained hove to off the strange island for the best part of a week. Hendricks and a squad of marines landed on the island and gathered many supplies in the slow days that passed. The pirate had commandeered several of the French ships which had sailed away with him, but Mudd had promised he would return them. Eventually the pirate fleet reappeared over the horizon and as they sailed closer they signalled for the Admiral to meet them aboard one of the French vessels.

Marching down into the 'tween decks of the newly acquired ship beside the huge pirate Admiral Philip Saunders froze in his tracks once he reached her storage sections, completely lost for words. The ship's hold was full to the brim with treasure. Wandering around the Admiral picked up bars of both silver and gold before replacing them in amazement. He tried to calculate the treasure's worth, but gave up and turned to the gaunt pirate instead.

"What is this?" he asked, and Mudd's face creased in a wicked grin that still managed to send shivers down the Admiral's spine.

"This, Philip, is a peace treaty between my country and yours," he said, before pulling a letter from his jacket and handing it to the Admiral. "Please give this to Rupert Knightly. Now, take your men back to England."

Saunders took the envelope from the pirate's bony hand and admired the wax seal on it for a brief moment before looking up into the man's truly terrifying eyes for the very last time.

"Thank you. I vow to you that my countrymen will trouble you no more," Saunders promised, and then both men climbed back up on deck of the ship. A short while later the notorious – and definitely living – pirate disappeared forever as his huge fleet sailed towards the horizon.

Chapter Fifty Three

The journey back to England took the best part of six months, and like the outbound journey before it, the return leg had its fair share of difficult moments. The treasure stored deep in the hold of the French warship was securely locked away. Admiral Philip Saunders kept both its existence and the fact that Alfred Mudd lived a secret from his men, including all of his officers. Only Benny Swift and Lieutenant Lucas knew the truth, and both men he would have trusted with his life. As for the crew that had risked their lives many times during the treacherous journey, the Admiral offered them all the prize money they deserved. The mission's success had added half a dozen warships to the British fleet, and that was before the treasure was even considered. Philip Saunders would make sure that each and every sailor received a generous reward for the contribution they'd made. As a result, the mood aboard the returning ships was full of cheer, as men dreamed of finally seeing their loved ones and the money they would spoil them with.

Philip Saunders often wondered about the content of the letter the pirate had asked him to deliver to the spymaster in London. The Admiral had considered opening it on several occasions, but had stared at the wax seal for a long time and had eventually stored the letter away. Philip Saunders considered the pirate and the spymaster to be the two most dangerous people he'd ever met. In many ways they were complete opposites, but in other ways they were definitely akin. Both were extremely intelligent, and the Admiral didn't want to risk getting on the wrong side of either of them.

Eventually Saunders' augmented squadron of eleven tall ships sailed into the English Channel and dropped anchor in a safe stretch of water known as the Downs. A messenger was sent ashore to carry the news that the squadron would arrive in London the next day. That night Benjamin Swift spent many hours on deck with the friends he'd made during the journey, occasionally glancing over at the faint lights showing where the small town of Deal nestled on the familiar coastline.

When the squadron sailed up the Thames estuary it was met with a hero's welcome. Hundreds of people crowded the banks of the mighty river cheering at the British victory over the French and welcoming the newly acquired ships to the city of London. The squadron navigated into the Royal Docks at Deptford completing its journey to the other side of the world and back. Sailors poured down the gangplanks where they were met by their families with open arms and many tears. Admiral Saunders remained on the deck of the Romulus watching this with pride and thinking of his father. At least an hour passed before the dockyards returned to normality and Rupert Knightly appeared. The spymaster and the Royal Navy's 1st Sea Lord Sir Robert Burns were piped up the Romulus' gangplank, and, unlike the meeting at the Somerset Club over a year before, Saunders' superior looked untroubled. Both men were flanked by over a dozen of Rupert Knightly's trusted agents. As the group reached Saunders they stopped in their tracks and saluted him, making the Admiral feel incredibly proud.

After a brief chat with Knightly, Philip Saunders led the man below decks and towards the ship's storeroom, enjoying the look of curiosity on the spymaster's face. The Admiral had known Rupert for many years and had never had the privilege of knowing something that the spymaster didn't. On reaching the thick timber door the Admiral stopped and pulled the envelope from his jacket. Rupert Knightly pushed the spectacles he wore up the bridge of his nose before taking the envelope.

"What's this?" he asked, and Philip Saunders took great pleasure informing his friend it was a letter for him from Alfred Mudd, and then savoured the look of surprise on Knightly's face. "He lives?" the spymaster asked, and Saunders nodded. Tearing the seal from the envelope Rupert Knightly read the long letter to himself, as the Admiral's curiosity grew and grew. Eventually Rupert read the end of the letter aloud: "Forever your loyal friend and ally, Alfred Mudd."

Saunders wanted to know more, but whatever message had been relayed it was for Rupert Knightly's eyes only and the Admiral respected that. Turning the key in the lock Philip Saunders swung the thick door open revealing the immense bounty of treasure and watched the spymaster gasp in shock. It was a moment Philip Saunders would treasure for the rest of his life.

The next day down on the Kent coast the stagecoach carrying Benjamin Swift and several other smugglers who'd fled the town two years earlier trotted along the promenade overlooking the town's shingle beach. The old fisherman stared out at the English Channel where he'd worked as a fisherman for most of his life, observing the white water breaking in the distance on the Goodwin Sands and all the wrecks that Benny knew so well, and he smiled to himself. After an adventure that had taken him around the world and back he'd finally arrived home.

When the coach pulled up in the large square in the southern section of Deal, Benny was hit by a wave of pain as memories of the son he'd lost came flooding back. Jacob was dead, a fact he'd eventually come to terms with, but a fact he'd always struggle to accept.

Stepping out of the carriage into the bustle he'd missed so much he stood for a moment taking it all in, watching the street urchins as they ran around jostling the town's wealthy who were busying themselves preparing to board coaches to a hundred different destinations, whilst sailors staggered from tavern to tavern and wenches plied their trade. Benjamin Swift took a deep breath of salty air and chuckled. The cobbled streets of Deal hadn't changed, but Benny had. Before his capture and involvement in the most important mission in the history of the British Navy he'd spent his entire life in this town. It was all he knew. Now he'd helped navigate a squadron through several seas, faced terrors and hardships, and seen things he could never have imagined. Stepping into the hubbub, Benny Swift began to stroll towards a drinking den he'd often visited a lifetime ago, a small tavern known as The Seagull, to wet his whistle.

On the other side of the square a group of men were gazing out at the crowd and chatting amongst themselves. The leaders name was Michael Swan, a tough local man who's only sister Elizabeth had once married a local legend known as The Boy, who people still spoke of in awe. Spotting Benny, a face he knew well, he stopped in mid-sentence and stared in shock. His friends turned round, curious to know what had captured his attention.

"What's up? You look like you've just seen a ghost!" one of them said, before Michael looked over at him.

"I reckon I have. Go get my sister, now!" he ordered, and several of the men disappeared into the town's labyrinth of streets.

Benny Swift continued to stroll along the cobbled streets that he knew so well, watching the crowds of people as they went about their business. Approaching the tavern he'd often frequented he suddenly stopped dead in his tracks as a little boy broke through the crowd. The toddler stood for a moment as the old fisherman stared at his blonde hair and blue eyes, and Benjamin Swift found a lump in his throat. The boy was the mirror image of a child Benny had once raised, a child that had grown into a powerful smuggling gang leader and a man Benny missed every day.

"Jake, slow down!" a woman's voice called, and a second later she appeared from the crowd, grabbing her son's hand. Elizabeth Swift spotted her father-in-law and rushed over and hugged him. It was several minutes before she was able to speak and she wasted no time introducing the old fisherman to his only grandson, Jacob Swift, son of the greatest smuggler to ever control the Kent coast.

Other books by the author

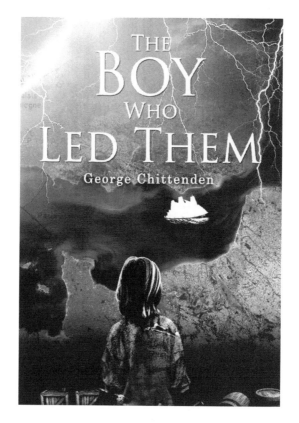

Raised by a fisherman on the English Channel and taken under the wing of the fearsome Billy Bates, Jacob Swift was leading the country's most successful smuggling gang at fifteen, landing cargoes of brandy, tobacco and silk along the Kent coast whilst fighting battles with rival gangs and customs officers on land and sea. But when the king of smugglers gets caught up in a plot to steal a priceless treasure he makes an enemy with enough power to bring his empire to its knees. This is a story of honour, loyalty and England's troubled past. A story of treasure lost and finally found.

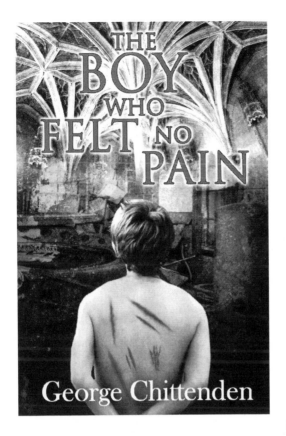

THE BOY WHO FELT NO PAIN

George Chittenden

1760, The coastal town of Deal is a dangerous place, ruled by bare knuckle fighter Dale Jenkins and his ruthless gang of thugs who demand money from anyone forced to live on the wrong side of the law. But when Dale dies a battle for leadership between his brother and youngest son, Ronnie begins. As the townsfolk hold their breath in anticipation of trouble, local fisherman turned smuggler, Billy Bates spots an opportunity to end the Jenkins reign of terror and gathers an army out of the clan's enemies, an army of misfits including a daring young thief called Alfred Bicks and a mysterious orphan whose past has destroyed his very soul. Risking everything Bill steps out of the shadows challenging the clan for control of the town's criminal underworld and all out war erupts in the streets.